I0577215

Nathaniel Hawthorne

Tanglewood tales and biographical stories

Nathaniel Hawthorne

Tanglewood tales and biographical stories

ISBN/EAN: 9783337174262

Printed in Europe, USA, Canada, Australia, Japan

Cover: Foto ©Andreas Hilbeck / pixelio.de

More available books at **www.hansebooks.com**

Hawthorne's Works.

ILLUSTRATED LIBRARY EDITION.

TANGLEWOOD TALES,

AND

BIOGRAPHICAL STORIES.

BY

NATHANIEL HAWTHORNE.

TWO VOLUMES IN ONE.

BOSTON:

HOUGHTON, MIFFLIN AND COMPANY.

The Riverside Press, Cambridge.

1881.

TANGLEWOOD TALES

FOR GIRLS AND BOYS.

BEING

A SECOND WONDER-BOOK.

CONTENTS.

THE WAYSIDE.

INTRODUCTORY.

A SHORT time ago, I was favored with a flying visit from my young friend Eustace Bright,
whom I had not before met with since quitting
the breezy mountains of Berkshire. It being
the winter vacation at his college, Eustace was
allowing himself a little relaxation, in the hope,
he told me, of repairing the inroads which severe
application to study had made upon his health;
and I was happy to conclude, from the excellent
physical condition in which I saw him, that the
remedy had already been attended with very de-
sirable success. He had now run up from Boston by the noon train, partly impelled by the
friendly regard with which he is pleased to honor
me, and partly, as I soon found, on a matter of
literary business.

It delighted me to receive Mr. Bright, for the
first time, under a roof, though a very humble

one, which I could really call my own. Nor did
I fail (as is the custom of landed proprietors all
about the world) to parade the poor fellow up
and down over my half a dozen acres; secretly
rejoicing, nevertheless, that the disarray of the
inclement season, and particularly the six inches
of snow then upon the ground, prevented him
from observing the ragged neglect of soil and
shrubbery into which the place has lapsed.   It
was idle, however, to imagine that an airy guest
from Monument Mountain, Bald Summit, and
old Graylock, shaggy with primeval forests,
could see any thing to admire in my poor little
hillside, with its growth of frail and insect-
eaten locust trees.   Eustace very frankly called
the view from my hill top tame; and so, no
doubt, it was, after rough, broken, rugged, headlong Berkshire, and especially the northern parts
of the county, with which his college residence
had made him familiar.   But to me there is a
peculiar, quiet charm in these broad meadows
and gentle eminences.   They are better than
mountains, because they do not stamp and
stereotype themselves into the brain, and thus
grow wearisome with the same strong impres-

sion, repeated day after day. A few summer weeks among mountains, a lifetime among green meadows and placid slopes, with outlines forever new, because continually fading out of the memory — such would be my sober choice.

I doubt whether Eustace did not internally pronounce the whole thing a bore, until I led him to my predecessor's little ruined, rustic summer house, midway on the hillside. It is a mere skeleton of slender, decaying tree trunks, with neither walls nor a roof; nothing but a tracery of branches and twigs, which the next wintry blast will be very likely to scatter in fragments along the terrace. It looks, and is, as evanescent as a dream; and yet, in its rustic network of boughs, it has somehow enclosed a hint of spiritual beauty, and has become a true emblem of the subtile and ethereal mind that planned it. I made Eustace Bright sit down on a snow bank, which had heaped itself over the mossy seat, and gazing through the arched window opposite, he acknowledged that the scene at once grew picturesque.

"Simple as it looks," said he, "this little edifice seems to be the work of magic. It is full of suggestiveness, and, in its way, is as good as a cathedral. Ah, it would be just the spot for one to sit in, of a summer afternoon, and tell the children some more of those wild stories from the classic myths!"

"It would, indeed," answered I. "The summer house itself, so airy and so broken, is like one of those old tales, imperfectly remembered; and these living branches of the Baldwin apple tree, thrusting themselves so rudely in, are like your unwarrantable interpolations. But, by the by, have you added any more legends to the series, since the publication of the Wonder Book?"

"Many more," said Eustace; "Primrose, Periwinkle, and the rest of them, allow me no comfort of my life, unless I tell them a story every day or two. I have run away from home partly to escape the importunity of those little wretches. But I have written out six of the new stories, and have brought them for you to look over."

"Are they as good as the first?" I inquired.

"Better chosen, and better handled," replied

Eustace Bright. " You will say so when you read them."

" Possibly not," I remarked. " I know, from my own experience, that an author's last work is always his best one, in his own estimate, until it quite loses the red heat of composition. After that, it falls into its true place, quietly enough. But let us adjourn to my study, and examine these new stories. It would hardly be doing yourself justice, were you to bring me acquainted with them, sitting here on this snow bank ! "

So we descended the hill to my small, old cottage, and shut ourselves up in the south-eastern room, where the sunshine comes in, warmly and brightly, through the better half of a winter's day. Eustace put his bundle of manuscript into my hands ; and I skimmed through it pretty rapidly, trying to find out its merits and demerits by the touch of my fingers, as a veteran story teller ought to know how to do.

It will be remembered, that Mr. Bright condescended to avail himself of my literary experience by constituting me editor of the Wonder Book. As he had no reason to complain of

the reception of that erudite work, by the public
he was now disposed to retain me in a similar
position, with respect to the present volume,
which he entitled " TANGLEWOOD TALES." Not,
as Eustace hinted, that there was any real
necessity for my services as introductor, inasmuch as his own name had become established,
in some good degree of favor, with the literary
world. But the connection with myself, he was
kind enough to say, had been highly agreeable;
nor was he by any means desirous, as most
people are, of kicking away the ladder that had
perhaps helped him to reach his present eleva-
tion. My young friend was willing, in short,
that the fresh verdure of his growing reputation
should spread over my straggling and half-
naked boughs; even as I have sometimes thought
of training a vine, with its broad leafiness, and
purple fruitage, over the worm-eaten posts and
rafters of the rustic summer house. I was not
insensible to the advantages of his proposal, and
gladly assured him of my acceptance.

Merely from the titles of the stories, I saw at
once that the subjects were not less rich than
those of the former volume; nor did I at all

doubt that **Mr.** Bright's audacity (so far as that endowment might avail) had enabled him to take full advantage of whatever capabilities they offered. Yet, in spite of my experience of his free way of handling them, I did not quite see, I confess, how he could have obviated all the difficulties in the way of rendering them presentable to children. These old legends, so brimming over with every thing that is most abhorrent to our Christianized moral sense — some of them so hideous, others so melancholy and miserable, amid which the Greek tragedians sought their themes, and moulded them into the sternest forms of grief that ever the world saw; was such material the stuff that children's playthings should be made of! How were they to be purified? How was the blessed sunshine to be thrown into them?

But Eustace told me that these myths were the most singular things in the world, and that he was invariably astonished, whenever he began to relate one, by the readiness with which it adapted itself to the childish purity of his auditors. The objectionable characteristics seem to be a parasitical growth, having no essential

connection with the original fable. They fall
away, and are thought of no more, the instant
he puts his imagination in sympathy with the
innocent little circle, whose wide-open eyes are
fixed so eagerly upon him. Thus the stories
(not by any strained effort of the narrator's, but
in harmony with their inherent germ) transform
themselves, and reassume the shapes which
they might be supposed to possess in the pure
childhood of the world. When the first poet
or romancer told these marvellous legends, (such
is Eustace Bright's opinion,) it was still the
Golden Age. Evil had never yet existed; and
sorrow, misfortune, crime, were mere shadows
which the mind fancifully created for itself, as
a shelter against too sunny realities ; or, at
most, but prophetic dreams, to which the dream-
er himself did not yield a waking credence.
Children are now the only representatives of
the men and women of that happy era; and
therefore it is that we must raise the intellect
and fancy to the level of childhood, in order to
re-create the original myths.

I let the youthful author talk as much and
as extravagantly as he pleased, and was glad

to see him commencing life with such confidence in himself and his performances. A few years will do all that is necessary towards showing him the truth in both respects. Meanwhile, it is but right to say, he does really appear to have overcome the moral objections against these fables, although at the expense of such liberties with their structure as must be left to plead their own excuse, without any help from me. Indeed, except that there was a necessity for it, — and that the inner life of the legends cannot be come at save by making them entirely one's own property, — there is no defence to be made.

Eustace informed me that he had told his stories to the children in various situations — in the woods, on the shore of the lake, in the dell of Shadow Brook, in the play room, at Tanglewood fireside, and in a magnificent palace of snow, with ice windows, which he helped his little friends to build. His auditors were even more delighted with the contents of the present volume than with the specimens which have already been given to the world. The classically learned Mr. Pringle, too, had listened to two

or three of the tales, and censured them even
more bitterly than he did THE THREE GOLDEN
APPLES; so that, what with praise, and what
with criticism, Eustace Bright thinks that there
is good hope of at least as much success with
the public as in the case of the Wonder Book.

I made all sorts of inquiries about the chil
dren, not doubting that there would be great
eagerness to hear of their welfare, among some
good little folks who have written to me, to ask
for another volume of myths. They are all, I
am happy to say, (unless we except Clover,) in
excellent health and spirits. Primrose is now
almost a young lady, and, Eustace tells me, is
just as saucy as ever. She pretends to consider
herself quite beyond the age to be interested
by such idle stories as these; but, for all that,
whenever a story is to be told, Primrose never
fails to be one of the listeners, and to make fun
of it when finished. Periwinkle is very much
grown, and is expected to shut up her baby
house and throw away her doll in a month or
two more. Sweet Fern has learned to read and
write, and has put on a jacket and pair of pan-
taloons — all of which improvements I am sorry

for. Squash Blossom, Blue Eye, Plantain, and Buttercup have had the scarlet fever, but came easily through it. Huckleberry, Milkweed, and Dandelion were attacked with the hooping cough, but bore it bravely, and kept out of doors whenever the sun shone. Cowslip, dur- ing the autumn, had either the measles, or some eruption that looked very much like it, but was hardly sick a day. Poor Clover has been a good deal troubled with her second teeth, which have made her meagre in aspect and rather fractious in temper; nor, even when she smiles, is the matter much mended, since it discloses a gap just within her lips, almost as wide as the barn door. But all this will pass over, and it is predicted that she will turn out a very pretty girl.

As for Mr. Bright himself, he is now in his senior year at Williams College, and has a pros- pect of graduating with some degree of honor- able distinction at the next commencement. In his oration for the bachelor's degree, he gives me to understand, he will treat of the classical myths, viewed in the aspect of baby stories, and has a great mind to discuss the expediency of

2

using up the whole of ancient history, for the same purpose. I do not know what he means to do with himself after leaving college, but trust that, by dabbling so early with the danger-ous and seductive business of autnorship, he will not be tempted to become an author by profession. If so, I shall be very sorry for the little that I have had to do with the matter, in encouraging these first beginnings.

I wish there were any likelihood of my soon seeing Primrose, Periwinkle, Dandelion, Sweet Fern, Clover, Plantain, Huckleberry, Milkweed, Cowslip, Buttercup, Blue Eye, and Squash Blos-som again. But as I do not know when I shall revisit Tanglewood, and as Eustace Bright probably will not ask me to edit a third Wonder Book, the public of little folks must not expect to hear any more about those dear children from me. Heaven bless them, and every body else, whether grown people or children!

THE WAYSIDE, CONCORD, (MASS.,)
March 13, 1853.

THE MINOTAUR.

In the old city of Trœzene, at the foot of a lofty mountain, there lived, a very long time ago, a little boy named Theseus. His grandfather, King Pittheus, was the sovereign of that country, and was reckoned a very wise man; so that Theseus, being brought up in the royal palace, and being naturally a bright lad, could hardly fail of profiting by the old king's instructions. His mother's name was Æthra. As for his father, the boy had never seen him. But, from his earliest remembrance, Æthra used to go with little Theseus into a wood, and sit down upon a moss-grown rock, which was deeply sunken into the earth. Here she often talked with her son about his father, and said that he was called Ægeus, and that he was a great king, and ruled over Attica, and dwelt at Athens,

which was as famous a city as any in the world.
Theseus was very fond of hearing about King
Ægeus, and often asked his good mother Æthra
why he did not come and live with them at
Trœzene.

"Ah, my dear son," answered Æthra, with a
sigh, "a monarch has his people to take care of.
The men and women over whom he rules are
in the place of children to him; and he can seldom spare time to love his own children as other
parents do. Your father will never be able to
leave his kingdom for the sake of seeing his
little boy."

"Well, but, dear mother," asked the boy, "why
cannot I go to this famous city of Athens, and
tell King Ægeus that I am his son?"

"That may happen by and by," said Æthra.
"Be patient, and we shall see. You are not yet
big and strong enough to set out on such an
errand."

"And how soon shall I be strong enough?"
Theseus persisted in inquiring.

"You are but a tiny boy as yet," replied his
mother. "See if you can lift this rock on which
we are sitting?"

The little fellow had a great opinion of his own strength. So, grasping the rough protuberances of the rock, he tugged and toiled amain, and got himself quite out of breath, without being able to stir the heavy stone. It seemed to be rooted into the ground. No wonder he could not move it; for it would have taken all the force of a very strong man to lift it out of its earthy bed.

His mother stood looking on, with a sad kind of a smile on her lips and in her eyes, to see the zealous and yet puny efforts of her little boy. She could not help being sorrowful at finding him already so impatient to begin his adventures in the world.

" You see how it is, my dear Theseus," said she. " You must possess far more strength than now before I can trust you to go to Athens, and tell King Ægeus that you are his son. But when you can lift this rock, and show me what is hidden beneath it, I promise you my permission to depart."

Often and often, after this, did Theseus ask his mother whether it was yet time for him to go to Athens, and still his mother pointed to the

rock, and told him that, for years to come, he
could not be strong enough to move it. And
again and again the rosy-cheeked and curly
headed boy would tug and strain at the huge
mass of stone, striving, child as he was, to do
what a giant could hardly have done without
taking both of his great hands to the task.
Meanwhile the rock seemed to be sinking farther and farther into the ground. The moss
grew over it thicker and thicker, until at last it
looked almost like a soft green seat, with only a
few gray knobs of granite peeping out. The
overhanging trees, also, shed their brown leaves
upon it, as often as the autumn came ; and at
its base grew ferns and wild flowers, some of
which crept quite over its surface. To all appearance, the rock was as firmly fastened as any
other portion of the earth's substance.

But, difficult as the matter looked, Theseus
was now growing up to be such a vigorous
youth, that, in his own opinion, the time would
quickly come when he might hope to get the
upper hand of this ponderous lump of stone.

"Mother, I do believe it has started!" cried
he, after one of his attempts. "The earth
around it is certainly a little cracked!"

' No, no, child!" his mother hastily answered.
' It is not possible you can have moved it,
such a boy as you still are!"

Nor would she be convinced, although Theseus showed her the place where he fancied that
the stem of a flower had been partly uprooted
by the movement of the rock. But Æthra
sighed, and looked disquieted; for, no doubt,
she began to be conscious that her son was
no longer a child, and that, in a little while
hence, she must send him forth among the
perils and troubles of the world.

It was not more than a year afterwards when
they were again sitting on the moss-covered
stone. Æthra had once more told him the oft-
repeated story of his father, and how gladly he
would receive Theseus at his stately palace, and
how he would present him to his courtiers and
the people, and tell them that here was the heir
of his dominions. The eyes of Theseus glowed
with enthusiasm, and he would hardly sit still to
hear his mother speak.

" Dear mother Æthra," he exclaimed, " I never
felt half so strong as now! I am no longer a
child, nor a boy, nor a mere youth! I feel my-

self a man! It is now time to make one earnest
trial to remove the stone."

"Ah, my dearest Theseus," replied his mother,
" not yet! not yet!"

" Yes, mother," said he, resolutely, " the time
has come."

Then Theseus bent himself in good earnest to
the task, and strained every sinew, with manly
strength and resolution. He put his whole brave
heart into the effort. He wrestled with the big
and sluggish stone, as if it had been a living
enemy. He heaved, he lifted, he resolved now
to succeed, or else to perish there, and let the
rock be his monument forever! Æthra stood
gazing at him, and clasped her hands, partly
with a mother's pride, and partly with a mother's
sorrow. The great rock stirred! Yes, it was
raised slowly from the bedded moss and earth,
uprooting the shrubs and flowers along with it,
and was turned upon its side. Theseus had
conquered!

While taking breath, he looked joyfully at his
mother, and she smiled upon him through her
tears.

" Yes, Theseus," she said, " the time has come

and you must stay no longer at my side! See
what King Ægeus, your royal father, left for
you, beneath the stone, when he lifted it in his
mighty arms, and laid it on the spot whence
you have now removed it."

Theseus looked, and saw that the rock had
been placed over another slab of stone, containing a cavity within it; so that it somewhat
resembled a roughly-made chest or coffer, of
which the upper mass had served as the lid.
Within the cavity lay a sword, with a golden
hilt, and a pair of sandals.

" That was your father's sword," said Æthra,
" and those were his sandals. When he went to
be king of Athens, he bade me treat you as a
child until you should prove yourself a man by
lifting this heavy stone. That task being accomplished, you are to put on his sandals, in order
to follow in your father's footsteps, and to gird
on his sword, so that you may fight giants and
dragons, as King Ægeus did in his youth."

" I will set out for Athens this very day!"
cried Theseus.

. But his mother persuaded him to stay a day
or two longer, while she got ready some neces-

sary articles for his journey. When his grand
father, the wise King Pittheus, heard that The·
seus intended to present himself at his father's
palace, he earnestly advised him to get on board
of a vessel, and go by sea; because he might
thus arrive within fifteen miles of Athens, with·
out either fatigue or danger.

" The roads are very bad by land," quoth the
venerable king; " and they are terribly infested
with robbers and monsters. A mere lad, like
Theseus, is not fit to be trusted on such a perilous journey, all by himself. No, no; let him go
by sea ! "

But when Theseus heard of robbers and monsters, he pricked up his ears, and was so much
the more eager to take the road along which
they were to be met with. On the third day,
therefore, he bade a respectful farewell to his
grandfather, thanking him for all his kindness;
and, after affectionately embracing his mother,
he set forth, with a good many of her tears glistening on his cheeks, and some, if the truth
must be told, that had gushed out of his own
eyes. But he let the sun and wind dry them,
and walked stoutly on, playing with the golden

hilt of his sword, and taking very manly strides in his father's sandals.

I cannot stop to tell you hardly any of the adventures that befell Theseus on the road to Athens It is enough to say, that he quite cleared that part of the country of the robbers, about whom King Pittheus had been so much alarmed. One of these bad people was named Procrustes; and he was indeed a terrible fellow, and had an ugly way of making fun of the poor travellers who happened to fall into his clutches. In his cavern he had a bed, on which, with great pretence of hospitality, he invited his guests to lie down; but if they happened to be shorter than the bed, this wicked villain stretched them out by main force; or, if they were too tall, he lopped off their heads or feet, and laughed at what he had done, as an excellent joke. Thus, however weary a man might be, he never liked to lie in the bed of Procrustes. Another of these robbers, named Scinis, must likewise have been a very great scoundrel. He was in the habit of flinging his victims off a hign cliff into the sea; and, in order to give him exactly his deserts, Theseus tossed him off the very same place. But if yon

will believe me, the sea would not pollute itself
by receiving such a bad person into its bosom
neither would the earth, having once got rid of
him, consent to take him back; so that, between
the cliff and the sea, Scinis stuck fast in the air,
which was forced to bear the burden of his
naughtiness.

After these memorable deeds, Theseus heard
of an enormous sow, which ran wild, and was
the terror of all the farmers round about; and,
as he did not consider himself above doing any
good thing that came in his way, he killed this
monstrous creature, and gave the carcass to the
poor people for bacon.   The great sow had been
an awful beast, while ramping about the woods
and fields, but was a pleasant object enough
when cut up into joints, and smoking on I
know not how many dinner tables.

Thus, by the time he reached his journey's
end, Theseus had done many valiant feats
with his father's golden-hilted sword, and had
gained the renown of being one of the bravest
young men of the day. His fame travelled
faster than he did, and reached Athens before
him. As he entered the city, he heard th

inhabitants talking at the street corners, and saying that Hercules was brave, and Jason too, and Castor and Pollux likewise, but that Theseus, the son of their own king, would turn out as great a hero as the best of them. Theseus took longer strides on hearing this, and fancied himself sure of a magnificent reception at his father's court, since he came thither with Fame to blow her trumpet before him, and cry to King Ægeus, " Behold your son ! "

He little suspected, innocent youth that he was, that here, in this very Athens, where his father reigned, a greater danger awaited him than any which he had encountered on the road. Yet this was the truth. You must understand that the father of Theseus, though not very old in years, was almost worn out with the cares of government, and had thus grown aged before his time. His nephews, not expecting him to live a very great while, intended to get all the power of the kingdom into their own hands. But when they heard that Theseus had arrived in Athens, and learned what a gallant young man he was, they saw that he would not be at all the kind of person to let them steal away his father's crown and sceptre, which ought to be his own by right of inheritance. Thus these bad-hearteo nephews of King Ægeus, who were the own cousins of Theseus, at once became his enemies. A still more dangerous enemy was Medea, the wicked enchantress; for she was now the king's wife, and wanted to give the kingdom to her son Medus, instead of letting it be given to the son of Æthra, whom she hated.

It so happened that the king's nephews met Theseus, and found out who he was, just as he reached the entrance of the royal palace. With all their evil designs against him, they pretended to be their cousin's best friends, and expressed great joy at making his acquaintance. They proposed to him that he should come into the king's presence as a stranger, in order to try whether Ægeus would discover in the young man's features any likeness either to himself or his mother Æthra, and thus recognize him for a son. Theseus consented; for he fancied that his father would know him in a moment, by the love that was in his heart. But, while he waited at the door, the nephews ran and told King Ægeus that a young man had arrived in Athens who, to their certain knowledge, intended to put him to death, and get possession of his royal crown.

" And he is now waiting for admission to your majesty's presence," added they.

" Aha! " cried the old king, on hearing this. " Why, he must be a very wicked young fellow indeed! Pray, what would you advise me to do with him ? "

In reply to this question, the wicked Medea put in her word. As I have already told you, she was a famous enchantress. According to some stories, she was in the habit of boiling old people in a large caldron, under pretence of making them young again ; but King Ægeus, I suppose, did not fancy such an uncomfortable way of growing young, or perhaps was contented to be old, and therefore would never let himself be popped into the caldron. If there were time to spare from more important matters, I should be glad to tell you of Medea's fiery chariot, drawn by winged dragons, in which the enchantress used often to take an airing among the clouds. This chariot, in fact, was the vehicle that first brought her to Athens, where she had done nothing but

mischief ever since her arrival. But these and
many other wonders must be left untold; and it
is enough to say, that Medea, amongst a thousand other bad things, knew how to prepare a
poison, that was instantly fatal to whomsoever
might so much as touch it with his lips.

So, when the king asked what he should do
with Theseus, this naughty woman had an
answer ready at her tongue's end.

"Leave that to me, please your majesty," she
replied. "Only admit this evil-minded young
man to your presence, treat him civilly, and in-
vite him to drink a goblet of wine. Your majesty is well aware that I sometimes amuse
myself with distilling very powerful medicines
Here is one of them in this small phial. As to
what it is made of, that is one of my secrets of
state. Do but let me put a single drop into the
goblet, and let the young man taste it; and I
will answer for it, he shall quite lay aside the
bad designs with which he comes hither."

As she said this, Medea smiled; but, for all
her smiling face, she meant nothing less than to
poison the poor innocent Theseus, before his
father's eyes. And King Ægeus, like most other

kings thought any punishment mild enough for
a person who was accused of plotting against
his life. He therefore made little or no objec-
tion to Medea's scheme, and as soon as the
poisonous wine was ready, gave orders that the
young stranger should be admitted into his
presence. The goblet was set on a table
beside the king's throne; and a fly, meaning
just to sip a little from the brim, immediately
tumbled into it, dead. Observing this, Medea
looked round at the nephews, and smiled again.

When Theseus was ushered into the royal
apartment, the only object that he seemed to
behold was the white-bearded old king. There
he sat on his magnificent throne, a dazzling
crown on his head, and a sceptre in his hand.
His aspect was stately and majestic, although
his years and infirmities weighed heavily upon
him, as if each year were a lump of lead, and
each infirmity a ponderous stone, and all were
bundled up together, and laid upon his weary
shoulders. The tears both of joy and sorrow
sprang into the young man's eyes; for he thought
how sad it was to see his dear father so infirm,
and how sweet it would be to support him with

3

his own youthful strength, and to cheer him up
with the alacrity of his loving spirit.   When a
son takes his father into his warm heart, it
renews the old man's youth in a better way
than by the heat of Medea's magic caldron.
And this was what Theseus resolved to do.   He
could scarcely wait to see whether King Ægeus
would recognize him, so eager was he to throw
himself into his arms.

Advancing to the foot of the throne, he attempted to make a little speech, which he had
been thinking about, as he came up the stairs.
But he was almost choked by a great many
tender feelings that gushed out of his heart
and swelled into his throat, all struggling to find
utterance together.   And therefore, unless he
could have laid his full, over-brimming heart
into the king's hand, poor Theseus knew not
what to do or say.   The cunning Medea observed what was passing in the young man's
mind.   She was more wicked at that moment
than ever she had been before; for (and it makes
me tremble to tell you of it) she did her worst
to turn all this unspeakable love with which
Theseus was agitated, to his own ruin and
destruction.

" Does your majesty see his confusion?" she whispered in the king's ear. " He is so con scious of guilt, that he trembles and cannot speak. The wretch lives too long! Quick! offer him the wine!"

Now King Ægeus had been gazing earnestly at the young stranger, as he drew near the throne. There was something, he knew not what, either in his white brow, or in the fine expression of his mouth, or in his beautiful and tender eyes, that made him indistinctly feel as if he had seen this youth before; as if, indeed, he had trotted him on his knee when a baby, and had beheld him growing to be a stalwart man, while he himself grew old. But Medea guessed how the king felt, and would not suffer him to yield to these natural sensibilities; although they were the voice of his deepest heart, telling him, as plainly as it could speak, that here was our dear son, and Æthra's son, coming to claim him for a father. The enchantress again whispered in the king's ear, and compelled him, by her witchcraft, to see every thing under a false aspect.

He made up his mind, therefore, to let Theseus drink off the poisoned wine.

"Young man," said he, "you are welcome !
I am proud to show hospitality to so heroic a
youth. Do me the favor to drink the contents
of this goblet. It is brimming over, as you see,
with delicious wine, such as I bestow only on
those who are worthy of it! None is more worthy to quaff it than yourself!"

So saying, King Ægeus took the golden goblet from the table, and was about to offer it to
Theseus. But, partly through his infirmities,
and partly because it seemed so sad a thing to
take away this young man's life, however wicked
he might be, and partly, no doubt, because his
heart was wiser than his head, and quaked within him at the thought of what he was going to
do — for all these reasons, the king's hand trembled so much that a great deal of the wine
slopped over. In order to strengthen his purpose, and fearing lest the whole of the precious
poison should be wasted, one of his nephews
now whispered to him, —

"Has your majesty any doubt of this stranger's guilt? There is the very sword with
which he meant to slay you. How sharp, and
bright, and terrible it is! Quick! — let him

taste the wine; or perhaps he may do the deed even yet."

At these words, Ægeus drove every thought and feeling out of his breast, except the one idea of how justly the young man deserved to be put to death. He sat erect on his throne, and held out the goblet of wine with a steady hand, and bent on Theseus a frown of kingly severity; for, after all, he had too noble a spirit to murder even a treacherous enemy with a deceitful smile upon his face.

"Drink!" said he, in the stern tone with which he was wont to condemn a criminal to be be-headed. "You have well deserved of me such wine as this!"

Theseus held out his hand to take the wine. But, before he touched it, King Ægeus trembled again. His eyes had fallen on the gold-hilted sword that hung at the young man's side. He drew back the goblet.

"That sword!" he exclaimed; "how came you by it?"

"It was my father's sword," replied Theseus with a tremulous voice. "These were his san-dals. My dear mother (her name is Æthra) told me his story while I was yet a little child. But it is only a month since I grew strong enough to lift the heavy stone, and take the sword and sandals from beneath it, and come to Athens to seek my father."

"My son! my son!" cried King Ægeus, flinging away the fatal goblet, and tottering down from the throne to fall into the arms of Theseus. "Yes, these are Æthra's eyes. It is my son."

I have quite forgotten what became of the king's nephews. But when the wicked Medea saw this new turn of affairs, she hurried out of the room, and going to her private chamber, lost no time in setting her enchantments at work. In a few moments, she heard a great noise of hissing snakes outside of the chamber window; and, behold! there was her fiery chariot, and four huge winged serpents, wriggling and twisting in the air, flourishing their tails higher than the top of the palace, and all ready to set off on an aerial journey. Medea staid only long enough to take her son with her, and to steal the crown jewels, together with the king's best robes, and whatever other valuable things she could lay hands on; and getting into the chariot, she whipped up the snakes, and ascended high over the city.

The king, hearing the hiss of the serpents, scrambled as fast as he could to the window, and bawled out to the abominable enchantress never to come back. The whole people of Athens, too, who had run out of doors to see this wonderful spectacle, set up a shout of joy at the prospect of getting rid of her. Medea, almost bursting with rage, uttered precisely such a hiss as one of her own snakes, only ten times more venomous and spiteful; and glaring fiercely out of the blaze of the chariot, she shook her hands over the multitude below, as if she were scattering a million of curses among them. In so doing, however, she unintentionally let fall about five hundred diamonds of the first water, together with a thousand great pearls, and two thousand emeralds, rubies, sapphires, opals, and topazes, to which she had helped herself out of the king's strong box. All these came pelting down, like a shower of many-colored hailstones, upon the heads of grown people and children, who forthwith gathered them up, and carried them back to the palace. But King Ægeus told

them that they were welcome to the whole, and
to twice as many more, if he had them, for the
sake of his delight at finding his son, and losing
the wicked Medea. And, indeed, if you had
seen how hateful was her last look, as the flam·
ing chariot flew upward, you would not have
wondered that both king and people should
think her departure a good riddance.

And now Prince Theseus was taken into great
favor by his royal father. The old king was
never weary of having him sit beside him on his
throne, (which was quite wide enough for two,)
and of hearing him tell about his dear mother,
and his childhood, and his many boyish efforts
to lift the ponderous stone. Theseus, however,
was much too brave and active a young man to
be willing to spend all his time in relating things
which had already happened. His ambition
was to perform other and more heroic deeds,
which should be better worth telling in prose
and verse. Nor had he been long in Athens be·
fore he caught and chained a terrible mad bull,
and made a public show of him, greatly to the
wonder and admiration of good King Ægeus
and his subjects. But pretty soon, he undertook

an affair that made all his foregone adventures seem like mere boy's play. The occasion of it was as follows: —

One morning, when Prince Theseus awoke, he fancied that he must have had a very sorrowful dream, and that it was still running in his mind, even now that his eyes were open. For it appeared as if the air was full of a melancholy wail; and when he listened more attentively, he could hear sobs, and groans, and screams of woe, mingled with deep, quiet sighs, which came from the king's palace, and from the streets, and from the temples, and from every habitation in the city. And all these mournful noises, issuing out of thousands of separate hearts, united themselves into the one great sound of affliction, which had startled Theseus from slumber. He put on his clothes as quickly as he could, (not forgetting his sandals and gold-hilted sword,) and hastening to the king, inquired what it all meant.

"Alas! my son," quoth King Ægeus, heaving a long sigh, "here is a very lamentable matter in hand! This is the wofulest anniversary in the whole year   It is the day when we annually draw lots to see which of the youths and maidens of Athens shall go to be devoured by the horrible Minotaur!"

" The Minotaur!" exclaimed Prince Theseus · and like a brave young prince as he was, he put his hand to the hilt of his sword. " What kind of a monster may that be? Is it not possible, at the risk of one's life, to slay him?"

But King Ægeus shook his venerable head, and to convince Theseus that it was quite a hopeless case, he gave him an explanation of the whole affair. It seems that in the Island of Crete there lived a certain dreadful monster, called a Minotaur, which was shaped partly like a man and partly like a bull, and was altogether such a hideous sort of a creature that it is really disagreeable to think of him. If he were suffered to exist at all, it should have been on some desert island, or in the duskiness of some deep cavern, where nobody would ever be tormented by his abominable aspect. But King Minos, who reigned over Crete, laid out a vast deal of money in building a habitation for the Minotaur, and took great care of his health and comfort, merely for mischief's sake. A

few years before this time, there had been a
war between the city of Athens and the island
of Crete, in which the Athenians were beaten,
and compelled to beg for peace. No peace
could they obtain, however, except on condition
that they should send seven young men and
seven maidens, every year, to be devoured
by the pet monster of the cruel King Minos.
For three years past, this grievous calamity
had been borne. And the sobs, and groans,
and shrieks, with which the city was now filled,
were caused by the people's woe, because the
fatal day had come again, when the fourteen
victims were to be chosen by lot; and the old
people feared lest their sons or daughters might
be taken, and the youths and damsels dreaded
lest they themselves might be destined to glut
the ravenous maw of that detestable man-
brute.

But when Theseus heard the story, he straight-
ened himself up, so that he seemed taller than
ever before; and as for his face, it was indig-
nant, despiteful, bold, tender, and compassion-
ate, all in one look.

"Let the people of Athens, this year, draw

lots for only six young men, instead of seven," said he. "I will myself be the seventh; and let the Minotaur devour me, if he can!"

"O my dear son," cried King Ægeus, "why should you expose yourself to this horrible fate? You are a royal prince, and have a right to hold yourself above the destinies of common men."

"It is because I am a prince, your son, and the rightful heir of your kingdom, that I freely take upon me the calamity of your subjects," answered Theseus. "And you my father, being king over this people, and answerable to Heaven for their welfare, are bound to sacrifice what is dearest to you, rather than that the son or daughter of the poorest citizen should come to any harm."

The old king shed tears, and besought Theseus not to leave him desolate in his old age, more especially as he had but just begun to know the happiness of possessing a good and valiant son. Theseus, however, felt that he was in the right, and therefore would not give up his resolution But he assured his father that he did not intend to be eaten up, unresistingly, like a sheep, and that, if the Minotaur devoured him, it should not be without a battle for his dinner. And finally, since he could not help it, King Ægeus consented to let him go. So a vessel was got ready, and rigged with black sails; and Theseus, with six other young men, and seven tender and beautiful damsels, came down to the harbor to embark. A sorrowful multitude accompanied them to the shore. There was the poor old king, too, leaning on his son's arm, and looking as if his single heart held all the grief of Athens.

Just as Prince Theseus was going on board, his father bethought himself of one last word to say.

"My beloved son," said he, grasping the prince's hand, "you observe that the sails of this vessel are black; as indeed they ought to be, since it goes upon a voyage of sorrow and despair. Now, being weighed down with infirmities, I know not whether I can survive till the vessel shall return. But, as long as I do live, I shall creep daily to the top of yonder cliff, to watch if there be a sail upon the sea. And, dearest Theseus, if, by some happy chance, you should escape the jaws of the Minotaur,

then tear down those dismal sails, and hoist
others that shall be bright as the sunshine.
Beholding them on the horizon, myself and all
the people will know that you are coming back
victorious, and will welcome you with such a
festal uproar as Athens never heard before."

Theseus promised that he would do so. Then,
going on board, the mariners trimmed the vessel's black sails to the wind, which blew faintly
off the shore, being pretty much made up of
the sighs that every body kept pouring forth on
this melancholy occasion. But by and by,
when they had got fairly out to sea, there came
a stiff breeze from the north-west, and drove
them along as merrily over the white-capped
waves as if they had been going on the most
delightful errand imaginable. And though it
was a sad business enough, I rather question
whether fourteen young people, without any
old persons to keep them in order, could continue to spend the whole time of the voyage
in being miserable. There had been some few
dances upon the undulating deck, I suspect,
and some hearty bursts of laughter, and other
such unseasonable merriment among the vic-

tims, before the high, blue mountains of Crete began to show themselves among the far-off clouds. That sight, to be sure, made them all very grave again.

Theseus stood among the sailors, gazing eagerly towards the land; although, as yet, it seemed hardly more substantial than the clouds, amidst which the mountains were looming up. Once or twice, he fancied that he saw a glare of some bright object, a long way off, flinging a gleam across the waves.

" Did you see that flash of light? " he inquired of the master of the vessel.

" No, prince; but I have seen it before," answered the master. " It came from Talus, I suppose."

As the breeze came fresher just then, the master was busy with trimming his sails, and had no more time to answer questions. But while the vessel flew faster and faster towards Crete, Theseus was astonished to behold a human figure, gigantic in size, which appeared to be striding, with a measured movement, along the margin of the island. It stepped from cliff to cliff, and sometimes from one headland to

another, while the sea foamed and thundered on
the shore beneath, and dashed its jets of spray
over the giant's feet.   What was still more remarkable, whenever the sun shone on this huge
figure, it flickered and glimmered; its vast countenance, too, had a metallic lustre, and threw
great flashes of splendor through the air.   The
folds of its garments, moreover, instead of waving
in the wind, fell heavily over its limbs, as if
woven of some kind of metal.

The nigher the vessel came, the more Theseus
wondered what this immense giant could be
and whether it actually had life or no.   For
though it walked, and made other lifelike mo
tions, there yet was a kind of jerk in its gait,
which, together with its brazen aspect, caused
the young prince to suspect that it was no true
giant, but only a wonderful piece of machinery.
The figure looked all the more terrible because
it carried an enormous brass club on its shoulder.

"What is this wonder?" Theseus asked of
the master of the vessel, who was now at leisure
to answer him.

"It is Talus, the Man of Brass," said the
master.

"And is he a live giant, or a brazen image?" asked Theseus.

"That, truly," replied the master, "is the point which has always perplexed me. Some say, indeed, that this Talus was hammered out for King Minos by Vulcan himself, the skilfulest of all workers in metal. But who ever saw a brazen image that had sense enough to walk round an island three times a day, as this giant walks round the Island of Crete, challenging every vessel that comes nigh the shore? And, on the other hand, what living thing, unless his sinews were made of brass, would not be weary of marching eighteen hundred miles in the twenty-four hours, as Talus does, without ever sitting down to rest? He is a puzzler, take him how you will."

Still the vessel went bounding onward; and now Theseus could hear the brazen clangor of the giant's footsteps, as he trod heavily upon the sea-beaten rocks, some of which were seen to crack and crumble into the foamy waves beneath his weight. As they approached the entrance of the port, the giant straddled clear across it, with a foot firmly planted on each

headland, and uplifting his club to such a height
that its but-end was hidden in a cloud, he stood
in that formidable posture, with the sun gleaming all over his metallic surface.   There seemed
nothing else to be expected but that, the next
moment, he would fetch his great club down,
slam bang, and smash the vessel into a thousand
pieces, without heeding how many innccent
people he might destroy; for there is seldom any
mercy in a giant, you know, and quite as little
in a piece of brass clockwork.   But just when
Theseus and his companions thought the blow
was coming, the brazen lips unclosed themselves,
and the figure spoke.

" Whence come you, strangers ? "

And when the ringing voice ceased, there was
just such a reverberation as you may have heard
within a great church bell, for a moment or two
after the stroke of the hammer.

" From Athens!" shouted the master in reply.

" On what errand ? " thundered the Man of
Brass.

And he whirled his club aloft more threaten
ingly than ever, as if he were about to smite
them with a thunderstroke right amidships, be

cause Athens, so little while ago, had been at war witn Crete.

" We bring the seven youths and the seven maidens," answered the master, " to be devoured by the Minotaur ! "

" Pass ! " cried the brazen giant.

That one loud word rolled all about the sky, while again there was a booming reverberation within the figure's breast. The vessel glided between the headlands of the port, and the giant resumed his march. In a few moments, this wondrous sentinel was far away, flashing in the distant sunshine, and revolving with im mense strides around the Island of Crete, as it was his never-ceasing task to do.

No sooner had they entered the harbor than a party of the guards of King Minos came down to the water side, and took charge of the fourteen young men and damsels. Surrounded by these armed warriors, Prince Theseus and his companions were led to the king's palace, and ushered into his presence. Now, Minos was a stern and pitiless king. If the figure that guarded Crete was made of brass, then the monarch, who ruled over it, might be thought to have a still harder metal in his breast, and might have been called a man of iron. He bent his shaggy brows upon the poor Athenian victims. Any other mortal, beholding their fresh and tender beauty, and their innocent looks, would have felt himself sitting on thorns until he had made every soul of them happy, by bidding them go free as the summer wind. But this immitigable Minos cared only to examine whether they were plump enough to satisfy the Minotaur's appetite. For my part, I wish he himself had been the only victim ; and the monster would have found him a pretty tough one.

One after another, King Minos called these pale, frightened youths and sobbing maidens to his footstool, gave them each a poke in the ribs with his sceptre, (to try whether they were in good flesh or no,) and dismissed them with a nod to his guards. But when his eyes rested on Theseus, the king looked at him more attentively, because his face was calm and brave.

" Young man," asked he, with his stern voice, " are you not appalled at the certainty of being devoured by this terrible Minotaur ? "

" I have offered my life in a good cause."

answered Theseus, " and therefore I give it freely and gladly. But thou, King Minos, art thou not thyself appalled, who, year after year, hast perpetrated this dreadful wrong, by giving seven innocent youths and as many maidens to be devoured by a monster? Dost thou not tremble, wicked king, to turn thine eyes inward on thine own heart? Sitting there on thy golden throne, and in thy robes of majesty, I tell thee to thy face, King Minos, thou art a more hideous monster than the Minotaur himself!"

" Aha! do you think me so?" cried the king, laughing in his cruel way. " To-morrow, at breakfast time, you shall have an opportunity of judging which is the greater monster, the Minotaur or the king! Take them away, guards; and let this free-spoken youth be the Minotaur's first morsel!"

Near the king's throne (though I had no time to tell you so before) stood his daughter Ariadne. She was a beautiful and tender-hearted maiden, and looked at these poor doomed captives with very different feelings from those of the iron-breasted King Minos. She really wept, indeed, at the idea of how much human

happiness would be needlessly thrown away, **by**
giving so many young people, in the first **bloom**
and rose blossom of their lives, to be eaten **up**
by a creature who, no doubt, would have **pre-**
ferred a fat ox, or even a large pig, **to the**
plumpest of them.   And when she beheld **the**
brave, spirited figure of Prince Theseus bearing
himself so calmly in his terrible peril, she grew
a hundred times more pitiful than before.   As
the guards were taking him away, she flung
herself at the king's feet, and besought him to
set all the captives free, and especially this one
young man.

   " Peace, foolish girl!" answered King Minos.
" What hast thou to do with an affair like this?
It is a matter of state policy, and therefore quite
beyond thy weak comprehension.   Go water
thy flowers, and think no more of these Athenian caitiffs, whom the Minotaur shall as cer
tainly eat up for breakfast as I will eat a par-
tridge for my supper."

   So saying, the king looked cruel enough to
devour Theseus and all the rest of the captives,
himself, had there been no Minotaur to save him
the trouble.   As he would hear not another

word in their favor, the prisoners were now led away, and clapped into a dungeon, where the jailer advised them to go to sleep as soon as possible, because the Minotaur was in the habit of calling for breakfast early. The seven maidens and six of the young men soon sobbed themselves to slumber. But Theseus was not like them. He felt conscious that he was wiser, and braver, and stronger than his companions, and that therefore he had the responsibility of all their lives upon him, and must consider whether there was no way to save them, even in this last extremity. So he kept himself awake, and paced to and fro across the gloomy dungeon in which they were shut up.

Just before midnight, the door was softly unbarred, and the gentle Ariadne showed herself, with a torch in her hand.

" Are you awake, Prince Theseus ? " she whispered.

" Yes," answered Theseus. " With so little time to live, I do not choose to waste any of it in sleep."

" Then follow me," said Ariadne, " and tread softly."

What had become of the jailer and the guards, Theseus never knew. But, however that might be, Ariadne opened all the doors, and led him forth from the darksome prison into the pleasant moonlight.

"Theseus," said the maiden, "you can now get on board your vessel, and sail away for Athens."

"No," answered the young man; "I will never leave Crete unless I can first slay the Minotaur, and save my poor companions, and deliver Athens from this cruel tribute."

"I knew that this would be your resolution," said Ariadne. "Come, then, with me, brave Theseus. Here is your own sword, which the guards deprived you of. You will need it; and pray Heaven you may use it well."

Then she led Theseus along by the hand until they came to a dark, shadowy grove, where the moonlight wasted itself on the tops of the trees, without shedding hardly so much as a glimmering beam upon their pathway. After going a good way through this obscurity, they reached a high, marble wall, which was overgrown with creeping plants, that made it shaggy with their verdure. The wall seemed to have no door, nor any. windows, but rose up, lofty, and massive, and mysterious, and was neither to be clambered over, nor, so far as Theseus could perceive, to be passed through. Nevertheless, Ariadne did but press one of her soft little fingers against a particular block of marble, and, though it looked as solid as any other part of the wall, it yielded to her touch, disclosing an entrance just wide enough to admit them. They crept through, and the marble stone swung back into its place.

"We are now," said Ariadne, "in the famous labyrinth which Dædalus built before he made himself a pair of wings, and flew away from our island like a bird. That Dædalus was a very cunning workman; but of all his artful con- trivances, this labyrinth is the most wondrous Were we to take but a few steps from the door- way, we might wander about all our lifetime, and never find it again. Yet in the very centre of this labyrinth is the Minotaur; and, Theseus, you must go thither to seek him."

"But how shall I ever find him," asked The- seus, "if the labyrinth so bewilders me as you say it will?"

Just as he spoke, they heard a rough and very disagreeable roar, which greatly resembled the lowing of a fierce bull, but yet had some sort of sound like the human voice. Theseus even fancied a rude articulation in it, as if the creature that uttered it were trying to shape his hoarse breath into words. It was at some distance, however, and he really could not tell whether it sounded most like a bull's roar or a man's harsh voice.

"That is the Minotaur's noise," whispered Ariadne, closely grasping the hand of Theseus, and pressing one of her own hands to her heart, which was all in a tremble. "You must follow that sound through the windings of the labyrinth, and, by and by, you will find him. Stay! take the end of this silken string; I will hold the other end; and then, if you win the victory, it will lead you again to this spot. Farewell, brave Theseus."

So the young man took the end of the silken string in his left hand, and his gold-hilted sword, ready drawn from its scabbard, in the other, and trod boldly into the inscrutable labyrinth. How this labyrinth was built is more than I can tel you. But so cunningly contrived a mizmaze

was never seen in the world, before nor since.
There can be nothing else so intricate, unless it
were the brain of a man like Dædalus, who
planned it, or the heart of any ordinary man;
which last, to be sure, is ten times as great a
mystery as the labyrinth of Crete. Theseus had
not taken five steps before he lost sight of Ariadne; and in five more his head was growing
dizzy. But still he went on; now creeping
through a low arch, now ascending a flight of
steps, now in one crooked passage, and now in
another, with here a door opening before him,
and there one banging behind, until it really
seemed as if the walls spun round, and whirled
him round along with them. And all the while,
through these hollow avenues, now nearer, now
farther off again, resounded the cry of the Minotaur; and the sound was so fierce, so cruel, so
ugly, so like a bull's roar, and withal so like a
human voice, and yet like neither of them, that
the brave heart of Theseus grew sterner and
angrier at every step; for he felt it an insult
to the moon and sky, and to our affectionate
and simple Mother Earth, that such a monster
should have the audacity to exist.

As he passed onward, the clouds gathered over the moon, and the labyrinth grew so dusky that Theseus could no longer discern the bewilderment through which he was passing. He would have felt quite lost, and utterly hopeless of ever again walking in a straight path, if, every little while, he had not been conscious of a gentle twitch at the silken cord. Then he knew that the tender-hearted Ariadne was still holding the other end, and that she was fearing for him, and hoping for him, and giving him just as much of her sympathy as if she were close by his side. O, indeed, I can assure you, there was a vast deal of human sympathy running along that slender thread of silk. But still he followed the dreadful roar of the Minotaur, which now grew louder and louder, and finally so very loud that Theseus fully expected to come close upon him, at every new zigzag and wriggle of the path. And at last, in an open space, at the very centre of the labyrinth, he did discern the hideous creature.

Sure enough, what an ugly monster it was! Only his horned head belonged to a bull; and yet, somehow or other, he looked like a bull all

over, preposterously waddling on his hind legs;
or if you happened to view him in another way,
he seemed wholly a man, and all the more monstrous for being so.   And there he was, the
wretched thing, with no society, no companion,
no kind of a mate, living only to do mischief,
and incapable of knowing what affection means.
Theseus hated him, and shuddered at him, and
yet could not but be sensible of some sort of
pity; and all the more, the uglier and more detestable the creature was.   For he kept striding
to and fro, in a solitary frenzy of rage, continually emitting a hoarse roar, which was oddly
mixed up with half-shaped words; and, after
listening a while, Theseus understood that the
Minotaur was saying to himself how miserable
he was, and how hungry, and how he hated
every body, and how he longed to eat up the
human race alive.

Ah, the bull-headed villain!   And O, my good
little people, you will perhaps see, one of these
days, as I do now, that every human being who
suffers any thing evil to get into his nature, or
to remain there, is a kind of Minotaur, an enemy of his fellow-creatures, and separated from

all good companionship, as this poor monster
was.

Was Theseus afraid? By no means, my dear
auditors. What! a hero like Theseus afraid!
Not had the Minotaur had twenty bull heads
instead of one. Bold as he was, however, I
rather fancy that it strengthened his valiant
heart, just at this crisis, to feel a tremulous
twitch at the silken cord, which he was still holding in his left hand. It was as if Ariadne were
giving him all her might and courage; and,
much as he already had, and little as she had
to give, it made his own seem twice as much.
And to confess the honest truth, he needed the
whole; for now the Minotaur, turning suddenly
about, caught sight of Theseus, and instantly
lowered his horribly sharp horns, exactly as a
mad bull does when he means to rush against
an enemy. At the same time, he belched forth
a tremendous roar, in which there was something like the words of human language, but
all disjointed and shaken to pieces by passing
through the gullet of a miserably enraged brute.

Theseus could only guess what the creature
intended to say, and that rather by his gestures

than his words; for the Minotaur's horns were sharper than his wits, and of a great deal more service to him than his tongue. But probably this was the sense of what he uttered : —

" Ah, wretch of a human being! I'll stick my horns through you, and toss you fifty feet high, and eat you up the moment you come down."

" Come on, then, and try it!" was all that Theseus deigned to reply; for he was far too magnanimous to assault his enemy with insolent language.

Without more words on either side, there ensued the most awful fight between Theseus and the Minotaur that ever happened beneath the sun or moon. I really know not how it might have turned out, if the monster, in his first headlong rush against Theseus, had not missed him, by a hair's breadth, and broken one of his horns short off against the stone wall. On this mishap, he bellowed so intolerably that a part of the labyrinth tumbled down, and all the inhabitants of Crete mistook the noise for an uncommonly heavy thunder storm. Smarting with the pain, he galloped around the open space in so ridiculous a way that Theseus

laughed at it, long afterwards, though not precisely at the moment. After this, the two an-
tagonists stood valiantly up to one another, and
fought, sword to horn, for a long while. At
last, the Minotaur made a run at Theseus,
grazed his left side with his horn, and flung him
down; and thinking that he had stabbed him to
the heart, he cut a great caper in the air, opened
his bull mouth from ear to ear, and prepared to
snap his head off. But Theseus by this time
had leaped up, and caught the monster off his
guard. Fetching a sword stroke at him with
all his force, he hit him fair upon the neck, and
made his bull head skip six yards from his human body, which fell down flat upon the ground.

So now the battle was ended. Immediately
the moon shone out as brightly as if all the
troubles of the world, and all the wickedness and
the ugliness that infest human life, were past
and gone forever. And Theseus, as he leaned
on his sword, taking breath, felt another twitch
of the silken cord; for all through the terrible
encounter, he had held it fast in his left hand.
Eager to let Ariadne know of his success,
he followed the guidance of the thread, and

soon found himself at the entrance of the labyrinth.

"Thou hast slain the monster," cried Ariadne, clasping her hands.

"Thanks to thee, dear Ariadne," answered Theseus, "I return victorious."

"Then," said Ariadne, "we must quickly summon thy friends, and get them and thyself on board the vessel before dawn. If morning finds thee here, my father will avenge the Minotaur."

To make my story short, the poor captives were awakened, and, hardly knowing whether it was not a joyful dream, were told of what Theseus had done, and that they must set sail for Athens before daybreak. Hastening down to the vessel, they all clambered on board, except Prince Theseus, who lingered behind them, on the strand, holding Ariadne's hand clasped in his own.

"Dear maiden," said he, "thou wilt surely go with us. Thou art too gentle and sweet a child for such an iron-hearted father as King Minos. He cares no more for thee than a granite rock cares for the little flower that grows in one of its crevices. But my father, King Ægeus, and my dear mother, Æthra, and all the fathers and mothers in Athens, and all the sons and daughters too, will love and honor thee as their benefactress. Come with us, then; for King Minos will be very angry when he knows what thou hast done."

Now, some low-minded people, who pretend to tell the story of Theseus and Ariadne, have the face to say that this royal and honorable maiden did really flee away, under cover of the night, with the young stranger whose life she had preserved. They say, too, that Prince Theseus (who would have died sooner than wrong the meanest creature in the world) ungratefully deserted Ariadne, on a solitary island, where the vessel touched on its voyage to Athens. But, had the noble Theseus heard these falsehoods, he would have served their slanderous authors as he served the Minotaur! Here is what Ariadne answered, when the brave prince of Athens besought her to accompany him : —

"No, Theseus," the maiden said, pressing his hand, and then drawing back a step or two.

"I cannot go with you. My father is old, and has nobody but myself to love him. Hard as you think his heart is, it would break to lose me. At first, King Minos will be angry; but he will soon forgive his only child; and, by and by, he will rejoice, I know, that no more youths and maidens must come from Athens to be devoured by the Minotaur. I have saved you, Theseus, as much for my father's sake as for your own. Farewell! Heaven bless you!"

All this was so true, and so maiden-like, and was spoken with so sweet a dignity, that Theseus would have blushed to urge her any longer. Nothing remained for him, therefore, but to bid Ariadne an affectionate farewell, and to go on board the vessel, and set sail.

In a few moments the white foam was boiling up before their prow, as Prince Theseus and his companions sailed out of the harbor, with a whistling breeze behind them. Talus, the brazen giant, on his never-ceasing sentinel's march, happened to be approaching that part of the coast; and they saw him, by the glimmering of the moonbeams on his polished surface, while he was yet a great way off. As the figure moved like clockwork, however, and could neither hasten his enormous strides nor retard them, he arrived at the port when they were just beyond the reach of his club. Nevertheless, straddling from headland to headland, as his custom was, Talus attempted to strike a blow at the vessel, and, overreaching himself, tumbled at full length into the sea, which splashed high over his gigantic shape, as when an iceberg turns a somerset. There he lies yet; and whoever desires to enrich himself by means of brass had better go thither with a diving bell, and fish up Talus.

On the homeward voyage, the fourteen youths and damsels were in excellent spirits, as you will easily suppose. They spent most of their time in dancing, unless when the sidelong breeze made the deck slope too much. In due season, they came within sight of the coast of Attica, which was their native country. But here, I am grieved to tell you, happened a sad misfortune.

You will remember (what Theseus unfortunately forgot) that his father, King Ægeus. had enjoined it upon him to hoist sunshin sails, instead of black ones, in case he shou.d overcome the Minotaur, and return victorious. In the joy of their success, however, and amidst the sports, dancing, and other merriment, with which these young folks wore away the time, they never once thought whether their sails were black, white, or rainbow colored, and, indeed, left it entirely to the mariners whether they had any sails at all. Thus the vessel returned, like a raven, with the same sable wings that had wafted her away. But poor King Ægeus, day after day, infirm as he was, had clambered to the summit of a cliff that overhung the sea, and there sat watching for Prince Theseus, homeward bound ; and no sooner did he behold the fatal blackness of the sails, than he concluded that his dear son, whom he loved so much, and felt so proud of, had been eaten by the Minotaur. He could not bear the thought of living any longer; so, first flinging his crown and sceptre into the sea, (useless bawbles that they were to him now!) King Ægeus merely stooped forward, and fell headlong over the cliff, and was drowned, poor soul, in the waves that foamed at its base !

This was melancholy news for Prince Theseus, who, when he stepped ashore, found himself king of all the country, whether he would or no; and such a turn of fortune was enough to make any young man feel very much out of spirits. However, he sent for his dear mother to Athens, and, by taking her advice in matters of state, became a very excellent monarch, and was greatly beloved by his people.

THE PYGMIES.

A GREAT while ago, when the world was full of wonders, there lived an earth-born Giant, named Antæus, and a million or more of curious little earth-born people, who were called Pygmies. This Giant and these Pygmies being children of the same mother, (that is to say, our good old Grandmother Earth,) were all brethren, and dwelt together in a very friendly and affectionate manner, far, far off, in the middle of hot Africa. The Pygmies were so small, and there were so many sandy deserts and such high mountains between them and the rest of mankind, that nobody could get a peep at them oftener than once in a hundred years. As for the Giant, being of a very lofty stature, it was easy enough to see him, but safest to keep out of his sight.

Among the Pygmies, I suppose, if one of them grew to the height of six or eight inches, he was reckoned a prodigiously tall man. It must have been very pretty to behold their little cities, with streets two or three feet wide, paved with the smallest pebbles, and . bordered by habitations about as big as a squirrel's cage. The king's palace attained to the stupendous magnitude of Periwinkle's baby house, and stood in the centre of a spacious square, which could hardly have been covered by our hearth rug. Their principal temple, or cathedral, was as lofty as yonder bureau, and was looked upon as a wonderfully sublime and magnificent edifice. All these structures were built neither of stone nor wood. They were neatly plastered together by the Pygmy workmen, pretty much like birds' nests, out of straw, feathers, egg shells, and other small bits of stuff, with stiff clay instead of mortar; and when the hot sun had dried them, they were just as snug and comfortable as a Pygmy could desire.

The country round about was conveniently laid out in fields, the largest of which was nearly of the same extent as one of Sweet Fern's flower

beds. Here the **Pygmies** used to plant wheat
and other kinds of grain, which, when it grew
up and ripened, overshadowed these tiny people,
as the pines, and the oaks, and the walnut and
chestnut trees overshadow you and me, when
we walk in our own tracts of woodland. At
harvest time, they were forced to go with their
little axes and cut down the grain, exactly as a
woodcutter makes a clearing in the forest; and
when a stalk of wheat, with its overburdened
top, chanced to come crashing down upon an
unfortunate Pygmy, it was apt to be a very sad
affair. If it did not smash him all to pieces, at
least, I am sure, it must have made the poor
little fellow's head ache. And O, my stars! if
the fathers and mothers were so small, what
must the children and babies have been? A
whole family of them might have been put to
bed in a shoe, or have crept into an old glove,
and played at hide and seek in its thumb and
fingers. You might have hidden a year-old baby
under a thimble.

Now these funny Pygmies, as I told you before, had a Giant for their neighbor and brother,
who was bigger, if possible, than they were little.

He was so very tall that he carried a pine tree,
which was eight feet through the but, for a walk
ing stick.   It took a far-sighted Pygmy, I can
assure you, to discern his summit without the
help of a telescope; and sometimes, in misty
weather, they could not see his upper half, but
only his long legs, which seemed to be striding
about by themselves. But at noonday, in a
clear atmosphere, when the sun shone brightly
over him, the Giant Antæus presented a very
grand spectacle.   There he used to stand, a perfect mountain of a man, with his great countenance smiling down upon his little brothers, and
his one vast eye (which was as big as a cart
wheel, and placed right in the centre of his forehead) giving a friendly wink to the whole nation
at once.

The Pygmies loved to talk with Antæus; and
fifty times a day, one or another of them would
turn up his head, and shout through the hollow
of his fists, "Halloo, brother Antæus! How
are you, my good fellow?" And when the
small, distant squeak of their voices reached his
ear, the Giant would make answer, "Pretty
well, brother Pygmy, I thank you," in a thun-

derous roar that would have shaken down the walls of their strongest temple, only that it came from so far aloft.

It was a happy circumstance that Antæus was the Pygmy people's friend; for there was more strength in his little finger than in ten million of such bodies as this. If he had been as ill natured to them as he was to every body else, he might have beaten down their biggest city at one kick, and hardly have known that he did it. With the tornado of his breath, he could have stripped the roofs from a hundred dwellings, and sent thousands of the inhabitants whirling through the air. He might have set his immense foot upon a multitude; and when he took it up again, there would have been a pitiful sight, to be sure. But, being the son of Mother Earth, as they likewise were, the Giant gave them his brotherly kindness, and loved them with as big a love as it was possible to feel for creatures so very small. And, on their parts, the Pygmies loved Antæus with as much affection as their tiny hearts could hold. He was always ready to do them any good offices that lay in his power; as for example, when they

wanted a breeze to turn their wind mills, the
Giant would set all the sails a-going with the
mere natural respiration of his lungs. When
the sun was too hot, he often sat himself down,
and let his shadow fall over the kingdom, from
one frontier to the other; and as for matters in
general, he was wise enough to let them alone,
and leave the Pygmies to manage their own
affairs — which, after all, is about the best thing
that great people can do for little ones.

In short, as I said before, Antæus loved the
Pygmies, and the Pygmies loved Antæus. The
Giant's life being as long as his body was large,
while the lifetime of a Pygmy was but a span,
this friendly intercourse had been going on for
innumerable generations and ages. It was
written about in the Pygmy histories, and
talked about in their ancient traditions. The
most venerable and white-bearded Pygmy had
never heard of a time, even in his greatest of
grandfather's days, when the Giant was not
their enormous friend. Once, to be sure, (as
was recorded on an obelisk, three feet high,
erected on the place of the catastrophe,) Antæus
sat down upon about five thousand Pygmies,

who were assembled at a military review. But this was one of those unlucky accidents for which nobody is to blame; so that the small folks never took it to heart, and only requested the Giant to be careful forever afterwards to examine the acre of ground where he intended to squat himself.

It is a very pleasant picture to imagine Antæus standing among the Pygmies, like the spire of the tallest cathedral that ever was built, while they ran about like pismires at his feet, and to think that, in spite of their difference in size, there were affection and sympathy between them and him! Indeed, it has always seemed to me that the Giant needed the little people more than the Pygmies needed the Giant. For, unless they had been his neighbors and well wishers, and, as we may say, his playfellows, Antæus would not have had a single friend in the world. No other being like himself had ever been created. No creature of his own size had ever talked with him, in thunder-like accents, face to face. When he stood with his head among the clouds, he was quite alone, and had been so for hundreds of years, and would be so forever. Even if he had met another Giant, Antæus would have fancied the world not big enough for two such vast personages, and, instead of being friends with him. would have fought him till one of the two was kiiled. But with the Pygmies he was the most sportive, and humorous, and merry-hearted, and sweet-tempered old Giant that ever washed his face in a wet cloud.

His little friends, like all other small people, had a great opinion of their own importance, and used to assume quite a patronizing air towards the Giant.

"Poor creature!" they said one to another. "He has a very dull time of it, all by himself; and we ought not to grudge wasting a little of our precious time to amuse him. He is not half so bright as we are, to be sure; and, for that reason, he needs us to look after his comfort and happiness. Let us be kind to the old fellow. Why, if Mother Earth had not been very kind to ourselves, we might all have been Giants too"

On all their holiaays, the Pygmies had ex· cellent sport with Antæus He often stretched

himself out at full length on the ground, where
he looked like the long ridge of a hill; and it
was a good hour's walk, no doubt, for a short-
legged Pygmy to journey from head to foot of
the Giant. He would lay down his great hand
flat on the grass, and challenge the tallest of
them to clamber upon it, and straddle from
finger to finger. So fearless were they, that
they made nothing of creeping in among the
folds of his garments. When his head lay
sidewise on the earth, they would march boldly
up, and peep into the great cavern of his mouth,
and take it all as a joke (as indeed it was
meant) when Antæus gave a sudden snap with
his jaws, as if he were going to swallow fifty of
them at once. You would have laughed to see
the children dodging in and out among his hair,
or swinging from his beard. It is impossible
to tell half of the funny tricks that they played
with their huge comrade; but I do not know
that any thing was more curious than when
a party of boys were seen running races on his
forehead, to try which of them could get first
round the circle of his one great eye. It was
another favorite feat with them to march along

the bridge of his nose, and jump down upon his upper lip.

If the truth must be told, they were sometimes as troublesome to the Giant as a swarm of ants or mosquitoes, especially as they had a fondness for mischief, and liked to prick his skin with their little swords and lances, to see how thick and tough it was. But Antæus took it all kindly enough; although, once in a while, when he happened to be sleepy, he would grumble out a peevish word or two, like the muttering of a tempest, and ask them to have done with their nonsense. A great deal oftener, however, he watched their merriment and gambols until his huge, heavy, clumsy wits were completely stirred up by them; and then would he roar out such a tremendous volume of immeasurable laughter, that the whole nation of Pygmies had to put their hands to their ears, else it would certainly have deafened them.

" Ho! ho! ho!" quoth the Giant, shaking his mountainous sides. " What a funny thing it is to be little! If I were not Antæus, I should like to be a Pygmy, just for the joke's sake."

The Pygmies had but one thing to trouble

them in the world. They were constantly at
war with the cranes, and had always been so,
ever since the long-lived Giant could remember.
From time to time, very terrible battles had been
fought, in which sometimes the little men won
the victory, and sometimes the cranes. According to some historians, the Pygmies used to go
to the battle, mounted on the backs of goats and
rams; but such animals as these must have been
far too big for Pygmies to ride upon; so that, I
rather suppose, they rode on squirrelback, or rab-
bitback, or ratback, or perhaps got upon hedge-
hogs, whose prickly quills would be very terrible
to the enemy. However this might be, and
whatever creatures the Pygmies rode upon, I do
not doubt that they made a formidable appearance, armed with sword and spear, and bow and
arrow, blowing their tiny trumpet, and shouting
their little war cry. They never failed to exhort
one another to fight bravely, and recollect that
the world had its eyes upon them; although, in
simple truth, the only spectator was the Giant
Antæus, with his one, great, stupid eye, in the
middle of his forehead.

When the two armies joined battle, the cranes

6

would rush forward, flapping their wings and
stretching out their necks, and would perhaps
snatch up some of the Pygmies crosswise in
their beaks. Whenever this happened, it was
truly an awful spectacle to see those little men
of might kicking and sprawling in the air,
and at last disappearing down the crane's long,
crooked throat, swallowed up alive. A hero,
you know, must hold himself in readiness for any
kind of fate; and doubtless the glory of the
thing was a consolation to him, even in the
crane's gizzard. If Antæus observed that the
battle was going hard against his little allies,
he generally stopped laughing, and ran with
mile-long strides to their assistance, flourishing
his club aloft and shouting at the cranes, who
quacked and croaked, and retreated as fast as
they could.   Then the Pygmy army would
march homeward in triumph, attributing the victory entirely to their own valor, and to the warlike skill and strategy of whomsoever happened
to be captain general; and for a tedious while
afterwards, nothing would be heard of but grand
processions, and public banquets, and brilliant
illuminations, and shows of waxwork, with like-

nesses of the distinguished officers, as small as life.

In the above-described warfare, if a Pygmy chanced to pluck out a crane's tail feather, it proved a very great feather in his cap. Once or twice, if you will believe me, a little man was made chief ruler of the nation for no other merit in the world than bringing home such a feather.

But I have now said enough to let you see what a gallant little people these were, and how happily they and their forefathers, for nobody knows how many generations, had lived with the immeasurable Giant Antæus. In the remaining part of the story, I shall tell you of a far more astonishing battle than any that was fought between the Pygmies and the cranes.

One day the mighty Antæus was lolling at full length among his little friends. His pine tree walking stick lay on the ground, close by his side. His head was in one part of the kingdom, and his feet extended across the boundaries of another part ; and he was taking whatever comfort he could get, while the Pygmies scrambled over him, and peeped into his cavernous mouth, and

played among his hair. Sometimes, for a min·
ute or two, the Giant dropped asleep, and snorea
like the rush of a whirlwind. During one of these
little bits of slumber, a Pygmy chanced to climb
upon his shoulder, and took a view around the
horizon, as from the summit of a hill; and he
beheld something, a long way off, which made
him rub the bright specks of his eyes, and look
sharper than before. At first he mistook it for
a mountain, and wondered how it had grown up
so suddenly out of the earth. But soon he
saw the mountain move. As it came nearer and
nearer, what should it turn out to be but a human shape, not so big as Antæus, it is true,
although a very enormous figure, in comparison
with Pygmies, and a vast deal bigger than the
men whom we see nowadays.

When the Pygmy was quite satisfied that his
eyes had not deceived him, he scampered, as fast
as his legs would carry him, to the Giant's ear,
and stooping over its cavity, shouted lustily
into it, —

"Halloo, brother Antæus! Get up this min·
ute, and take your pine tree walking stick in
your hand. Here comes another Giant to have
a tussle with you."

"Poh, poh!" grumbled Antæus, only half awake. "None of your nonsense, my little fellow! Don't you see I'm sleepy. There is not a Giant on earth for whom I would take the trouble to get up."

But the Pygmy looked again, and now perceived that the stranger was coming directly towards the prostrate form of Antæus. With every step, he looked less like a blue mountain, and more like an immensely large man. He was soon so nigh, that there could be no possible mistake about the matter. There he was, with the sun flaming on his golden helmet, and flashing from his polished breastplate; he had a sword by his side, and a lion's skin over his back, and on his right shoulder he carried a club, which looked bulkier and heavier than the pine-tree walking stick of Antæus.

By this time, the whole nation of Pygmies had seen the new wonder, and a million of them set up a shout, all together; so that it really made quite an audible squeak.

"Get up, Antæus! Bestir yourself, you lazy old Giant! Here comes another Giant, as strong as you are, to fight with you."

" Nonsense, nonsense!" growled the sleepy
Giant. " I'll have my nap out, come who
may."

Still the stranger drew nearer; and now the
Pygmies could plainly discern that, if his stature
were less lofty than the Giant's, yet his shoulders were even broader. And, in truth, what a
pair of shoulders they must have been! As I
told you, a long while ago, they once upheld the
sky. The Pygmies, being ten times as viva-
cious as their great numskull of a brother, could
nôt abide the Giant's slow movements, and
were determined to have him on his feet. So
they kept shouting to him, and even went so far
as to prick him with their swords.

" Get up, get up, get up!" they cried. " Up
with you, lazy bones! The strange Giant's club
is bigger than your own, his shoulders are the
broadest, and we think him the stronger of
the two."

Antæus could not endure to have it said that
any mortal was half so mighty as himself. This
latter remark of the Pygmies pricked him deeper
than their swords, and, sitting up, in rather a
sulky humor, he gave a gape of several yards

wide, rubbed his eyes, and finally turned his stupid head in the direction whither his little friends were eagerly pointing.

No sooner did he set eyes on the stranger, than, leaping on his feet, and seizing his walking stick, he strode a mile or two to meet him; all the while brandishing the sturdy pine tree, so that it whistled through the air.

" Who are you?" thundered the Giant. "And what do you want in my dominions?"

There was one strange thing about Antæus, of which I have not yet told you, lest, hearing of so many wonders all in a lump, you might not believe much more than half of them. You are to know, then, that whenever this redoubtable Giant touched the ground, either with his hand, his foot, or any other part of his body, he grew stronger than ever he had been before. The Earth, you remember, was his mother, and was very fond of him, as being almost the biggest of her children; and so she took this method of keeping him always in full vigor. Some persons affirm that he grew ten times stronger at every touch; others say that it was only twice as strong. But only think of it! Whenever

Antæus took a walk, supposing it were but ten
miles, and that he stepped a hundred yards at a
stride, you may try to cipher out how much
mightier he was, on sitting down again, than
when he first started. And whenever he flung
himself on the earth to take a little repose, even
if he got up the very next instant, he would be
as strong as exactly ten just such giants as his
former self. It was well for the world that Antæus happened to be of a sluggish disposition,
and liked ease better than exercise; for, if he
had frisked about like the Pygmies, and touched
the earth as often as they did, he would long
ago have been strong enough to pull down the
sky about people's ears. But these great lub-
berly fellows resemble mountains, not only in
bulk, but in their disinclination to move.

Any other mortal man, except the very one
whom Antæus had now encountered, would have
been half frightened to death by the Giant's
ferocious aspect and terrible voice. But the
stranger did not seem at all disturbed. He care-
lessly lifted his club, and balanced it in his hand
measuring Antæus with his eye, from head to
foot, not as if wonder-smitten at his stature, but

as if he had seen a great many Giants before, and this was by no means the biggest of them. In fact, if the Giant had been no bigger than the Pygmies, (who stood pricking up their ears, and looking and listening to what was going forward,) the stranger could not have been less afraid of him.

"Who are you, I say?" roared Antæus again. "What's your name? Why do you come hither? Speak, you vagabond, or I'll try the thickness of your skull with my walking stick."

"You are a very discourteous Giant," answered the stranger, quietly, "and I shall probably have to teach you a little civility, before we part. As for my name, it is Hercules. I have come hither because this is my most convenient road to the garden of the Hesperides, whither I am going to get three of the golden apples for King Eurystheus."

"Caitiff, you shall go no farther!" bellowed Antæus, putting on a grimmer look than before; for he had heard of the mighty Hercules, and hated him because he was said to be so strong. "Neither shall you go back whence you came!"

" How will you prevent me," asked Hercules,
" from going whither I please ? "

" By hitting you a rap with this pine tree
here," shouted Antæus, scowling so that he
made himself the ugliest monster in Africa.
" I am fifty times stronger than you; and, now
that I stamp my foot upon the ground, I am
five hundred times stronger ! I am ashamed to
kill such a puny little dwarf as you seem to be.
I will make a slave of you, and you shall likewise be the slave of my brethren, here, the
Pygmies. So throw down your club and your
other weapons ; and as for that lion's skin, I
intend to have a pair of gloves made of it."

" Come and take it off my shoulders, then,"
answered Hercules, lifting his club.

Then the Giant, grinning with rage, strode
tower-like towards the stranger, (ten times
strengthened at every step,) and fetched a monstrous blow at him with his pine tree, which
Hercules caught upon his club ; and being more
skilful than Antæus, he paid him back such a
rap upon the sconce, that down tumbled the
great lumbering man-mountain, flat upon the
ground. The poor little Pygmies (who really

never dreamed that any body in the world was half so strong as their brother Antæus) were a good deal dismayed at this. But no sooner was the Giant down, than up he bounced again, with tenfold might, and such a furious visage as was horrible to behold. He aimed another blow at Hercules, but struck awry, being blinded with wrath, and only hit his poor innocent Mother Earth, who groaned and trembled at the stroke. His pine tree went so deep into the ground, and stuck there so fast, that, before Antæus could get it out, Hercules brought down his club across his shoulders with a mighty thwack, which made the Giant roar as if all sorts of intolerable noises had come screeching and rumbling out of his immeasurable lungs in that one cry. Away it went, over mountains and valleys, and, for aught I know, was heard on the other side of the African deserts.

As for the Pygmies, their capital city was laid in ruins by the concussion and vibration of the air; and, though there was uproar enough without their help, they all set up a shriek out of three millions of little throats, fancying, no doubt, that they swelled the Giant's bellow by at least ten times as much. Meanwhile, Antæus had scrambled upon his feet again, and pulled his pine tree out of the earth; and, all a-flame with fury, and more outrageously strong than ever, he ran at Hercules, and brought down another blow.

"This time, rascal," shouted he, "you shall not escape me."

But once more Hercules warded off the stroke with his club, and the Giant's pine tree was shattered into a thousand splinters, most of which flew among the Pygmies, and did them more mischief than I like to think about. Before Antæus could get out of the way, Hercules let drive again, and gave him another knock-down blow, which sent him heels over head, but served only to increase his already enormous and insufferable strength. As for his rage, there is no telling what a fiery furnace it had now got to be. His one eye was nothing but a circle of red flame. Having now no weapons but his fists, he doubled them up, (each bigger than a hogshead,) smote one against the other, and danced up and down with absolute frenzy, flourishing his immense arms about, as if he meant not merely to kill Hercules, but to smash the whole world to pieces.

"Come on!" roared this thundering Giant. " Let me hit you but one box on the ear, and you'll never have the headache again."

Now Hercules (though strong enough, as you already know, to hold the sky up) began to be sensible that he should never win the victory, if he kept on knocking Antæus down; for, by and by, if he hit him such hard blows, the Giant would inevitably, by the help of his Mother Earth, become stronger than the mighty Hercules himself. So, throwing down his club, with which he had fought so many dreadful battles, the hero stood ready to receive his antagonist with naked arms.

"Step forward," cried he. "Since I've broken your pine tree, we'll try which is the better man at a wrestling match."

"Aha! then I'll soon satisfy you," shouted the Giant; for, if there was one thing on which he prided himself more than another, it was his skill in wrestling. " Villain, I'll fling

you where you can never pick yourself **up**
again."

On came Antæus, hopping and capering with
the scorching heat of his rage, and getting new
vigor wherewith to wreak his passion, every
time he hopped. But Hercules, you must understand, was wiser than this numskull of a
Giant, and had thought of a way to fight him, .
— huge, earth-born monster that he was,— and
to conquer him too, in spite of all that his
Mother Earth could do for him. Watching his
opportunity, as the mad Giant made a rush
at him, Hercules caught him round the middle
with both hands, lifted him high into the air,
and held him aloft overhead.

Just imagine it, my dear little friends! What
a spectacle it must have been, to see this monstrous fellow sprawling in the air, face down-
ward, kicking out his long legs and wriggling
his whole vast body, like a baby when its father
holds it at arm's length towards the ceiling.

But the most wonderful thing was, that, as
soon as Antæus was fairly off the earth, he
began to lose the vigor which he had gained
by touching it. Hercules very soon perceived

that his troublesome enemy was growing weaker, both because he struggled and kicked with
less violence, and because the thunder of his big
voice subsided into a grumble. The truth was,
that, unless the Giant touched Mother Earth as
often as once in five minutes, not only his overgrown strength, but the very breath of his life,
would depart from him. Hercules had guessed
this secret; and it may be well for us all to
remember it, in case we should ever have to
fight a battle with a fellow like Antæus. For
these earth-born creatures are only difficult
to conquer on their own ground, but may
easily be managed if we can contrive to lift
them into a loftier and purer region. So
it proved with the poor Giant, whom I am
really a little sorry for, notwithstanding his
uncivil way of treating strangers who came
to visit him.

When his strength and breath were quite
gone, Hercules gave his huge body a toss, and
flung it about a mile off, where it fell heavily,
and lay with no more motion than a sand hill.
It was too late for the Giant's Mother Earth to
help him now; and I should not wonder if his

ponderous bones were lying on the same spot
to this very day, and were mistaken for those of
an uncommonly large elephant.

But, alas me! What a wailing did the poor
little Pygmies set up when they saw their enormous brother treated in this terrible manner!
If Hercules heard their shrieks, however, he took
no notice, and perhaps fancied them only the
shrill, plaintive twittering of small birds that
had been frightened from their nests by the
uproar of the battle between himself and Antæus. Indeed, his thoughts had been so much
taken up with the Giant, that he had never
once looked at the Pygmies, nor even knew that
there was such a funny little nation in the world
And now, as he had travelled a good way, and
was also rather weary with his exertions in the
fight, he spread out his lion's skin on the
ground, and reclining himself upon it, fell fast
asleep.

As soon as the Pygmies saw Hercules preparing for a nap, they nodded their little heads
at one another, and winked with their little eyes
And when his deep, regular breathing gave
them notice that he was asleep, they assembled

together in an immense crowd, spreading over
a space of about twenty-seven feet square. One
of their most eloquent orators (and a valiant
warrior enough, besides, though hardly so good
at any other weapon as he was with his tongue)
climbed upon a toadstool, and, from that elevated position, addressed the multitude. His
sentiments were pretty much as follows; or, at
all events, something like this was probably the
upshot of his speech : —

"Tall Pygmies and mighty little men! You
and all of us have seen what a public calamity
has been brought to pass, and what an insult has
here been offered to the majesty of our nation.
Yonder lies Antæus, our great friend and brother,
slain, within our territory, by a miscreant who
took him at disadvantage, and fought him (if
fighting it can be called) in a way that neither
man, nor Giant, nor Pygmy ever dreamed of
fighting, until this hour. And, adding a grievous
contumely to the wrong already done us, the
miscreant has now fallen asleep as quietly as
if nothing were to be dreaded from our wrath!
It behooves you, fellow-countrymen, to consider
in what aspect we shall stand before the world,

and what will be the verdict of impartial history, should we suffer these accumulated outrages to go unavenged.

"Antæus was our brother, born of that same beloved parent to whom we owe the thews and sinews, as well as the courageous heaits, which made him proud of our relationship. He was our faithful ally, and fell fighting as much for our national rights and immunities as for his own personal ones. We and our forefathers have dwelt in friendship with him, and held affectionate intercourse, as man to man, througn immemorial generations. You remember how often our entire people have reposed in his great shadow, and how our little ones have played at hide and seek in the tangles of his hair, and how his mighty footsteps have familiarly gone to and fro among us, and never trodden upon any of our toes. And there lies this dear brother — this sweet and amiable friend — this brave and faithful ally — this virtuous Giant — this blameless and excellent Antæus — dead! Dead. Silent! Powerless! A mere mountain of clay! Forgive my tears! Nay, I behold your own: Were we to drown the world with them, could the world blame us?

"But to resume : Shall we, my countrymen, suffer this wicked stranger to depart unharmed, and triumph in his treacherous victory, among distant communities of the earth? Shall we not rather compel him to leave his bones here on our soil, by the side of our slain brother's bones? so that, while one skeleton shall remain as the ever-lasting monument of our sorrow, the other shall endure as long, exhibiting to the whole human race a terrible example of Pygmy vengeance! Such is the question. I put it to you in full confidence of a response that shall be worthy of our national character, and calculated to increase, rather than diminish, the glory which our ancestors have transmitted to us, and which we ourselves have proudly vindicated in our warfare with the cranes."

The orator was here interrupted by a burst of irrepressible enthusiasm ; every individual Pygmy crying out that the national honor must be preserved at all hazards. He bowed, and making a gesture for silence, wound up his harangue in the following admirable manner :—

"It only remains for us, then, to decide whether we shall carry on the war in our national capacity, — one united people against a common enemy, — or whether some champion, famous in former fights, shall be selected to defy the slayer of our brother Antæus to single combat.   In the latter case, though not unconscious that there may be taller men among you, I hereby offer myself for that enviable duty.   And, believe me, dear countrymen, whether I live or die, the honor of this great country, and the fame bequeathed us by our heroic progenitors, shall suffer no diminution in my hands.   Never, while I can wield this sword, of which I now fling away the scabbard — never, never, never, even if the crimson hand that slew the great Antæus shall lay me prostrate, like him, on the soil which I give my life to defend."

So saying, this valiant Pygmy drew out his weapon, (which was terrible to behold, being as long as the blade of a penknife,) and sent the scabbard whirling over the heads of the multitude. His speech was followed by an uproar of applause, as its patriotism and self-devotion unquestionably deserved; and the shouts and clapping of hands would have been greatly prolonged, had they not been rendered quite inaudi ble by a deep respiration, vulgarly called a snore, from the sleeping Hercules.

It was finally decided that the whole nation of Pygmies should set to work to destroy Hercules; not, be it understood, from any doubt that a single champion would be capable of putting him to the sword, but because he was a public enemy, and all were desirous of sharing in the glory of his defeat. There was a debate whether the national honor did not demand that a herald should be sent with a trumpet, to stand over the ear of Hercules, and, after blowing a blast right into it, to defy him to the combat by formal proclamation. But two or three venerable and sagacious Pygmies, well versed in state affairs, gave it as their opinion that war already existed, and that it was their rightful privilege to take the enemy by surprise. Moreover, if awakened, and allowed to get upon his feet, Hercules might happen to do them a mischief before he could be beaten down again. For, as these sage counsellors remarked, the stranger's club was really very big, and had rattled like a thunderbolt against the skull of Antæus. So the Pygmies resolved to set aside all foolish punctilios, and assail their antagonist at once.

Accordingly, all the fighting men of the nation took their weapons, and went boldly up to Hercules, who still lay fast asleep, little dreaming of the harm which the Pygmies meant to do him. A body of twenty thousand archers marched in front, with their little bows all ready, and the arrows on the string. The same number were ordered to clamber upon Hercules, some with spades, to dig his eyes out, and others with bundles of hay, and all manner of rubbish, with which they intended to plug up his mouth and nostrils, so that he might perish for lack of breath. These last, however, could by no means perform their appointed duty; inasmuch as the enemy's breath rushed out of his nose in an obstreperous hurricane and whirlwind, which blew the Pygmies away as fast as they came nigh. It was found necessary, therefore, to hit upon some other method of carrying on the war.

After holding a council, the captains ordered their troops to collect sticks, straws, dry weeds, and whatever combustible stuff they could find, and make a pile of it, heaping it high around

the head of Hercules. As a great many thousand Pygmies were employed in this task, they
soon brought together several bushels of inflam-
matory matter, and raised so tall a heap, that,
mounting on its summit, they were quite upon
a level with the sleeper's face. The archers,
meanwhile, were stationed within bow shot, with
orders to let fly at Hercules the instant that he
stirred. Every thing being in readiness, a torch
was applied to the pile, which immediately burst
into flames, and soon waxed hot enough to roast
the enemy, had he but chosen to lie still. A
Pygmy, you know, though so very small, might
set the world on fire, just as easily as a Giant
could; so that this was certainly the very best
way of dealing with their foe, provided they
could have kept him quiet while the conflagra
tion was going forward.

But no sooner did Hercules begin to be
scorched, than up he started, with his hair in a
red blaze.

"What's all this?" he cried, bewildered with
sleep, and staring about him as if he expected
to see another Giant.

At that moment the twenty thousand archers

twanged their bowstrings, and the arrows came whizzing, like so many winged mosquitoes, right into the face of Hercules. But I doubt whether more than half a dozen of them punctured the skin, which was remarkably tough, as you know the skin of a hero has good need to be.

" Villain!" shouted all the Pygmies at once. " You have killed the Giant Antæus, our great brother, and the ally of our nation. We declare bloody war against you, and will slay you on the spot."

Surprised at the shrill piping of so many little voices, Hercules, after putting out the conflagration of his hair, gazed all round about, but could see nothing. At last, however, looking narrowly on the ground, he espied the innumerable assemblage of Pygmies at his feet. He stooped down, and taking up the nearest one between his thumb and finger, set him on the palm of his left hand, and held him at a proper distance for examination. It chanced to be the very identical Pygmy who had spoken from the top of the toadstool, and had offered himself as a champion to meet Hercules in single combat.

" What in the world, my little fellow," ejacu-lated Hercules, " may you be ? "

" I am your enemy," answered the valiant Pygmy, in his mightiest squeak. " You have slain the enormous Antæus, our brother by the mother's side, and for ages the faithful ally of our illustrious nation. We are determined to put you to death; and for my own part, I chal-lenge you to instant battle, on equal ground."

Hercules was so tickled with the Pygmy's big words and warlike gestures, that he burst into a great explosion of laughter, and almost dropped the poor little mite of a creature off the palm of his hand, through the ecstasy and convulsion of his merriment.

" Upon my word," cried he, " I thought I had seen wonders before to-day — hydras with nine heads, stags with golden horns, six-legged men, three-headed dogs, giants with furnaces in their stomachs, and nobody knows what besides. But here, on the palm of my hand, stands a wonder that outdoes them all ' Your body, my little friend, is about the size of an ordinary man's fin-ger. Pray, how big may your soul be ? "

" As big as your own!" said the Pygmy.

Hercules was touched with the little man's dauntless courage, and could not help acknowledging such a brotherhood with him as one hero feels for another.

"My good little people," said he, making a low obeisance to the grand nation, "not for all the world would I do an intentional injury to such brave fellows as you! Your hearts seem to me so exceedingly great, that, upon my honor, I marvel how your small bodies can contain them. I sue for peace, and, as a condition of it, will take five strides, and be out of your kingdom at the sixth. Good by. I shall pick my steps carefully, for fear of treading upon some fifty of you, without knowing it. Ha, ha, ha! Ho, ho, ho! For once, Hercules acknowledges himself vanquished."

Some writers say, that Hercules gathered up the whole race of Pygmies in his lion's skin, and carried them home to Greece, for the children of King Eurystheus to play with. But this is a mistake. He left them, one and all, within their own territory, where, for aught I can tell, their descendants are alive to the present day, building their little nouses, cultivating their little

fields, spanking their little children, waging their
little warfare with the cranes, doing their little
business, whatever it may be, and reading their
little histories of ancient times. In those histories, perhaps, it stands recorded, that, a great
many centuries ago, the valiant Pygmies avenged
the death of the Giant Antæus by scaring away
the mighty Hercules.

THE DRAGON'S TEETH.

CADMUS, Phœnix, and Cilix, the three sons of King Agenor, and their little sister Europa, (who was a very beautiful child,) were at play togeth· er, near the sea shore, in their father's kingdom of Phœnicia.   They had rambled to some dis- tance from the palace where their parents dwelt, and were now in a verdant meadow, on one side of which lay the sea, all sparkling and dimpling in the sunshine, and murmuring gently against the beach.   The three boys were very happy, gathering flowers, and twining them into gar- lands, with which they adorned the little Europa. Seated on the grass, the child was almost hid· den under an abundance of buds and blossoms, whence her rosy face peeped merrily out, and, as Cadmus said, was the prettiest of all the flowers.

Just then, there came a splendid butterfly,

fluttering along the meadow; and Cadmus, Phœnix, and Cilix set off in pursuit of it, crying out that it was a flower with wings. Europa, who was a little wearied with playing all day long, did not chase the butterfly with her brothers, but sat still where they had left her, and closed her eyes. For a while, she listened to the pleasant murmur of the sea, which was like a voice saying "Hush!" and bidding her go to sleep. But the pretty child, if she slept at all, could not have slept more than a moment, when she heard something trample on the grass, not far from her, and peeping out from the heap of flowers, beheld a snow-white bull.

And whence could this bull have come? Europa and her brothers had been a long time playing in the meadow, and had seen no cattle, nor other living thing, either there or on the neighboring hills.

"Brother Cadmus!" cried Europa, starting up out of the midst of the roses and lilies. "Phœnix! Cilix! Where are you all? Help! Help! Come and drive away this bull!"

But her brothers were too far off to hear; especially as the fright took away Europa's

voice, and hindered her from calling very loudly
So there she stood, with her pretty mouth wide
open, as pale as the white lilies that were twisted
among the other flowers in her garlands.

Nevertheless, it was the suddenness with
which she had perceived the bull, rather than
any thing frightful in his appearance, that
caused Europa so much alarm. On looking at
him more attentively, she began to see that he
was a beautiful animal, and even fancied a particularly amiable expression in his face. As for
his breath, — the breath of cattle, you know, is
always sweet, — it was as fragrant as if he had
been grazing on no other food than rosebuds, or,
at least, the most delicate of clover blossoms.
Never before did a bull have such bright and
tender eyes, and such smooth horns of ivory, as
this one. And the bull ran little races, and
capered sportively around the child ; so that she
quite forgot how big and strong he was, and,
from the gentleness and playfulness of his ac-
tions, soon came to consider him as innocent a
creature as a pet lamb.

Thus, frightened as she at first was, you
might by and by have seen Europa stroking the

bull's forehead with her small white hand, and
taking the garlands off her own head to hang
them on his neck and ivory horns. Then she
pulled up some blades of grass, and he ate them
out of her hand, not as if he were hungry, but
because he wanted to be friends with the child,
and took pleasure in eating what she had
touched. Well, my stars! was there ever such
a gentle, sweet, pretty, and amiable creature as
this bull, and ever such a nice playmate for a
little girl?

When the animal saw, (for the bull had so
much intelligence that it is really wonderful to
think of,) when he saw that Europa was no
longer afraid of him, he grew overjoyed, and
could hardly contain himself for delight. He
frisked about the meadow, now here, now there,
making sprightly leaps, with as little effort as a
bird expends in hopping from twig to twig. Indeed, his motion was as light as if he were flying
through the air, and his hoofs seemed hardly to
leave their print in the grassy soil over which he
trod. With his spotless hue, he resembled a
snow drift, wafted along by the wind. Once he
galloped so far away that Europa feared lest

she might never see him again; so, setting **up**
her childish voice, she called him back.

"Come back, pretty creature!" she cried.
"Here is a nice clover blossom."

And then it was delightful to witness the
gratitude of this amiable bull, and how he was
so full of joy and thankfulness that he capered
higher than ever. He came running, and bowed
his head before Europa, as if he knew her to be
a king's daughter, or else recognized the important truth that a little girl is every body's queen.
And not only did the bull bend his neck, he
absolutely knelt down at her feet, and made
such intelligent nods, and other inviting gestures,
that Europa understood what he meant just as
well as if he had put it in so many words.

"Come, dear child," was what he wanted to
say, "let me give you a ride on my back."

At the first thought of such a thing, Europa
drew back. But then she considered in her
wise little head that there could be no possible harm in taking just one gallop on the back
of this docile and friendly animal, who would
certainly set her down the very instant she desired it. And how it would surprise her brothers

to see her riding across the green meadow! And what merry times they might have, either taking turns for a gallop, or clambering on the gentle creature, all four children together, and careering round the field with shouts of laughter that would be heard as far off as King Agenor's palace!

"I think I will do it," said the child to herself.

And, indeed, why not? She cast a glance around, and caught a glimpse of Cadmus, Phœnix, and Cilix, who were still in pursuit of the butterfly, almost at the other end of the meadow. It would be the quickest way of rejoining them, to get upon the white bull's back. She came a step nearer to him therefore; and — sociable creature that he was — he showed so much joy at this mark of her confidence, that the child could not find in her heart to hesitate any longer. Making one bound, (for this little princess was as active as a squirrel,) there sat Europa on the beautiful bull, holding an ivory horn in each hand, lest she should fall off.

"Softly, pretty bull, softly!" she said, rather frightened at what she had done. "Do not gallop too fast."

8

Having got the child on his back, the animal
gave a leap into the air, and came down so like
a feather that Europa did not know when his
hoofs touched the ground. He then began a
race to that part of the flowery plain where her
three brothers were, and where they had just
caught their splendid butterfly. Europa screamed
with delight; and Phœnix, Cilix, and Cadmus
stood gaping at the spectacle of their sister
mounted on a white bull, not knowing whether
to be frightened or to wish the same good luck
for themselves. The gentle and innocent creature (for who could possibly doubt that he was
so?) pranced round among the children as sportively as a kitten. Europa all the while looked
down upon her brothers, nodding and laughing,
but yet with a sort of stateliness in her rosy little
face. As the bull wheeled about to take another
gallop across the meadow, the child waved her
hand, and said, "Good by," playfully pretending that she was now bound on a distant journey, and might not see her brothers again for
nobody could tell how long.

"Good by," shouted Cadmus, Phœnix, and
Cilix, all in one breath.

But, together with her enjoyment of the sport, there was still a little remnant of fear in the child's heart; so that her last look at the three boys was a troubled one, and made them feel as if their dear sister were really leaving them for-ever. And what do you think the snowy bull did next? Why, he set off, as swift as the wind, straight down to the sea shore, scampered across the sand, took an airy leap, and plunged right in among the foaming billows. The white spray rose in a shower over him and little Europa, and fell spattering down upon the water.

Then what a scream of terror did the poor child send forth! The three brothers screamed man-fully, likewise, and ran to the shore as fast as their legs would carry them, with Cadmus at their head. But it was too late. When they reached the margin of the sand, the treacherous animal was already far away in the wide blue sea, with only his snowy head and tail emerging, and poor little Europa between them, stretching out one hand towards her dear brothers, while she grasped the bull's ivory horn with the other. And there stood Cadmus, Phœnix, and Cilix, gazing at this sad spectacle, through their tears,

until they could no longer distinguish the bull's
snowy head from the white-capped billows that
seemed to boil up out of the sea's depths around
him.   Nothing more was ever seen of the white
bull — nothing more of the beautiful child.

This was a mournful story, as you may well
think, for the three boys to carry home to their
parents.   King Agenor, their father, was the
ruler of the whole country; but he loved his
little daughter Europa better than his kingdom,
or than all his other children, or than any thing
else in the world.   Therefore, when Cadmus and
his two brothers came crying home, and told him
how that a white bull had carried off their sister,
and swam with her over the sea, the king was
quite beside himself with grief and rage.   Although it was now twilight, and fast growing
dark, he bade them set out instantly in search
of her.

"Never shall you see my face again," he cried,
"unless you bring me back my little Europa, to
gladden me with her smiles and her pretty ways.
Begone, and enter my presence no more, till you
come leading her by the hand."

As King Agenor said this, his eyes flashed fire

(for he was a very passionate king,) and he looked so terribly angry that the poor boys did not even venture to ask for their suppers, but slunk away out of the palace, and only paused on the steps a moment to consult whither they should go first While they were standing there, all in dismay, their mother, Queen Telephassa, (who happened not to be by when they told the story to the king,) came hurrying after them, and said that she too would go in quest of her daughter.

" O, no, mother!" cried the boys. " The night is dark, and there is no knowing what troubles and perils we may meet with."

" Alas! my dear children," answered poor Queen Telephassa, weeping bitterly, "that is only another reason why I should go with you. If I should lose you, too, as well as my little Europa, what would become of me!"

" And let me go likewise!" said their playfellow Thasus, who came running to join them.

Thasus was the son of a seafaring person in the neighborhood; he had been brought up with the young princes, and was their intimate friend, and loved Europa very much; so they consented that he should accompany them. The whole party, therefore, set forth together. Cadmus, Phœnix, Cilix, and Thasus clustered round Queen Telephassa, grasping her skirts, and begging her to lean upon their shoulders, whenever she felt weary. In this manner they went down the palace steps, and began a journey, which turned out to be a great deal longer than they dreamed of. The last that they saw of King Agenor, he came to the door, with a servant holding a torch beside him, and called after them into the gathering darkness : —

"Remember! Never ascend these steps again without the child!"

"Never!" sobbed Queen Telephassa ; and the three brothers and Thasus answered, "Never Never! Never! Never!"

And they kept their word. Year after year King Agenor sat in the solitude of his beautiful palace, listening in vain for their returning footsteps, hoping to hear the familiar voice of the queen, and the cheerful talk of his sons and their playfellow Thasus, entering the door together, and the sweet, childish accents of little Europa in the midst of them. But so long a time went by, that, at last, if they had really come, the king would not have known that this was the voice of Telephassa, and these the younger voices that used to make such joyful echoes, when the children were playing about the palace. We must now leave King Agenor to sit on his throne, and must go along with Queen Telephassa and her four youthful companions.

They went on and on, and travelled a long way, and passed over mountains and rivers, and sailed over seas. Here, and there, and every where, they made continual inquiry if any person could tell them what had become of Europa. The rustic people, of whom they asked this question, paused a little while from their labors in the field, and looked very much surprised. They thought it strange to behold a woman in the garb of a queen, (for Telephassa, in her haste, had forgotten to take off her crown and her royal robes,) roaming about the country, with four lads around her, on such an errand as this seemed to be. But nobody could give them any tidings of Europa; nobody had seen a little girl dressed like a princess, and mounted on a snow-white bull, which galloped as swiftly as the wind.

I cannot tell you how long Queen Telephassa,

and Cadmus, Phœnix, and Cilix, her three sons, and Thasus, their playfellow, went wandering along the highways and bypaths, or through the pathless wildernesses of the earth, in this manner. But certain it is, that, before they reached any place of rest, their splendid garments were quite worn out. They all looked very much travel-stained, and would have had the dust of many countries on their shoes, if the streams, through which they waded, had not washed it all away. When they had been gone a year, Telephassa threw away her crown, because it chafed her forehead.

" It has given me many a headache," said the poor queen, " and it cannot cure my heartache."

As fast as their princely robes got torn and tattered, they exchanged them for such mean attire as ordinary people wore. By and by, they came to have a wild and homeless aspect; so that you would much sooner have taken them for a gypsy family than a queen and three princes, and a young nobleman, who had once a palace for their home, and a train of servants to do their bidding. The four boys grew up to be tall young men, with sunburnt faces. Each

of them girded on a sword, to defend themselves against the perils of the way. When the
husbandmen, at whose farm houses they sought
hospitality, needed their assistance in the harvest
field, they gave it willingly; and Queen Telephassa (who had done no work in her palace,
save to braid silk threads with golden ones)
came behind them to bind the sheaves. If pay-
ment was offered, they shook their heads, and
only asked for tidings of Europa.

"There are bulls enough in my pasture," the
old farmers would reply; "but I never heard of
one like this you tell me of. A snow-white bull
with a little princess on his back! Ho! ho! I
ask your pardon, good folks; but there never
was such a sight seen hereabouts."

At last, when his upper lip began to have the
down on it, Phœnix grew weary of rambling
hither and thither to no purpose. So, one day,
when they happened to be passing through a
pleasant and solitary tract of country, he sat
himself down on a heap of moss.

"I can go no farther," said Phœnix. "It is a
mere foolish waste of life, to spend it, as we do,
in always wandering up and down, and never

coming to any home at nightfall.   Our sister is
lost, and never will be found.   She probably
perished in the sea; or, to whatever shore the
white bull may have carried her, it is now so
many years ago, that there would be neither
love nor acquaintance between us, should we
meet again.   My father has forbidden us to return to his palace; so I shall build me a hut
of branches, and dwell here."

   " Well, son Phœnix," said Telephassa, sorrowfully, "you have grown to be a man, and must
do as you judge best.   But, for my part, I will
still go in quest of my poor child."

   " And we three will go along with you!" cried
Cadmus and Cilix, and their faithful friend
Thasus.

   But, before setting out, they all helped Phœnix to build a habitation.   When completed, it
was a sweet rural bower, roofed overhead with
an arch of living boughs.   Inside there were
two pleasant rooms, one of which had a soft
heap of moss for a bed, while the other was
furnished with a rustic seat or two, curiously
fashioned out of the crooked roots of trees.   So
comfortable and home-like did it seem, that

Telephassa and her three companions could not help sighing, to think that they must still roam about the world, instead of spending the remainder of their lives in some such cheerful abode as they had here built for Phœnix. But, when they bade him farewell, Phœnix shed tears, and probably regretted that he was no longer to keep them company.

However, he had fixed upon an admirable place to dwell in. And by and by there came other people, who chanced to have no homes; and, seeing how pleasant a spot it was, they built themselves huts in the neighborhood of Phœnix's habitation. Thus, before many years went by, a city had grown up there, in the centre of which was seen a stately palace of marble, wherein dwelt Phœnix, clothed in a purple robe, and wearing a golden crown upon his head. For the inhabitants of the new city, finding that he had royal blood in his veins, had chosen him to be their king. The very first decree of state which King Phœnix issued was, that, if a maiden happened to arrive in the kingdom, mounted on a snow-white bull, and calling herself Europa, his subjects should treat her with

the greatest kindness and respect, and imme
diately bring her to the palace. You may see,
by this, that Phœnix's conscience never quite
ceased to trouble him, for giving up the quest of
his dear sister, and sitting himself down to be
comfortable, while his mother and her companions went onward.

But often and often, at the close of a weary
day's journey, did Telephassa and Cadmus, Cilix and Thasus, remember the pleasant spot in
which they had left Phœnix. It was a sorrowful prospect for these wanderers, that on the
morrow they must again set forth, and that,
after many nightfalls, they would perhaps be no
nearer the close of their toilsome pilgrimage than
now. These thoughts made them all melancholy at times, but appeared to torment Cilix
more than the rest of the party At length,
one morning, when they were taking their
staffs in hand to set out. he thus addressed
them : —

" My dear mother, and you good brother Cad
mus, and my friend Thasus, methinks we are
like people in a dream. There is no substance
in the life which we are leading. It is such a

dreary length of time since the white bull carried off my sister Europa, that I have quite forgotten how she looked, and the tones of her voice, and, indeed, almost doubt whether such a little girl ever lived in the world. And whether she once lived or no, I am convinced that she no longer survives, and that therefore it is the merest folly to waste our own lives and happiness in seeking her. Were we to find her, she would now be a woman grown, and would look upon us all as strangers. So, to tell you the truth, I have resolved to take up my abode here; and I entreat you, mother, brother, and friend, to follow my example."

" Not I, for one," said Telephassa; although the poor queen, firmly as she spoke, was so travel-worn that she could hardly put her foot to the ground. " Not I for one! In the depths of my heart, little Europa is still the rosy child who ran to gather flowers so many years ago. She has not grown to womanhood, nor forgotten me. At noon, at night, journeying onward, sitting down to rest, her childish voice is always in my ears, calling ' Mother! mother!' Stop here who may, there is no repose for me.'

"Nor for me," said Cadmus, "while my dear mother pleases to go onward."

And the faithful Thasus, too, was resolved to bear them company. They remained with Cilix a few days, however, and helped him to build a rustic bower, resembling the one which they had formerly built for Phœnix.

When they were bidding him farewell, Cilix burst into tears, and told his mother that it seemed just as melancholy a dream to stay there, in solitude, as to go onward. If she really believed that they would ever find Europa, he was willing to continue the search with them, even now. But Telephassa bade him remain there, and be happy, if his own heart would let him. So the pilgrims took their leave of him, and departed, and were hardly out of sight before some other wandering people came along that way, and saw Cilix's habitation, and were greatly delighted with the appearance of the place. There being abundance of unoccupied ground in the neighborhood, these strangers built huts for themselves, and were soon joined by a multitude of new settlers, who quickly formed a city. In the middle of it was seen a magnificent palace of colored marble, on the balcony of which, every noontide, appeared Cilix, in a long purple robe, and with a jewelled crown upon his head ; for the inhabit ants, when they found out that he was a king's son, had considered him the fittest of all men to be a king himself.

One of the first acts of King Cilix's government was to send out an expedition, consisting of a grave ambassador and an escort of bold and hardy young men, with orders to visit the principal kingdoms of the earth, and inquire whether a young maiden had passed through those regions, galloping swiftly on a white bull. It is, therefore, plain to my mind, that Cilix secretly blamed himself for giving up the search for Europa, as long as he was able to put one foot before the other.

As for Telephassa, and Cadmus, and the good Thasus, it grieves me to think of them, still keeping up that weary pilgrimage. The two young men did their best for the poor queen, helping her over the rough places, often carrying her across rivulets in their faithful arms, and seeking to shelter her at nightfall, even when they themselves lay on the ground. Sad, sad it was to hear them asking of every passer by if he had seen Europa, so long after the white bull had carried her away. But, though the gray years thrust themselves between, and made the child's figure dim in their remembrance, neither of these true-hearted three ever dreamed of giving up the search.

One morning, however, poor Thasus found that he had sprained his ankle, and could not possibly go a step farther.

"After a few days, to be sure," said he, mournfully, "I might make shift to hobble along with a stick. But that would only delay you, and perhaps hinder you from finding dear little Europa, after all your pains and trouble. Do you go forward, therefore, my beloved companions, and leave me to follow as I may."

"Thou hast been a true friend, dear Thasus," said Queen Telephassa, kissing his forehead. "Being neither my son, nor the brother of our lost Europa, thou hast shown thyself truer to me and her than Phœnix and Cilix did, whom we have left behind us. Without thy loving help, and that of my son Cadmus, my limbs could not have borne me half so far as this. Now,

take thy rest, and be at peace. For — and it is
the first time I have owned it to myself — I begin
to question whether we shall ever find my be·
loved daughter in this world."

Saying this, the poor queen shed tears, because
it was a grievous trial to the mother's heart to
confess that her hopes were growing faint. From
that day forward, Cadmus noticed that she never
travelled with the same alacrity of spirit that had
heretofore supported her. Her weight was heav·
·er upon his arm.

Before setting out, Cadmus helped Thasus
build a bower ; while Telephassa, being too in·
firm to give any great assistance, advised them
how to fit it up and furnish it, so that it might
be as comfortable as a hut of branches could.
Thasus, however, did not spend all his days in
this green bower. For it happened to him, as to
Phœnix and Cilix, that other homeless people
visited the spot, and liked it, and built them·
selves habitations in the neighborhood. So here,
in the course of a few years, was another thriv·
ing city, with a red freestone palace in the centre
of it, where Thasus sat upon a throne, doing
justice to the people, with a purple robe over his

9

shoulders, a sceptre in his hand, and a crown
upon his head. The inhabitants had made him
king, not for the sake of any royal blood, (for
none was in his veins,) but because Thasus was
an upright, true-hearted, and courageous man,
and therefore fit to rule.

But, when the affairs of his kingdom were all
settled, King Thasus laid aside his purple robe,
and crown, and sceptre, and bade his worthiest
subject distribute justice to the people in his
stead. Then, grasping the pilgrim's staff that
had supported him so long, he set forth again,
hoping still to discover some hoof mark of the
snow-white bull, some trace of the vanished
child. He returned, after a lengthened absence,
and sat down wearily upon his throne. To his
latest hour, nevertheless, King Thasus showed
his true-hearted remembrance of Europa, by or-
dering that a fire should always be kept burning
in his palace, and a bath steaming hot, and food
ready to be served up, and a bed with snow
white sheets, in case the maiden should arrive,
and require immediate refreshment. And though
Europa never came, the good Thasus had the
blessings of many a poor traveller, who profited

by the food and lodging which were meant for the little playmate of the king's boyhood.

Telephassa and Cadmus were now pursuing their weary way, with no companion but each other. The queen leaned heavily upon her son's arm, and could walk only a few miles a day. But for all her weakness and weariness, she would not be persuaded to give up the search. It was enough to bring tears into the eyes of bearded men to hear the melancholy tone with which she inquired of every stranger whether he could tell her any news of the lost child.

" Have you seen a little girl — no, no, I mean a young maiden of full growth — passing by this way, mounted on a snow-white bull, which gallops as swiftly as the wind ? "

" We have seen no such wondrous sight," the people would reply; and very often, taking Cadmus aside, they whispered to him, " Is this stately and sad-looking woman your mother? Surely she is not in her right mind; and you ought to take her home, and make her comfortable, and do your best to get this dream out of her fancy."

" It is no dream," said Cadmus. " Every thing else is a dream, save that."

But, one day, Telephassa seemed feebler than usual, and leaned almost her whole weight on the arm of Cadmus, and walked more slowly than ever before. At last they reached a solitary spot, where she told her son that she must needs lie down, and take a good, long rest.

" A good, long rest!" she repeated, looking Cadmus tenderly in the face. " A good, long rest, thou dearest one!"

" As long as you please, dear mother," answered Cadmus.

Telephassa bade him sit down on the turf beside her, and then she took his hand.

" My son," said she, fixing her dim eyes most lovingly upon him, " this rest that I speak of will be very, long indeed! You must not wait till it is finished. Dear Cadmus, you do not comprehend me. You must make a grave here, and lay your mother's weary frame into it. My pilgrimage is over."

Cadmus burst into tears, and, for a long time, refused to believe that his dear mother was now to be taken from him. But Telephassa reasoned with him, and kissed him, and at length made him discern that it was better for her spirit to pass away out of the toil, the weariness, the grief, and disappointment which had burdened her on earth, ever since the child was lost. He therefore repressed his sorrow, and listened to her last words.

"Dearest Cadmus," said she, "thou hast been the truest son that ever mother had, and faithful to the very last. Who else would have borne with my infirmities as thou hast! It is owing to thy care, thou tenderest child, that my grave was not dug long years ago, in some valley or on some hillside, that lies far, far behind us. It is enough. Thou shalt wander no more on this hopeless search. But, when thou hast laid thy mother in the earth, then go, my son, to Delphi, and inquire of the oracle what thou shalt do next."

"O mother, mother," cried Cadmus, "couldst thou but have seen my sister before this hour!"

"It matters little now," answered Telephassa, and there was a smile upon her face. "I go now to the better world, and, sooner or later, shall find my daughter there."

I will not sadden you, my little hearers, with telling how Telephassa died and was buried, but will only say, that her dying smile grew brighter, instead of vanishing from her dead face; so that Cadmus felt' convinced that, at her very first step into the better world, she had caught Europa in her arms. He planted some flowers on his mother's grave, and left them to grow there, and make the place beautiful, when he should be far away.

After performing this last sorrowful duty, he set forth alone, and took the road towards the famous oracle of Delphi, as Telephassa had advised him. On his way thither, he still inquired of most people whom he met whether they had seen Europa; for, to say the truth, Cadmus had grown so accustomed to ask the question, that it came to his lips as readily as a remark about the weather. He received various answers. Some told him one thing, and some another. Among the rest, a mariner affirmed, that, many years before, in a distant country, he had heard a rumor about a white bull, which came swimming across the sea with a child on his back, dressed up in flowers that were blighted by the sea water. He did not know what had become of the child or the bull; and Cadmus suspected indeed, by a queer twinkle in the mariner's eyes, that he was putting a joke upon him, and had never really heard any thing about the matter.

Poor Cadmus found it more wearisome to travel alone than to bear all his dear mother's weight, while she had kept him company. His heart, you will understand, was now so heavy that it seemed impossible, sometimes, to carry it any farther. But his limbs were strong and active, and well accustomed to exercise. He walked swiftly along, thinking of King Agenor and Queen Telephassa, and his brothers, and the friendly Thasus, all of whom he had left behind him, at one point of his pilgrimage or another, and never expected to see them any more. Full of these remembrances, he came within sight of a lofty mountain, which the people thereabouts told him was called Parnassus. On the slope of Mount Parnassus was the famous Delphi, whither Cadmus was going.

This Delphi was supposed to be the very midmost spot of the whole world. The place of the oracle was a certain cavity in the mountain side, over which, when Cadmus came thither, he found a rude bower of branches. It reminded him of

those which he had helped to build for Phœnix
and Cilix, and afterwards for Thasus. In later
times, when multitudes of people came from great
distances to put questions to the oracle, a spacious
temple of marble was erected over the spot.
But in the days of Cadmus, as I have told you,
there was only this rustic bower, with its abundance of green foliage, and a tuft of shrubbery,
that ran wild over the mysterious hole in the
hillside.

When Cadmus had thrust a passage through
the tangled boughs, and made his way into the
bower, he did not at first discern the half-hidden
cavity. But soon he felt a cold stream of air
rushing out of it, with so much force that it
shook the ringlets on his cheek. Pulling away
the shrubbery which clustered over the hole, he
bent forward, and spoke in a distinct but reverential tone, as if addressing some unseen personage inside of the mountain.

" Sacred oracle of Delphi," said he, " whither
shall I go next in quest of my dear sister Eu
ropa ? "

There was at first a deep silence, and then a
rushing sound, or a noise like a long sigh

proceeding out of the interior of the earth. This cavity, you must know, was looked upon as a sort of fountain of truth, which sometimes gushed out in audible words; although, for the most part, these words were such a riddle that they might just as well have staid at the bottom of the hole. But Cadmus was more fortunate than many others who went to Delphi in search of truth. By and by, the rushing noise began to sound like articulate language. It repeated, over and over again, the following sentence, which, after all, was so like the vague whistle of a blast of air, that Cadmus really did not quite know whether it meant any thing or not: —

"Seek her no more! Seek her no more! Seek her no more!"

"What, then, shall I do?" asked Cadmus.

For, ever since he was a child, you know, it had been the great object of his life to find his sister. From the very hour that he left following the butterfly in the meadow, near his father's palace, he had done his best to follow Europa, over land and sea. And now, if he must give up the search, he seemed to have no more business in the world.

But again the sighing gust of air grew into something like a hoarse voice.

"Follow the cow!" it said. "Follow the cow! Follow the cow!"

And when these words had been repeated until Cadmus was tired of hearing them, (especially as he could not imagine what cow it was, or why he was to follow her,) the gusty hole gave vent to another sentence.

"Where the stray cow lies down, there is your home."

These words were pronounced but a single time, and died away into a whisper before Cadmus was fully satisfied that he had caught the meaning. He put other questions, but received no answer; only the gust of wind sighed continually out of the cavity, and blew the withered leaves rustling along the ground before it.

"Did there really come any words out of the hole?" thought Cadmus; "or have I been dreaming all this while?"

He turned away from the oracle, and thought himself no wiser than when he came thither. Caring little what might happen to him, he took the first path that offered itself, and went along at a sluggish pace; for, having no object in view, nor any reason to go one way more than another, it would certainly have been foolish to make haste. Whenever he met any body, the old question was at his tongue's end: —

" Have you seen a beautiful maiden, dressed like a king's daughter, and mounted on a snow-white bull, that gallops as swiftly as the wind?"

But, remembering what the oracle had said, he only half uttered the words, and then mumbled the rest indistinctly; and from his confusion, people must have imagined that this handsome young man had lost his wits.

I know not how far Cadmus had gone, nor could he himself have told you, when, at no great distance before him, he beheld a brindled cow. She was lying down by the wayside, and quietly chewing her cud; nor did she take any notice of the young man until he had approached pretty nigh. Then, getting leisurely upon her feet, and giving her head a gentle toss, she began to move along at a moderate pace, often pausing just long enough to crop a mouthful of grass. Cadmus loitered behind, whistling idly to himself, and scarcely noticing the cow; until the

thought occurred to him, whether this could possibly be the animal which, according to the oracle's response, was to serve him for a guide. But
he smiled at himself for fancying such a thing.
He could not seriously think that this was the
cow, because she went along so quietly, behaving
just like any other cow. Evidently she neither
knew nor cared so much as a wisp of hay about
Cadmus, and was only thinking how to get her
living along the wayside, where the herbage was
green and fresh. Perhaps she was going home
to be milked.

"Cow, cow, cow!" cried Cadmus. "Hey,
Brindle, hey! Stop, my good cow."

He wanted to come up with the cow, so as
to examine her, and see if she would appear to
know him, or whether there were any peculiarities to distinguish her from a thousand other
cows, whose only business is to fill the milk pail,
and sometimes kick it over. But still the brindled cow trudged on, whisking her tail to keep
the flies away, and taking as little notice of Cadmus as she well could. If he walked slowly, so
did the cow, and seized the opportunity to graze.
If he quickened his pace, the cow went just so

much the faster; and once, when Cadmus tried to catch her by running, she threw out her heels, stuck her tail straight on end, and set off at a gallop, looking as queerly as cows generally do, while putting themselves to their speed.

When Cadmus saw that it was impossible to come up with her, he walked on moderately, as before. The cow, too, went leisurely on, without looking behind. Wherever the grass was greenest, there she nibbled a mouthful or two. Where a brook glistened brightly across the path, there the cow drank, and breathed a comfortable sigh, and drank again, and trudged onward at the pace that best suited herself and Cadmus.

"I do believe," thought Cadmus, "that this may be the cow that was foretold me. If it be the one, I suppose she will lie down somewhere hereabouts."

Whether it were the oracular cow or some other one, it did not seem reasonable that she should travel a great way farther. So, whenever they reached a particularly pleasant spot on a breezy hiliside, or in a sheltered vale, or flowery meadow, on the shore of a calm lake, or along the bank of a clear stream, Cadmus looked

eagerly around to see if the situation would suit
him for a home.   But still, whether he liked the
place or no, the brindled cow never offered to lie
down.   On she went at the quiet pace of a cow
going homeward to the barn yard; and, every
moment, Cadmus expected to see a milkmaid approaching with a pail, or a herdsman running to
head the stray animal, and turn her back towards
the pasture.   But no milkmaid came; no herdsman drove her back; and Cadmus followed the
stray Brindle till he was almost ready to drop
down with fatigue.

"O, brindled cow," cried he, in a tone of despair, "do you never mean to stop?"

He had now grown too intent on following
her to think of lagging behind, however long
the way, and whatever might be his fatigue
Indeed, it seemed as if there were something
about the animal that bewitched people.   Several
persons who happened to see the brindled cow
and Cadmus following behind, began to trudge
after her, precisely as he did.   Cadmus was glad
of somebody to converse with, and therefore
talked very freely to these good people.   He told
them all his adventures, and how he had left

King Agenor in his palace, and Phœnix at one
place, and Cilix at another, and Thasus at a
third, and his dear mother, Queen Telephassa,
under a flowery sod; so that now he was quite
alone, both friendless and homeless. He mentioned, likewise, that the oracle had bidden him
be guided by a cow, and inquired of the strangers whether they supposed that this brindled
animal could be the one.

" Why, 'tis a very wonderful affair," answered
one of his new companions. " I am pretty well
acquainted with the ways of cattle, and I never
knew a cow, of her own accord, to go so far with
out stopping. If my legs will let me, I'll never
leave following the beast till she lies down."

" Nor I!" said a second.

" Nor I!" cried a third. " If she goes a hun
dred miles farther, I'm determined to see the end
of it."

The secret of it was, you must know, that the
cow was an enchanted cow, and that, without
their being conscious of it, she threw some of her
enchantment over every body that took so much
as half a dozen steps behind her. They could
not possibly help following her, though, all the

time, they fancied themselves doing it of their own accord. The cow was by no means very nice in choosing her path; so that sometimes they had to scramble over rocks, or wade through mud and mire, and were all in a terribly bedraggled condition, and tired to death, and very hungry, into the bargain. What a weary business it was!

But still they kept trudging stoutly forward, and talking as they went. The strangers grew very fond of Cadmus, and resolved never to leave him, but to help him build a city wherever the cow might lie down. In the centre of it there should be a noble palace, in which Cadmus might dwell, and be their king, with a throne, a crown, and sceptre, a purple robe, and every thing else that a king ought to have; for in him there was the royal blood, and the royal heart, and the head that knew how to rule.

While they were talking of these schemes and beguiling the tediousness of the way with laying out the plan of the new city, one of the company happened to look at the cow.

"Joy! joy!" cried he, clapping his hands. "Brindle is going to lie down."

They all looked; and, sure enough, the cow had stopped, and was staring leisurely about her, as other cows do when on the point of lying down. And slowly, slowly did she recline herself on the soft grass, first bending her fore legs, and then crouching her hind ones. When Cadmus and his companions came up with her, there was the brindled cow taking her ease, chewing her cud, and looking them quietly in the face; as if this was just the spot she had been seeking for, and as if it were all a matter of course.

"This, then," said Cadmus, gazing around him, "this is to be my home."

It was a fertile and lovely plain, with great trees flinging their sun-speckled shadows over it, and hills fencing it in from the rough weather. At no great distance, they beheld a river gleaming in the sunshine. A home feeling stole into the heart of poor Cadmus. He was very glad to know that here he might awake in the morning, without the necessity of putting on his dusty sandals to travel farther and farther. The days and the years would pass over him, and find him still in this pleasant spot. If he could

10

have had his brothers with him, and his friend Thasus, and could have seen his dear mother under a roof of his own, he might here have been happy, after all their disappointments. Some day or other, too, his sister Europa might have come quietly to the door of his home, and smiled round upon the familiar faces. But, indeed, since there was no hope of regaining the friends of his boyhood, or ever seeing his dear sister again, Cadmus resolved to make himself happy with these new companions, who had grown so fond of him while following the cow.

"Yes, my friends," said he to them, "this is to be our home. Here we will build our habitations. The brindled cow, which has led us hither, will supply us with milk. We will cultivate the neighboring soil, and lead an innocent and happy life."

His companions joyfully assented to this plan; and, in the first place, being very hungry and thirsty, they looked about them for the means of providing a comfortable meal. Not far off, they saw a tuft of trees, which appeared as if there might be a spring of water beneath them. They went thither to fetch some, leaving Cadmus stretched on the ground along with the brindled cow; for, now that he had found a place of rest, it seemed as if all the weariness of his pilgrimage, ever since he left King Agenor's palace, had fallen upon him at once. But his new friends had not long been gone, when he was suddenly startled by cries, shouts, and screams, and the noise of a terrible struggle, and in the midst of it all, a most awful hissing, which went right through his ears like a rough saw.

Running towards the tuft of trees, he beheld the head and fiery eyes of an immense serpent or dragon, with the widest jaws that ever a dragon had, and a vast many rows of horribly sharp teeth. Before Cadmus could reach the spot, this pitiless reptile had killed his poor companions, and was busily devouring them, making but a mouthful of each man.

It appears that the fountain of water was enchanted, and that the dragon had been set to guard it, so that no mortal might ever quench his thirst there. As the neighboring inhabitants carefully avoided the spot, it was now a long time (not less than a hundred years, or thereabouts) since the monster had broken his fast;

and, as was natural enough, his appetite had grown to be enormous, and was not half satisfied by the poor people whom he had just eaten up. When he caught sight of Cadmus, therefore, he set up another abominable hiss, and flung back his immense jaws, until his mouth looked like a great red cavern, at the farther end of which were seen the legs of his last victim, whom he had hardly had time to swallow.

But Cadmus was so enraged at the destruction of his friends, that he cared neither for the size of the dragon's jaws nor for his hundreds of sharp teeth. Drawing his sword, he rushed at the monster, and flung himself right into his cavernous mouth. This bold method of attacking him took the dragon by surprise; for, in fact, Cadmus had leaped so far down into his throat, that the rows of terrible teeth could not close upon him, nor do him the least harm in the world. Thus, though the struggle was a tremendous one, and though the dragon shattered the tuft of trees into small splinters by the lashing of his tail, yet, as Cadmus was all the while slashing and stabbing at his very vitals, it was not long before the scaly wretch bethought himse.f of slipping away. He had not gone his length, however, when the brave Cadmus gave him a sword thrust that finished the battle; and, creeping out of the gateway of the creature's jaws, there he beheld him still wriggling his vast bulk, although there was no longer life enough in him to harm a little child.

But do not you suppose that it made Cadmus sorrowful to think of the melancholy fate which had befallen those poor, friendly people, who had followed the cow along with him? It seemed as if he were doomed to lose every body whom he loved, or to see them perish in one way or another. And here he was, after all his toils and troubles, in a solitary place, with not a single human being to help him build a hut.

"What shall I do?" cried he aloud. "It were better for me to have been devoured by the dragon, as my poor companions were."

"Cadmus," said a voice — but whether it came from above or below him, or whether it spoke within his own breast, the young man could not tell — "Cadmus, pluck out the drag-on's teeth, and plant them in the earth."

This was a strange thing to do; nor was it

very easy, I should imagine, to dig out all those
deep-rooted fangs from the dead dragon's jaws.
But Cadmus toiled and tugged, and after pound-
ing the monstrous head almost to pieces with a
great stone, he at last collected as many teeth as
might have filled a bushel or two. The next
thing was to plant them. This, likewise, was a
tedious piece of work, especially as Cadmus was
already exhausted with killing the dragon and
knocking his head to pieces, and had nothing to
dig the earth with, that I know of, unless it were
his sword blade. Finally, however, a sufficiently
large tract of ground was turned up, and sown
with this new kind of seed ; although half of the
dragon's teeth still remained to be planted some
other day.

Cadmus, quite out of breath, stood leaning
upon his sword, and wondering what was to
happen next. He had waited but a few moments, when he began to see a sight, which was
as great a marvel as the most marvellous thing
I ever told you about.

The sun was shining slantwise over the field,
and showed all the moist, dark soil, just like any
other newly-planted piece of ground. All at

once, Cadmus fancied he saw something glisten very brightly, first at one spot, then at another, and then at a hundred and a thousand spots together. Soon he perceived them to be the steel heads of spears, sprouting up every where like so many stalks of grain, and continually growing taller and taller. Next appeared a vast number of bright sword blades, thrusting themselves up in the same way. A moment afterwards, the whole surface of the ground was broken by a multitude of polished brass helmets, coming up like a crop of enormous beans. So rapidly did they grow, that Cadmus now discerned the fierce countenance of a man beneath every one. In short, before he had time to think what a wonderful affair it was, he beheld an abundant harvest of what looked like human beings, armed with helmets and breastplates, shields, swords, and spears; and before they were well out of the earth, they brandished their weapons, and clashed them one against another, seeming to think, little while as they had yet lived, that they had wasted too much of life without a battle. Every tooth of the dragon had produced one of these sons of deadly mischief.

Up sprouted, also, a great many trumpeters;
and with the first breath that they drew, they
put their brazen trumpets to their lips, and
sounded a tremendous and ear-shattering blast;
so that the whole space, just now so quiet and
solitary, reverberated with the clash and clang
of arms, the bray of warlike music, and the
shouts of angry men. So enraged did they all
look, that Cadmus fully expected them to put
the whole world to the sword. How fortunate
would it be for a great conqueror, if he could get
a bushel of the dragon's teeth to sow!

" Cadmus," said the same voice which he had
before heard, " throw a stone into the midst of
the armed men."

So Cadmus seized a large stone, and, flinging
it into the middle of the earth army, saw it strike
the breastplate of a gigantic and fierce-looking
warrior. Immediately on feeling the blow, he
seemed to take it for granted that somebody
had struck him; and, uplifting his weapon, he
smote his next neighbor a blow that cleft his
helmet asunder, and stretched him on the ground.
In an instant, those nearest the fallen warrior
began to strike at one another with their swords.

and stab with their spears. The confusion spread wider and wider. Each man smote down his brother, and was himself smitten down before he had time to exult in his victory. The trumpeters, all the while, blew their blasts shriller and shriller; each soldier shouted a battle cry, and often fell with it on his lips. It was the strangest spectacle of causeless wrath, and of mischief for no good end, that had ever been witnessed; but, after all, it was neither more foolish nor more wicked than a thousand battles that have since been fought, in which men have slain their brothers with just as little reason as these children of the dragon's teeth. It ought to be considered, too, that the dragon people were made for nothing else; whereas other mortals were born to love and help one another.

Well, this memorable battle continued to rage until the ground was strewn with helmeted heads that had been cut off. Of all the thousands that began the fight, there were only five left standing. These now rushed from different parts of the field, and, meeting in the middle of it, clashed their swords, and struck at each other's hearts as fiercely as ever.

"Cadmus," said the voice again, "bid those five warriors sheathe their swords. They will help you to build the city."

Without hesitating an instant, Cadmus stepped forward, with the aspect of a king and a leader and extending his drawn sword amongst them, spoke to the warriors in a stern and command‧ ing voice.

"Sheathe your weapons!" said he.

And forthwith, feeling themselves bound to obey him, the five remaining sons of the drag‧ on's teeth made him a military salute with their swords, returned them to the scabbards, and stood before Cadmus in a rank, eying him as soldiers eye their captain, while awaiting the word of command.

These five men had probably sprung from the biggest of the dragon's teeth, and were the bold‧ est and strongest of the whole army. They were almost giants indeed, and had good need to be so, else they never could have lived through so terrible a fight. They still had a very furious look, and, if Cadmus happened to glance aside, would glare at one another, with fire flashing out of their eyes. It was strange, too, to ob‧

serve how the earth, out of which they had so lately grown, was incrusted, here and there, on their bright breastplates, and even begrimed their faces; just as you may have seen it clinging to beets and carrots, when pulled out of their native soil. Cadmus hardly knew whether to consider them as men, or some odd kind of vegetable although, on the whole, he concluded that there was human nature in them, because they were so fond of trumpets and weapons, and so ready to shed blood.

They looked him earnestly in the face, waiting for his next order, and evidently desiring no other employment than to follow him from one battle field to another, all over the wide world. But Cadmus was wiser than these earth-born creatures, with the dragon's fierceness in them, and knew better how to use their strength and hardihood.

"Come!" said he. "You are sturdy fellows. Make yourselves useful! Quarry some stones with those great swords of yours, and help me to build a city."

The five soldiers grumbled a little, and muttered that it was their business to overthrow cities, not to build them up. But Cadmus looked at them with a stern eye, and spoke to them in a tone of authority, so that they knew nim for their master, and never again thought of disobeying his commands. They set to work in good earnest, and toiled so diligently, that, in a very short time, a city began to make its appear- ance. At first, to be sure, the workmen showed a quarrelsome disposition. Like savage beasts, they would doubtless have done one another a mischief, if Cadmus had not kept watch over them, and quelled the fierce old serpent that lurked in their hearts, when he saw it gleaming out of their wild eyes. But, in course of time, they got accustomed to honest labor, and had sense enough to feel that there was more true enjoyment in living at peace, and doing good to one's neighbor, than in striking at him with a two-edged sword. It may not be too much to hope that the rest of mankind will by and by grow as wise and peaceable as these five earth begrimed warriors, who sprang from the drag on's teeth.

And now the city was built, and there was a home in it for each of the workmen. But the palace of Cadmus was not yet erected, because they had left it till the last, meaning to introduce all the new improvements of architecture, and make it very commodious, as well as stately and beautiful. After finishing the rest of their labors, they all went to bed betimes, in order to rise in the gray of the morning, and get at least the foundation of the edifice laid before nightfall. But, when Cadmus arose, and took his way towards the site where the palace was to be built, followed by his five sturdy workmen marching all in a row, what do you think he saw?

What should it be but the most magnificent palace that had ever been seen in the world. It was built of marble and other beautiful kinds of stone, and rose high into the air, with a splendid dome and a portico along the front, and carved pillars, and every thing else that befitted the habitation of a mighty king. It had grown up out of the earth in almost as short a time as it had taken the armed host to spring from the dragon's teeth; and what made the matter more strange, no seed of this stately edifice had ever been planted.

When the five workmen beheld the dome, with

the morning sunshine making it look golden and glorious, they gave a great shout.

"Long live King Cadmus," they cried, "in his beautiful palace."

And the new king, with his five faithful followers at his heels, shouldering their pickaxes and marching in a rank, (for they still had a soldierlike sort of behavior, as their nature was,) ascended the palace steps.   Halting at the entrance, they gazed through a long vista of lofty pillars, that were ranged from end to end of a great hall.   At the farther extremity of this hall, approaching slowly towards him, Cadmus beheld a female figure, wonderfully beautiful, and adorned with a royal robe, and a crown of diamonds over her golden ringlets, and the richest necklace that ever a queen wore.   His heart thrilled with delight.   He fancied it his long-lost sister Europa, now grown to womanhood, coming to make him happy, and to repay him with her sweet sisterly affection, for all those weary wanderings in quest of her since he left King Agenor's palace — for the tears that he had shed, on parting with Phœnix, and Cilix, and Thasus — for the heart-breakings that had made the whole world seem dismal to him over his dear mother's grave.

But, as Cadmus advanced to meet the beautiful stranger, he saw that her features were unknown to him, although, in the little time that it
required to tread along the hall, he had already
felt a sympathy betwixt himself and her.

"No, Cadmus," said the same voice that had
spoken to him in the field of the armed men,
"this is not that dear sister Europa whom you
have sought so faithfully all over the wide world.
This is Harmonia, a daughter of the sky, who
is given you instead of sister, and brothers, and
friend, and mother. You will find all those dear
ones in her alone."

So King Cadmus dwelt in the palace, with his
new friend Harmonia, and found a great deal of
comfort in his magnificent abode, but would
doubtless have found as much, if not more, in
the humblest cottage by the wayside. Before
many years went by, there was a group of rosy
little children (but how they came thither has
always been a mystery to me) sporting in the
great hall, and on the marble steps of the palace,
and running joyfully to meet King Cadmus when
affairs of state left him at leisure to play with
them. They called him father, and Queen

Harmonia mother. The five old soldiers of the dragon's teeth grew very fond of these small urchins, and were never weary of showing them how to shoulder sticks, flourish wooden swords, and march in military order, blowing a penny trumpet, or beating an abominable rub-a-dub upon a little drum.

But King Cadmus, lest there should be too much of the dragon's tooth in his children's disposition, used to find time from his kingly duties to teach them their A B C — which he invented for their benefit, and for which many little people, I am afraid, are not half so grateful to him as they ought to be.

CIRCE'S PALACE.

SOME of you have heard, no doubt, of the wise King Ulysses, and how he went to the siege of Troy, and how, after that famous city was taken and burned, he spent ten long years in trying to get back again to his own little kingdom of Ithaca. At one time in the course of this weary voyage, he arrived at an island that looked very green and pleasant, but the name of which was unknown to him. For, only a little while before he came thither, he had met with a terrible hurricane, or rather a great many hurricanes at once, which drove his fleet of vessels into a strange part of the sea, where neither himself nor any of his mariners had ever sailed. This misfortune was entirely owing to the foolish curiosity of his shipmates, who, while Ulysses lay asleep, had untied some very bulky leathern bags, in which they

11

supposed a valuable treasure to be concealed.
But in each of these stout bags, King Æolus,
the ruler of the winds, had tied up a tempest,
and had given it to Ulysses to keep, in order that
he might be sure of a favorable passage homeward to Ithaca ; and when the strings were
loosened, forth rushed the whistling blasts, like
air out of a blown bladder, whitening the sea
with foam, and scattering the vessels nobody
could tell whither.

Immediately after escaping from this peril, a
still greater one had befallen him. Scudding before the hurricane, he reached a place, which, as he
afterwards found, was called Læstrygonia, where
some monstrous giants had eaten up many of
his companions, and had sunk every one of his
vessels, except that in which he himself sailed,
by flinging great masses of rock at them, from
the cliffs along the shore. After going through
such troubles as these, you cannot wonder that
King Ulysses was glad to moor his tempest-
beaten bark in a quiet cove of the green island,
which I began with telling you about. But he
had encountered so many dangers from giants,
and one-eyed Cyclopes, and monsters of the sea

and land, that he could not help dreading some mischief, even in this pleasant and seemingly solitary spot. For two days, therefore, the poor weather-worn voyagers kept quiet, and either staid on board of their vessel, or merely crept along under the cliffs that bordered the shore; and to keep themselves alive, they dug shellfish out of the sand, and sought for any little rill of fresh water that might be running towards the sea.

Before the two days were spent, they grew very weary of this kind of life; for the followers of King Ulysses, as you will find it important to remember, were terrible gormandizers, and pretty sure to grumble if they missed their regular meals, and their irregular ones besides. Their stock of provisions was quite exhausted, and even the shellfish began to get scarce, so that they had now to choose between starving to death or venturing into the interior of the island, where perhaps some huge three-headed dragon, or other horrible monster, had his den. Such misshapen creatures were very numerous in those days; and nobody ever expected to make a voyage, or take a journey, without running more or less risk of being devoured by them.

But King Ulysses was a bold man as well as a prudent one; and on the third morning he determined to discover what sort of a place the island was, and whether it were possible to obtain a supply of food for the hungry mouths of his companions. So, taking a spear in his hand, he clambered to the summit of a cliff, and gazed round about him. At a distance, towards the centre of the island, he beheld the stately towers of what seemed to be a palace, built of snow-white marble, and rising in the midst of a grove of lofty trees. The thick branches of these trees stretched across the front of the edifice, and more than half concealed it, although, from the portion which he saw, Ulysses judged it to be spacious and exceedingly beautiful, and probably the residence of some great nobleman or prince. A blue smoke went curling up from the chimney, and was almost the pleasantest part of the spectacle to Ulysses. For, from the abundance of this smoke, it was reasonable to conclude that there was a good fire in the kitchen, and that, at dinner time, a plentiful banquet would be served up to the inhabitants of the palace, and to whatever guests might happen to drop in.

With so agreeable a prospect before him, Ulysses fancied that he could not do better than to go straight to the palace gate, and tell the master of it that there was a crew of poor ship-wrecked mariners, not far off, who had eaten nothing for a day or two, save a few clams and oysters, and would therefore be thankful for a little food. And the prince or nobleman must be a very stingy curmudgeon, to be sure, if, at least, when his own dinner was over, he would not bid them welcome to the broken victuals from the table.

Pleasing himself with this idea, King Ulysses had made a few steps in the direction of the palace, when there was a great twittering and chirping from the branch of a neighboring tree. A moment afterwards, a bird came flying to-wards him, and hovered in the air, so as al-most to brush his face with its wings. It was a very pretty little bird, with purple wings and body, and yellow legs, and a circle of golden feathers round its neck, and on its head a golden tuft, which looked like a king's crown in minia-ture. Ulysses tried to catch the bird. But it fluttered nimbly out of his reach, still chirping in a piteous tone, as if it could have told a lamentable story, had it only been gifted with human language. And when he attempted to drive it away, the bird flew no farther than the bough of the next tree, and again came fluttering about his head, with its doleful chirp, as soon as he showed a purpose of going forward.

"Have you any thing to tell me, little bird?" asked Ulysses.

And he was ready to listen attentively to whatever the bird might communicate; for, at the siege of Troy, and elsewhere, he had known such odd things to happen, that he would not have considered it much out of the common run had this little feathered creature talked as plainly as himself.

"Peep!" said the bird, "peep, peep, pe — weep!" And nothing else would it say, but only, "Peep, peep, pe — weep!" in a melancholy cadence, and over and over and over again. As often as Ulysses moved forward, however, the bird showed the greatest alarm, and did its best to drive him back, with the anxious flutter of its purple wings. Its unaccountable behavior made him conclude, at last, that the bird knew of some danger that awaited him, **and which must needs be** very terrible, **beyond all question,** since it moved even **a** little fowl to feel compassion for a human being. So he re-solved, for the present, to return to the vessel, and tell his companions what he had seen.

This appeared to satisfy the bird. As soon as Ulysses turned back, it ran up the trunk of a tree, and began to pick insects out of the bark with its long, sharp bill; for it was a kind of woodpecker, you must know, and had to get its living in the same manner as other birds of that species. But every little while, as it pecked at the bark of the tree, the purple bird bethought itself of some secret sorrow, and repeated its plaintive note of " Peep, peep, pe — weep!"

On his way to the shore, Ulysses had the good luck to kill a large stag by thrusting his spear into its back. Taking it on his shoulders, (for he was a remarkably strong man,) he lugged it along with him, and flung it down before his hungry companions. I have already hinted to you what gormandizers some of the comrades of King Ulysses were. From what is related of them, I reckon that their favorite diet was pork and that they had lived upon it until a good part of their physical substance was swine's flesh, and their tempers and dispositions were very much akin to the hog. A dish of venison, however, was no unacceptable meal to them, especially after feeding so long on oysters and clams. So, beholding the dead stag, they felt of its ribs, in a knowing way, and lost no time in kindling a fire, of driftwood, to cook it. The rest of the day was spent in feasting; and if these enormous eaters got up from table at sunset, it was only because they could not scrape another morsel off the poor animal's bones.

The next morning, their appetites were as sharp as ever. They looked at Ulysses, as if they expected him to clamber up the cliff again, and come back with another fat deer upon his shoulders. Instead of setting out, however, he summoned the whole crew together, and told them it was in vain to hope that he could kill a stag every day for their dinner, and therefore it was advisable to think of some other mode of satisfying their hunger.

"Now," said he, "when I was on the cliff, yesterday, I discovered that this island is inhabited. At a considerable distance from the shore stood a marble palace, which appeared to be very spacious, and had a great deal of· smoke curling out of one of its chimneys."

"Aha!" muttered some of his companions, smacking their lips. "That smoke must have come from the kitchen fire. There was a good dinner on the spit; and no doubt there will be as good a one to-day."

"But," continued the wise Ulysses, "you must remember, my good friends, our misadventure in the cavern of one-eyed Polyphemus, the Cyclops! Instead of his ordinary milk diet, did he not eat up two of our comrades for his supper, and a couple more for breakfast, and two at his supper again? Methinks I see him yet, the hideous monster, scanning us with that great red eye, in the middle of his forehead, to single out the fattest. And then, again, only a few days ago, did we not fall into the hands of the king of the Læstrygons, and those other horrible giants, his subjects, who devoured a great many more of us than are now left? To tell you the truth, if we go to yonder palace, there can be no question that we shall make our appearance at the dinner table; but whether seated as guests, or served up as food, is a point to be seriously considered."

"Either way," murmured some of the hungriest of the crew, "it will be better than starvation; particularly if one could be sure of being well fattened beforehand, and daintily cooked afterwards."

"That is a matter of taste," said King Ulysses, "and, for my own part, neither the most careful fattening nor the daintiest of cookery would reconcile me to being dished at last. My proposal is, therefore, that we divide ourselves into two equal parties, and ascertain, by drawing lots, which of the two shall go to the palace, and beg for food and assistance. If these can oe obtained, all is well. If not, and if the innabitants prove as inhospitable as Polyphemus, or the Læstrygons, then there will but half of us perish, and the remainder may set sail and escape."

As nobody objected to this scheme, Ulysses proceeded to count the whole band, and found that there were forty-six men, including himself. He then numbered off twenty-two of them, and put Eurylochus (who was one of his chief offi-

cers, and second only to himself in sagacity) at
their head. Ulysses took command of the remaining twenty-two men, in person. Then, taking off his helmet, he put two shells into it, on
one of which was written, "Go," and on the
other, "Stay." Another person now held the
helmet, while Ulysses and Eurylochus drew out
each a shell; and the word "Go" was found
written on that which Eurylochus had drawn.
In this manner, it was decided that Ulysses and
his twenty-two men were to remain at the sea-
side until the other party should have found out
what sort of treatment they might expect at the
mysterious palace. As there was no help for it,
Eurylochus immediately set forth at the head of
his twenty-two followers, who went off in a very
melancholy state of mind, leaving their friends
in hardly better spirits than themselves.

No sooner had they clambered up the cliff, than
they discerned the tall marble towers of the
palace, ascending, as white as snow, out of the
lovely green shadow of the trees which surrounded it. A gush of smoke came from a chimney in the rear of the edifice. This vapor rose
high in the air, and, meeting with a breeze, was

wafted seaward, and made to pass over the heads
of the hungry mariners. When people's appetites are keen, they have a very quick scent for
any thing savory in the wind.

"That smoke comes from the kitchen!" cried
one of them, turning up his nose as high as he
could, and snuffing eagerly. "And, as sure as
I'm a half-starved vagabond, I smell roast meat
in it."

"Pig, roast pig!" said another. "Ah, the
dainty little porker! My mouth waters for
him."

"Let us make haste," cried the others, "or we
shall be too late for the good cheer!"

But scarcely had they made half a dozen steps
from the edge of the cliff, when a bird came fluttering to meet them. It was the same pretty
little bird, with the purple wings and body, the
yellow legs, the golden collar round its neck, and
the crown-like tuft upon its head, whose behavior
had so much surprised Ulysses. It hovered
about Eurylochus, and almost brushed his face
with its wings.

"Peep, peep, pe — weep!" chirped the bird.

So plaintively intelligent was the sound, tha

it seemed as if the little creature were going to break its heart with some mighty secret that it had to tell, and only this one poor note to tell it with.

" My pretty bird," said Eurylochus, — for he was a wary person, and let no token of harm escape his notice, — " my pretty bird, who sent you hither? And what is the message which you bring?"

" Peep, peep, pe — weep!" replied the bird, very sorrowfully.

Then it flew towards the edge of the cliff, and looked round at them, as if exceedingly anxious that they should return whence they came. Eurylochus and a few of the others were inclined to turn back. They could not help suspecting that the purple bird must be aware of something mischievous that would befall them at the palace, and the knowledge of which affected its airy spirit with a human sympathy and sorrow. But the rest of the voyagers, snuffing up the smoke from the palace kitchen, ridiculed the idea of returning to the vessel. One of them (more brutal than his fellows, and the most notorious gormandizer in the whole crew) said such a cruel and wicked thing, that I wonder the mere thought did not turn him into a wild beast in shape, as he already was in his nature.

"This troublesome and impertinent little fowl," said he, "would make a delicate titbit to begin dinner with. Just one plump morsel, melting away between the teeth. If he comes within my reach, I'll catch him, and give him to the palace cook to be roasted on a skewer."

The words were hardly out of his mouth, before the purple bird flew away, crying, "Peep, peep, pe — weep," more dolorously than ever.

"That bird," remarked Eurylochus, "knows more than we do about what awaits us at the palace."

"Come on, then," cried his comrades, "and we'll soon know as much as he does."

The party, accordingly, went onward through the green and pleasant wood. Every little while they caught new glimpses of the marble palace, which looked more and more beautiful the nearer they approached it. They soon entered a broad pathway, which seemed to be very neatly kept, and which went winding along, with streaks of sunshine falling across it, and specks of light quivering among the deepest shadows that fell from the lofty trees. It was bordered, too, with a great many sweet-smelling flowers, such as the mariners had never seen before. So rich and beautiful they were, that, if the shrubs grew wild here, and were native in the soil, then this island was surely the flower garden of the whole earth; or, if transplanted from some other clime, it must have been from the Happy Islands that lay towards the golden sunset.

"There has been a great deal of pains foolishly wasted on these flowers," observed one of the company; and I tell you what he said, that you may keep in mind what gormandizers they were. "For my part, if I were the owner of the palace, I would bid my gardener cultivate nothing but savory pot herbs to make a stuffing for roast meat, or to flavor a stew with."

"Well said!" cried the others. "But I'll warrant you there's a kitchen garden in the rear of the palace."

At one place they came to a crystal spring, and paused to drink at it for want of liquor, which they liked better. Looking into its bosom, they beheld their own faces dimly reflected, but

so extravagantly distorted by the gush and motion of the water, that each one of them appeared
to be laughing at himself and all his companions.
So ridiculous were these images of themselves,
indeed, that they did really laugh aloud, and
could hardly be grave again as soon as they
wished. And after they had drank, they grew
still merrier than before.

" It has a twang of the wine cask in it," said
one, smacking his lips.

" Make haste!" cried his fellows; " we'll find
the wine cask itself at the palace; and that will
be better than a hundred crystal fountains."

Then they quickened their pace, and capered
for joy at the thought of the savory banquet at
which they hoped to be guests. But Eurylochus
told them that he felt as if he were walking in a
dream.

" If I am really awake," continued he, " then,
in my opinion, we are on the point of meeting
with some stranger adventure than any that
befell us in the cave of Polyphemus, or among
the gigantic man-eating Læstrygons, or in the
windy palace of King Æolus, which stands on a
brazen-walled island   This kind of dreamy feel-

ing always comes over me before any wonderful occurrence. If you take my advice, you will turn back."

" No, no," answered his comrades, snuffing the air, in which the scent from the palace kitchen was now very perceptible. " We would not turn back, though we were certain that the king of the Læstrygons, as big as a mountain, would sit at the head of the table, and huge Polyphemus, the one-eyed Cyclops, at its foot."

At length they came within full sight of the palace, which proved to be very large and lofty, with a great number of airy pinnacles upon its roof. Though it was now midday, and the sun shone brightly over the marble front, yet its snowy whiteness, and its fantastic style of architecture, made it look unreal, like the frostwork on a window pane, or like the shapes of castles which one sees among the clouds by moonlight. But, just then, a puff of wind brought down the smoke of the kitchen chimney among them, and caused each man to smell the odor of the dish that he liked best; and, after scenting it, they thought every thing else moonshine. and nothing real save this palace, and save the

12

banquet that was evidently ready to be served up in it.

So they hastened their steps towards the portal, but had not got half way across the wide lawn, when a pack of lions, tigers, and wolves came bounding to meet them. The terrified mariners started back, expecting no better fate than to be torn to pieces and devoured. To their surprise and joy, however, these wild beasts merely capered around them, wagging their tails, offering their heads to be stroked and patted, and behaving just like so many well-bred house dogs, when they wish to express their delight at meeting their master, or their master's friends. The biggest lion licked the feet of Eurylochus; and every other lion, and every wolf and tiger, singled out one of his two and twenty followers, whom the beast fondled as if he loved him better than a beef bone.

But, for all that, Eurylochus imagined that he saw something fierce and savage in their eyes; nor would he have been surprised, at any moment, to feel the big lion's terrible claws, or to see each of the tigers make a deadly spring, or each wolf leap at the throat of the man whom

he had fondled. Their mildness seemed un-
rea., and a mere freak; but their savage nature
was as true as their teeth and claws.

Nevertheless, the men went safely across the
lawn with the wild beasts frisking about them,
and doing no manner of harm; although, as
they mounted the steps of the palace, you might
possibly have heard a low growl, particularly
from the wolves; as if they thought it a pity,
after all, to let the strangers pass without so
much as tasting what they were made of.

Eurylochus and his followers now passed under a lofty portal, and looked through the open
doorway into the interior of the palace. The
first thing that they saw was a spacious hall,
and a fountain in the middle of it, gushing
up towards the ceiling out of a marble basin,
and falling back into it with a continual plash.
The water of this fountain, as it spouted upward, was constantly taking new shapes, not very
distinctly, but plainly enough for a nimble fancy
to recognize what they were. Now it was the
shape of a man in a long robe, the fleecy whiteness of which was made out of the fountain's
spray; now it was a lion, or a tiger, or a wolf

or an ass, or, as often as any thing else, a hog
wallowing in the marble basin as if it were his
sty.   It was either magic or some very curious
machinery that caused the gushing waterspout
to assume all these forms.   But, before the
strangers had time to look closely at this wonderful sight, their attention was drawn off by a
very sweet and agreeable sound.   A woman's
voice was singing melodiously in another room
of the palace, and with her voice was mingled
the noise of a loom, at which she was probably
seated, weaving a rich texture of cloth, and in-
tertwining the high and low sweetness of her
voice into a rich tissue of harmony.

By and by, the song came to an end; and
then, all at once, there were several feminine
voices, talking airily and cheerfully, with now
and then a merry burst of laughter, such as you
may always hear when three or four young
women sit at work together.

" What a sweet song that was! " exclaimed
one of the voyagers.

" Too sweet, indeed," answered Eurylochus,
shaking his head.   " Yet it was not so sweet
as the song of the Sirens, those bird-like damsels

who wanted to tempt us on the rocks, so that
our vessel might be wrecked, and our bones left
whitening along the shore."

"But just listen to the pleasant voices of those
maidens, and that buzz of the loom, as the shuttle passes to and fro," said another comrade
"What a domestic, household, home-like sound
it is! Ah, before that weary siege of Troy, 1
used to hear the buzzing loom and the women's
voices under my own roof. Shall I never hear
them again? nor taste those nice little savory
dishes which my dearest wife knew how to
serve up?"

"Tush! we shall fare better here," said another. "But how innocently those women are babbling together, without guessing that we over-
hear them! And mark that richest voice of all,
so pleasant and familiar, but which yet seems to
have the authority of a mistress among them.
Let us show ourselves at once. What harm
can the lady of the palace and her maidens do
to mariners and warriors like us?"

"Remember," said Eurylochus, "that it was
a young maiden who beguiled three of our friends
into the palace of the king of the Læstrygons.

who ate up one of them in the twinkling of an eye."

No warning or persuasion, however, had any effect on his companions. They went up to a pair of folding doors at the farther end of the hall, and throwing them wide open, passed into the next room. Eurylochus, meanwhile, had stepped behind a pillar. In the short moment while the folding doors opened and closed again, he caught a glimpse of a very beautiful woman rising from the loom, and coming to meet the poor weather-beaten wanderers, with a hospitable smile and her hand stretched out in welcome. There were four other young women, who joined their hands and danced merrily forward, making gestures of obeisance to the strangers. They were only less beautiful than the lady who seemed to be their mistress. Yet Eurylochus fancied that one of them had sea-green hair, and that the close-fitting bodice of a second looked like the bark of a tree, and that both the others had something odd in their aspect, although he could not quite determine what it was, in the little while that he had to examine them.

The folding doors swung quickly back, and

left him standing behind the pillar, in the soli·
tude of the outer hall.   There Eurylochus waited
until he was quite weary, and listened eagerly
to every sound, but without hearing any thing
that could help him to guess what had become
of his friends.   Footsteps, it is true, seemed to
be passing and repassing, in other parts of the
palace.   Then there was a clatter of silver dishes,
or golden ones, which made him imagine a rich
feast in a splendid banqueting hall.   But by and
by he heard a tremendous grunting and squealing, and then a sudden scampering, like that of
small, hard hoofs over a marble floor, while the
voices of the mistress and her four handmaidens
were screaming all together, in tones of anger
and derision.   Eurylochus could not conceive
what had happened, unless a drove of swine had
broken into the palace, attracted by the smell of
the feast.   Chancing to cast his eyes at the
fountain, he saw that it did not shift its shape, as
formerly, nor looked either like a long-robed man,
or a lion, a tiger, a wolf, or an ass.   It looked like
nothing but a hog, which lay wallowing in the
marble basin, and filled it from brim to brim.

But we must leave the prudent Eurylochus

waiting in the outer hall, and follow his friends into the inner secrecy of the palace. As soon as the beautiful woman saw them, she arose from the loom, as I have told you, and came forward, smiling, and stretching out her hand. She took the hand of the foremost among them, and bade him and the whole party welcome.

"You have been long expected, my good friends," said she. "I and my maidens are well acquainted with you, although you do not appear to recognize us. Look at this piece of tapestry, and judge if your faces must not have been familiar to us."

So the voyagers examined the web of cloth which the beautiful woman had been weaving in her loom; and, to their vast astonishment, they saw their own figures perfectly represented in different colored threads. It was a life-like picture of their recent adventures, showing them in the cave of Polyphemus, and how they had put out his one great moony eye; while in another part of the tapestry they were untying the leathern bags, puffed out with contrary winds; and farther on, they beheld themselves scampering away from the gigantic king of the

Læstrygons, who had caught one of them by the leg. Lastly, there they were, sitting on the desolate shore of this very island, hungry and downcast, and looking ruefully at the bare bones of the stag which they devoured yesterday. This was as far as the work had yet proceeded; but when the beautiful woman should again sit down at her loom, she would probably make a picture of what had since happened to the strangers, and of what was now going to happen.

"You see," she said, "that I know all about your troubles; and you cannot doubt that I desire to make you happy for as long a time as you may remain with me. For this purpose, my honored guests, I have ordered a banquet to be prepared. Fish, fowl, and flesh, roasted, and in luscious stews, and seasoned, I trust, to all your tastes, are ready to be served up. If your appetites tell you it is dinner time, then come with me to the festal saloon."

At this kind invitation, the hungry mariners were quite overjoyed; and one of them, taking upon himself to be spokesman, assured their hospitable hostess that any hour of the day was dinner time with them, whenever they could get

flesh to put in the pot, and fire to boil it with.
So the beautiful woman led the way; and the
four maidens, (one of them had sea-green hair,
another a bodice of oak bark, a third sprinkled a
shower of water drops from her fingers' ends, and
the fourth had some other oddity, which I have
forgotten,) all these followed behind, and hurried
the guests along, until they entered a magnificent saloon. It was built in a perfect oval, and
lighted from a crystal dome above. Around the
walls were ranged two and twenty thrones, overhung by canopies of crimson and gold, and provided with the softest of cushions, which were
tasselled and fringed with gold cord. Each of
the strangers was invited to sit down ; and there
they were, two and twenty storm-beaten mariners, in worn and tattered garb, sitting on two
and twenty cushioned and canopied thrones, so
rich and gorgeous that the proudest monarch
had nothing more splendid in his stateliest hall.

Then you might have seen the guests nodding,
winking with one eye, and leaning from one
throne to another, to communicate their satisfaction in hoarse whispers.

"Our good hostess has made kings of us all,"

said one. "Ha! do you smell the feast? I'll engage it will be fit to set before two and twenty kings."

"I hope," said another, "it will be, mainly, good substantial joints, surloins, spareribs, and hinder quarters, without too many kickshaws. If I thought the good lady would not take it amiss, I should call for a fat slice of fried bacon to begin with."

Ah, the gluttons and gormandizers! You see how it was with them. In the loftiest seats of dignity, on royal thrones, they could think of nothing but their greedy appetite, which was the portion of their nature that they shared with wolves and swine; so that they resembled those vilest of animals far more than they did kings — if, indeed, kings were what they ought to be.

But the beautiful woman now clapped her hands; and immediately there entered a train of two and twenty serving men, bringing dishes of the richest food, all hot from the kitchen fire, and sending up such a steam that it hung like a cloud below the crystal dome of the saloon. An equal number of attendants brought great flagons of wine, of various kinds, some of which

sparkled as it was poured out, and went babbling down the throat; while, of other sorts, the
purple liquor was so clear that you could see the
wrought figures at the bottom of the goblet.
While the servants supplied the two and twenty
guests with food and drink, the hostess and her
four maidens went from one throne to another,
exhorting them to eat their fill, and to quaff wine
abundantly, and thus to recompense themselves,
at this one banquet, for the many days when
they had gone without a dinner. But, whenever
the mariners were not looking at them, (which
was pretty often, as they looked chiefly into the
basins and platters,) the beautiful woman and
her damsels turned aside, and laughed. Even
the servants, as they knelt down to present the
dishes, might be seen to grin and sneer, while
the guests were helping themselves to the offered
dainties.

And, once in a while, the strangers seemed to
taste something that they did not like.

"Here is an odd kind of a spice in this dish,"
said one. "I can't say it quite suits my palate.
Down it goes, however."

"Send a good draught of wine down your

throat," said his comrade on the next throne.
" That is the stuff to make this sort of cookery
relish well.   Though I must needs say, the wine
has a queer taste too.   But the more I drink of
it, the better I like the flavor."

Whatever little fault they might find with the
dishes, they sat at dinner a prodigiously long
while ; and it would really have made you
ashamed to see how they swilled down the
liquor and gobbled up the food.   They sat on
golden thrones, to be sure ; but they behaved
like pigs in a sty; and, if they had had their
wits about them, they might have guessed that
this was the opinion of their beautiful hostess
and her maidens.   It brings a blush into my
face to reckon up, in my own mind, what mountains of meat and pudding, and what gallons
of wine, these two and twenty guzzlers and gormandizers ate and drank.   They forgot all about
their homes, and their wives and children, and
all about Ulysses, and every thing else, except this
banquet, at which they wanted to keep feasting forever.   But at length they began to give
over, from mere incapacity to hold any more.

" That last bit of fat is too much for me,"
said one.

"And I have not room for another morsel," said his next neighbor, heaving a sigh. "What a pity! My appetite is as sharp as ever."

In short, they all left off eating, and leaned back on their thrones, with such a stupid and helpless aspect as made them ridiculous to behold. When their hostess saw this, she laughed aloud; so did her four damsels; so did the two and twenty serving men that bore the dishes, and their two and twenty fellows that poured out the wine. And the louder they all laughed, the more stupid and helpless did the two and twenty gormandizers look. Then the beautiful woman took her stand in the middle of the saloon, and stretching out a slender rod, (it had been all the while in her hand, although they never noticed it till this moment,) she turned it from one guest to another, until each had felt it pointed at himself. Beautiful as her face was, and though there was a smile on it, it looked just as wicked and mischievous as the ugliest serpent that ever was seen; and fat-witted as the voyagers had made themselves, they began to suspect that they had fallen into the power of an evil-minded enchantress.

"Wretches," cried she, "you have abused a

lady's hospitality; and in this princely saloon
your behavior has been suited to a hogpen.
You are already swine in every thing but the human form, which you disgrace, and which I my·
self should be ashamed to keep a moment longer,
were you to share it with me. But it will require
only the slightest exercise of magic to make the
exterior conform to the hoggish disposition. As·
sume your proper shapes, gormandizers, and
begone to the sty!"

Uttering these last words, she waved her wand;
and stamping her foot imperiously, each of the
guests was struck aghast at beholding, instead
of his comrades in human shape, one and twenty
hogs sitting on the same number of golden
thrones. Each man (as he still supposed him·
self to be) essayed to give a cry of surprise, but
found that he could merely grunt, and that, in a
word, he was just such another beast as his com·
panions. It looked so intolerably absurd to see
hogs on cushioned thrones, that they made haste
to wallow down upon all fours, like other swine.
They tried to groan and beg for mercy, but
forthwith emitted the most awful grunting and
squealing that ever came out of swinish throats

They would have wrung their hands in despair,
but, attempting to do so, grew all the more
desperate for seeing themselves squatted on theil
hams, and pawing the air with their fore trotters.
Dear me! what pendulous ears they had! what
little red eyes, half buried in fat! and what long
snouts, instead of Grecian noses!

But brutes as they certainly were, they yet
had enough of human nature in them to be
shocked at their own hideousness; and, still in-
tending to groan, they uttered a viler grunt and
squeal than before. So harsh and ear-piercing
it was, that you would have fancied a butcher
was sticking his knife into each of their throats,
or, at the very least, that somebody was pulling
every hog by his funny little twist of a tail.

"Begone to your sty!" cried the enchantress,
giving them some smart strokes with her wand;
and then she turned to the serving men — "Drive
out these swine, and throw down some acorns
for them to eat."

The door of the saloon being flung open, the
drove of hogs ran in all directions save the right
one, in accordance with their hoggish perversity,
but were finally driven into the back yard of the

palace. It was a sight to bring tears into one's eyes, (and I hope none of you will be cruel enough to laugh at it,) to see the poor creatures go snuffing along, picking up here a cabbage leaf and there a turnip top, and rooting their noses in the earth for whatever they could find. In their sty, moreover, they behaved more piggishly than the pigs that had been born so; for they bit and snorted at one another, put their feet in the trough, and gobbled up their victuals in a ridiculous hurry; and, when there was nothing more to be had, they made a great pile of themselves among some unclean straw, and fell fast asleep. If they had any human reason left, it was just enough to keep them wondering when they should be slaughtered, and what quality of bacon they should make.

Meantime, as I told you before, Eurylochus had waited, and waited, and waited, in the entrance hall of the palace, without being able to comprehend what had befallen his friends. At last, when the swinish uproar resounded through the palace, and when he saw the image of a hog in the marble basin, he thought it best to hasten back to the vessel, and inform the wise Ulysses

13

of these marvellous occurrences   So he ran as fast as ɛc could down the steps, and nevei stopped to draw breath till he reached the shore.

"Why do you come alone?" asked King Ulysses, as soon as he saw him. "Where are your two and twenty comrades?"

At these questions, Eurylochus burst into tears.

"Alas!" cried he, "I greatly fear that we shall never see one of their faces again."

Then he told Ulysses all that had happened, as far as he knew it, and added that he suspected the beautiful woman to be a vile enchantress, and the marble palace, magnificent as it looked, to be only a dismal cavern in reality.   As for his companions, he could not imagine what had become of them, unless they had been given to the swine to be devoured alive.   At this intelligence, all the voyagers were greatly affrighted. But Ulysses lost no time in girding on his sword, and hanging his bow and quiver over his shoulders, and taking a spear in his right hand. When his followers saw their wise leader making these preparations, they inquired whither he was going, and earnestly besought him not to leave them.

" You are our king," cried they; "and what is more, you are the wisest man in the whole world, and nothing but your wisdom and courage can get us out of this danger. If you desert us, and go to the enchanted palace, you will suffer the same fate as our poor companions, and not a soul of us will ever see our dear Ithaca again."

" As I am your king," answered Ulysses, " and wiser than any of you, it is therefore the more my duty to see what has befallen our comrades, and whether any thing can yet be done to rescue them. Wait for me here until to-morrow. If I do not then return, you must hoist sail, and endeavor to find your way to our native land. For my part, I am answerable for the fate of these poor mariners, who have stood by my side in battle, and been so often drenched to the skin, along with me, by the same tempestuous surges. I will either bring them back with me, or perish."

Had his followers dared, they would have detained him by force. But King Ulysses frowned sternly on them, and shook his spear, and bade them stop him at their peril. Seeing him so determined, they let him go, and sat down on the sand, as disconsolate a set of people as could be, waiting and praying for his return.

It happened to Ulysses, just as before, that, when he had gone a few steps from the edge of the cliff, the purple bird came fluttering towards him, crying, " Peep, peep, pe — weep!" and using all the art it could to persuade him to go no farther.

" What mean you, little bird?" cried Ulysses. " You are arrayed like a king in purple and gold, and wear a golden crown upon your head. Is it because I too am a king, that you desire so earnestly to speak with me? If you can talk in human language, say what you would have me do."

" Peep!" answered the purple bird, very dolorously. " Peep, peep, pe — we — ep!"

Certainly there lay some heavy anguish at the little bird's heart; and it was a sorrowful predicament that he could not, at least, have the consolation of telling what it was. But Ulysses had no time to waste in trying to get at the mystery. He therefore quickened his pace, and had gone a good way along the pleasant wood path

when there met him a young man of very brisk
and intelligent aspect, and clad in a rather singular garb. He wore a short cloak, and a sort
of cap that seemed to be furnished with a pair
of wings; and from the lightness of his step,
you would have supposed that there might likewise be wings on his feet. To enable him to
walk still better, (for he was always on one journey or another,) he carried a winged staff, around
which two serpents were wriggling and twisting.
In short, I have said enough to make you guess
that it was Quicksilver; and Ulysses (who knew
him of old, and had learned a great deal of his
wisdom from him) recognized him in a moment.

" Whither are you going in such a hurry, wise
Ulysses?" asked Quicksilver. "Do you not know
that this island is enchanted? The wicked enchantress (whose name is Circe, the sister of King
Æetes) dwells in the marble palace which you
see yonder among the trees. By her magic arts,
she changes every human being into the brute
beast or fowl whom he happens most to resemble."

" That little bird, which met me at the edge
of the cliff," exclaimed Ulysses: " was he a
human being once?"

" Yes," answered Quicksilver. " He was once
a king, named Picus, and a pretty good sort of a
king too, only rather too proud of his purple
robe, and his crown, and the golden chain about
his neck ; so he was forced to take the shape of
a gaudy-feathered bird. The lions, and wolves,
and tigers, who will come running to meet you,
in front of the palace, were formerly fierce and
cruel men, resembling in their dispositions the
wild beasts whose forms they now rightfully
wear."

" And my poor companions," said Ulysses.
" Have they undergone a similar change, through
the arts of this wicked Circe ? "

" You well know what gormandizers they
were," replied Quicksilver; and rogue that he
was, he could not help laughing at the joke.
" So you will not be surprised to hear that they
have all taken the shapes of swine ! If Circe
had never done any thing worse, I really should
not think her so very much to blame."

" But can I do nothing to help them ? " inquired Ulysses.

" It will require all your wisdom," said Quicksilver, " and a little of my own into the bargain,

to keep your royal and sagacious self from being transformed into a fox. But do as I bid you; and the matter may end better than it has begun."

While he was speaking, Quicksilver seemed to be in search of something; he went stooping along the ground, and soon laid his hand on a little plant with a snow-white flower, which he plucked and smelt of. Ulysses had been looking at that very spot only just before; and it appeared to him that the plant had burst into full flower the instant when Quicksilver touched it with his fingers.

"Take this flower, King Ulysses," said he "Guard it as you do your eyesight; for I can assure you it is exceedingly rare and precious, and you might seek the whole earth over without ever finding another like it. Keep it in your hand, and smell of it frequently after you enter the palace, and while you are talking with the enchantress. Especially when she offers you food, or a draught of wine out of her goblet, be careful to fill your nostrils with the flower's fragrance. Follow these directions, and you may defy her magic arts to change you into a fox."

Quicksilver then gave him some further **advice**
how to behave, and bidding him be bold and
prudent, again assured him that, powerful **as**
Circe was, he would have a fair prospect of
coming safely out of her enchanted palace. After listening attentively, Ulysses thanked his
good friend, and resumed his way. But he had
taken only a few steps, when, recollecting some
other questions which he wished to ask, he turned
round again, and beheld nobody on the spot
where Quicksilver had stood ; for that winged
cap of his, and those winged shoes, with the help
of the winged staff, had carried him quickly out
of sight.

When Ulysses reached the lawn, in front of
the palace, the lions and other savage animals
came bounding to meet him, and would have
fawned upon him and licked his feet. But the
wise king struck at them with his long spear,
and sternly bade them begone out of his path ;
for he knew that they had once been bloodthirsty
men, and would now tear him limb from limb,
instead of fawning upon him, could they do the
mischief that was in their hearts. The wild
beasts yelped and glared at him, and stood

at a distance, while he ascended the palace steps.

On entering the hall, Ulysses saw the magic fountain in the centre of it. The up-gushing water had now again taken the shape of a man in a long, white, fleecy robe, who appeared to be · making gestures of welcome. The king like-wise heard the noise of the shuttle in the loom, and the sweet melody of the beautiful woman's song, and then the pleasant voices of herself and the four maidens talking together, with peals of merry laughter intermixed. But Ulysses did not waste much time in listening to the laughter or the song. He leaned his spear against one of the pillars of the hall, and then, after loosening his sword in the scabbard, stepped boldly forward, and threw the folding doors wide open. The moment she beheld his stately figure standing in the doorway, the beautiful woman rose from the loom, and ran to meet him with a glad smile throwing its sunshine over her face, and both her hands extended.

" Welcome, brave stranger!" cried she. " We were expecting you."

And the nymph with the sea-green hair made

a courtesy down to the ground, and likewise
bade him welcome; so did her sister with the
bodice of oaken bark, and she that sprinkled dewdrops from her fingers' ends, and the fourth one
with some oddity which I cannot remember.
And Circe, as the beautiful enchantress was
called, (who had deluded so many persons that
she did not doubt of being able to delude Ulysses, not imagining how wise he was,) again
addressed him: —

"Your companions," said she, "have already
been received into my palace, and have enjoyed
the hospitable treatment to which the propriety
of their behavior so well entitles them. If such
be your pleasure, you shall first take some refreshment, and then join them in the elegant apart-
:nent which they now occupy. See, I and my
maidens have been weaving their figures into
this piece of tapestry."

She pointed to the web of beautifully-woven
cloth in the loom. Circe and the four nymphs
must have been very diligently at work since the
arrival of the mariners; for a great many yards
of tapestry had now been wrought, in addition
to what I before described. In this new part,

Ulysses saw his two and twenty friends represented as sitting on cushioned and canopied
thrones, greedily devouring dainties, and quaffing
deep draughts of wine. The work had not yet
gone any further. O, no, indeed. The enchan
tress was far too cunning to let Ulysses see the
mischief which her magic arts had since brought
upon the gorman·lizers.

"As for yourself, valiant sir," said Circe,
"judging by the dignity of your aspect, I take
you to be nothing less than a king. Deign to
follow me, and you shall be treated as befits
your rank."

So Ulysses followed her into the oval saloon,
where his two and twenty comrades had devoured the banquet, which ended so disastrously
for themselves. But, all this while, he had held
the snow-white flower in his hand, and had constantly smelt of it while Circe was speaking;
and as he crossed the threshold of the saloon, he
took good care to inhale several long and deep
snuffs of its fragrance. Instead of two and
twenty thrones, which had before been ranged
around the wall, there was now only a single
throne, in the centre of the apartment But this

was surely the most magnificent seat that ever a king or an emperor reposed himself upon, all made of chased gold, studded with precious stones, with a cushion that looked like a soft heap of living roses, and overhung by a canopy of sun- light which Circe knew how to weave into drapery. The enchantress took Ulysses by the hand, and made him sit down upon this daz- zling throne. Then, clapping her hands, she summoned the chief butler.

"Bring hither," said she, "the goblet that is set apart for kings to drink out of. And fill it with the same delicious wine which my royal brother, King Æetes praised so highly, when he last visited me with my fair daughter Medea That good and amiable child! Were she now here, it would delight her to see me offering this wine to my honored guest."

But Ulysses, while the butler was gone for the wine, held the snow-white flower to his nose.

"Is it a wholesome wine?" he asked.

At this the four maidens tittered; whereupon the enchantress looked round at them, with an aspect of severity.

"It is the wholesomest juice that ever was

squeezed out of the grape," said she; "for, in-stead of disguising a man, as other liquor is apt to do, it brings him to his true self, and shows him as he ought to be."

The chief butler liked nothing better than to see people turned into swine, or making any kind of a beast of themselves; so he made haste to bring the royal goblet, filled with a liquid as bright as gold, and which kept sparkling upward, and throwing a sunny spray over the brim. But, delightfully as the wine looked, it was mingled with the most potent enchantments that Circe knew how to concoct. For every drop of the pure grape juice there were two drops of the pure mischief; and the danger of the thing was, that the mischief made it taste all the better. The mere smell of the bubbles, which effervesced at the brim, was enough to turn a man's beard into pig's bristles, or make a lion's claws grow out of his fingers, or a fox's brush behind him

"Drink, my noble guest," said Circe, smiling as she presented him with the goblet. "You will find in this draught a solace for all your troubles."

King Ulysses took the goblet with his right

hand, while with his left he held the snow-white flower to his nostrils, and drew in so long a breath that his lungs were quite filled with its pure and simple fragrance. Then, drinking off all the wine, he looked the enchantress calmly in the face.

"Wretch," cried Circe, giving him a smart stroke with her wand, "how dare you keep your human shape a moment longer? Take the form of the brute whom you most resemble. If a hog, go join your fellow-swine in the sty; if a lion, a wolf, a tiger, go howl with the wild beasts on the lawn; if a fox, go exercise your craft in stealing poultry. Thou hast quaffed off my wine, and canst be man no longer."

But, such was the virtue of the snow-white flower, instead of wallowing down from his throne in swinish shape, or taking any other brutal form, Ulysses looked even more manly and king-like than before. He gave the magic goblet a toss, and sent it clashing over the marble floor, to the farthest end of the saloon. Then, drawing his sword, he seized the enchantress by her beautiful ringlets, and made a gesture as if he meant to strike off her head at one blow.

"Wicked Circe," cried he, in a terrible voice, "this sword shall put an end to thy enchant-ments. Thou shalt die, vile witch, and do no more mischief in the world, by tempting human beings into the vices which make beasts of them."

The tone and countenance of Ulysses were so awful, and his sword gleamed so brightly, and seemed to have so intolerably keen an edge, that Circe was almost killed by the mere fright, with-out waiting for a blow. The chief butler scram-bled out of the saloon, picking up the golden goblet as he went; and the enchantress and the four maidens fell on their knees, wringing their hands, and screaming for mercy.

"Spare me!" cried Circe. "Spare me, royal and wise Ulysses. For now I know that thou art he of whom Quicksilver forewarned me, the most prudent of mortals, against whom no en-chantments can prevail. Thou only couldst have conquered Circe. Spare me, wisest of men. I will show thee true hospitality, and even give myself to be thy slave, and this mag-nificent palace to be henceforth thy home."

The four nymphs, meanwhile, were making a

most piteous ado; and especially the ocean
nymph, with the sea-green hair, wept a great
deal of salt water, and the fountain nymph, besides scattering dewdrops from her fingers' ends,
nearly melted away into tears. But Ulysses
would not be pacified until Circe had taken a
solemn oath to change back his companions,
and as many others as he should direct, from
their present forms of beast or bird into their
former shapes of men.

"On these conditions," said he, "I consent to
spare your life. Otherwise you must die upon
the spot."

With a drawn sword hanging over her, the enchantress would readily have consented to do as
much good as she had hitherto done mischief,
however little she might like such employment.
She therefore led Ulysses out of the back entrance of the palace, and showed him the swine
in their sty. There were about fifty of these
unclean beasts in the whole herd; and though
the greater part were hogs by birth and education, there was wonderfully little difference to be
seen betwixt them and their new brethren who
had so recently worn the human shape. To

speak critically, indeed, the latter rather carried the thing to excess, and seemed to make it a point to wallow in the miriest part of the sty, and otherwise to outdo the original swine in their own natural vocation. When men once turn to brutes, the trifle of man's wit that remains in them adds tenfold to their brutality.

The comrades of Ulysses, however, had not quite lost the remembrance of having formerly stood erect. When he approached the sty, two and twenty enormous swine separated them-selves from the herd, and scampered towards him, with such a chorus of horrible squealing as made him clap both hands to his ears. And yet they did not seem to know what they wanted, nor whether they were merely hungry, or misera-ble from some other cause. It was curious, in the midst of their distress, to observe them thrust-ing their noses into the mire, in quest of some-thing to eat. The nymph with the bodice of oaken bark (she was the hamadryad of an oak) threw a handful of acorns among them; and the two and twenty hogs scrambled and fought for the prize, as if they had tasted not so much as a noggin of sour milk for a twelvemonth.

14

" These must certainly be my comrades," said
Ulysses. " I recognize their dispositions. They
are hardly worth the trouble of changing them
into the human form again. Nevertheless, we
will have it done, lest their bad example should
corrupt the other hogs. Let them take their
original shapes, therefore, Dame Circe, if your
skill is equal to the task. It will require greater
magic, I trow, than it did to make swine of
them."

So Circe waved her wand again, and repeated
a few magic words, at the sound of which the
two and twenty hogs pricked up their pendulous
ears. It was a wonder to behold how their
snouts grew shorter and shorter, and their
mouths (which they seemed to be sorry for, because they could not gobble so expeditiously)
smaller and smaller, and how one and another
began to stand upon his hind legs, and scratch
his nose with his fore trotters. At first the spectators hardly knew whether to call them hogs
or men, but by and by came to the conclusion
that they rather resembled the latter. Finally
there stood the twenty-two comrades of Ulysses,
looking pretty much the same as when they left
the vessel.

You must not imagine, however, that the swinish quality had entirely gone out of them. When once it fastens itself into a person's character, it is very difficult getting rid of it. This was proved by the hamadryad, who, being exceedingly fond of mischief, threw another handful of acorns before the twenty-two newly restored people ; whereupon down they wallowed, in a moment, and gobbled them up in a very shameful way. Then, recollecting themselves, they scrambled to their feet, and looked more than commonly foolish.

"Thanks, noble Ulysses!" they cried. "From brute beasts you have restored us to the condition of men again."

"Do not put yourselves to the trouble of thanking me," said the wise king. "I fear I have done but little for you."

To say the truth, there was a suspicious kind of a grunt in their voices, and, for a long time afterwards, they spoke gruffly, and were apt to set up a squeal.

"It must depend on your own future behavior," added Ulysses, "whether you do not find your way back to the sty."

At this moment, the note of a bird sounded from the branch of a neighboring tree.

"Peep, peep, pe — wee — ep!"

It was the purple bird, who, all this while, had been sitting over their heads, watching what was going forward, and hoping that Ulysses would remember how he had done his utmost to keep him and his followers out of harm's way. Ulysses ordered Circe instantly to make a king of this good little fowl, and leave him exactly as she found him. Hardly were the words spoken, and before the bird had time to utter another "pe — weep," King Picus leaped down from the bough of the tree, as majestic a sovereign as any in the world, dressed in a long purple robe and gorgeous yellow stockings, with a splendidly wrought collar about his neck, and a golden crown upon his head. He and King Ulysses exchanged with one another the courtesies which belong to their elevated rank. But from that time forth, King Picus was no longer proud of his crown and his trappings of royalty, nor of the fact of his being a king; he felt himself merely the upper servant of his people, and that it must be his life-long labor to make them better and happier.

As for the ions, tigers, and wolves, (though Circe would have restored them to their former shapes at his slightest word,) Ulysses thought it advisable that they should remain as they now were. and thus give warning of their cruel dispositions, instead of going about under the guise of men, and pretending to human sympathies, while their hearts had the bloodthirstiness of wild beasts. So he let them howl as much as they liked, but never troubled his head about them. And, when every thing was settled according to his pleasure, he sent to summon the remainder of his comrades, whom he had left at the sea shore. These being arrived, with the prudent Eurylochus at their head, they all made themselves comfortable in Circe's enchanted palace, until quite rested and refreshed from the toils and hardships of their voyage.

THE POMEGRANATE SEEDS.

MOTHER CERES was exceedingly fond of her daughter Proserpina, and seldom let her go alone into the fields. But, just at the time when my story begins, the good lady was very busy, because she had the care of the wheat, and the Indian corn, and the rye and barley, and, in short, of the crops of every kind, all over the earth; and as the season had thus far been uncommonly backward, it was necessary to make the harvest ripen more speedily than usual. So she put on her turban, made of poppies, (a kind of flower which she was always noted for wearing,) and got into her car drawn by a pair of winged dragons, and was just ready to set off.

"Dear mother," said Proserpina, "I shall be very lonely while you are away. May I not run down to the shore, and ask some of the sea

nymphs to come up out of the waves and play
with me?"

" Yes, child," answered Mother Ceres. " The
sea nymphs are good creatures, and will never
lead you into any harm. But you must take
care not to stray away from them, nor go wandering about the fields by yourself. Young girls
without their mothers to take care of them, are
very apt to get into mischief."

The child promised to be as prudent as if she
were a grown-up woman ; and, by the time the
winged dragons had whirled the car out of sight,
she was already on the shore, calling to the sea
nymphs to come and play with her. They knew
Proserpina's voice, and were not long in showing
their glistening faces and sea-green hair above
the water, at the bottom of which was their
home. They brought along with them a great
many beautiful shells ; and sitting down on the
moist sand, where the surf wave broke over them,
'hey busied themselves in making a necklace,
which they hung round Proserpina's neck. By
way of showing her gratitude, the child besought them to go with her a little way into
the fields, so that they might gather abundance

of flowers, with which she would make each of
her kind playmates a wreath.

"O, no, dear Proserpina," cried the sea nymphs;
"we dare not go with you upon the dry land.
We are apt to grow faint, unless at every breath
we can snuff up the salt breeze of the ocean.
And don't you see how careful we are to let the
surf wave break over us every moment or two,
so as to keep ourselves comfortably moist? If
it were not for that, we should soon look like
bunches of uprooted seaweed dried in the sun."

"It is a great pity," said Proserpina. "But
do you wait for me here, and I will run and
gather my apron full of flowers, and be back
again before the surf wave has broken ten times
over you. I long to make you some wreaths
that shall be as lovely as this necklace of many-
colored shells."

"We will wait, then," answered the sea
nymphs. "But, while you are gone, we may as
well lie down on a bank of soft sponge, under
the water. The air to-day is a little too dry for
our comfort. But we will pop up our heads
every few minutes to see if you are coming."

The young Proserpina ran quickly to a spot

where, only the day before, she had seen a great many flowers. These, however, were now a little past their bloom; and wishing to give her friends the freshest and loveliest blossoms, she strayed farther into the fields, and found some that made her scream with delight. Never had she met with such exquisite flowers before — violets so large and fragrant — roses, with so rich and delicate a blush — such superb hyacinths and such aromatic pinks — and many others, some of which seemed to be of new shapes and colors. Two or three times, moreover, she could not help thinking that a tuft of most splendid flowers had suddenly sprouted out of the earth before her very eyes, as if on purpose to tempt her a few steps farther. Proserpina's apron was soon filled and brimming over with delightful blossoms. She was on the point of turning back in order to rejoin the sea nymphs, and sit with them on the moist sands, all twining wreaths together. But, a little farther on, what should she behold? It was a large shrub, completely covered with the most magnificent flowers in the world.

"The darlings!" cried Proserpina; and then

she thought to herself, "I was looking at that spot only a moment ago. How strange it is that I did not see the flowers!"

The nearer she approached the shrub, the more attractive it looked, until she came quite close to it; and then, although its beauty was richer than words can tell, she hardly knew whether to like it or not. It bore above a hundred flowers of the most brilliant hues, and each different from the others, but all having a kind of resemblance among themselves, which showed them to be sister blossoms. But there was a deep, glossy lustre on the leaves of the shrub, and on the petals of the flowers, that made Proserpina doubt whether they might not be poisonous. To tell you the truth, foolish as it may seem, she was half inclined to turn round and run away.

"What a silly child I am!" thought she, taking courage. "It is really the most beautiful shrub that ever sprang out of the earth. I will pull it up by the roots, and carry it home, and plant it in my mother's garden."

Holding up her apron full of flowers with her left hand, Proserpina seized the large shrub with the other, and pulled, and pulled, but was hardly able to loosen the soil about its roots. What a deep-rooted plant it was! Again the girl pulled with all her might, and observed that the earth began to stir and crack to some distance around the stem. She gave another pull, but relaxed her hold, fancying that there was a rumbling sound right beneath her feet. Did the roots extend down into some enchanted cavern? Then, laughing at herself for so childish a notion, she made another effort: up came the shrub, and Proserpina staggered back, holding the stem triumphantly in her hand, and gazing at the deep hole which its roots had left in the soil.

Much to her astonishment, this hole kept spreading wider and wider, and growing deeper and deeper, until it really seemed to have no bottom; and all the while, there came a rumbling noise out of its depths, louder and louder, and nearer and nearer, and sounding like the tramp of horses' hoofs and the rattling of wheels. Too much frightened to run away, she stood straining her eyes into this wonderful cavity, and soon saw a team of four sable horses, snorting smoke out of their nostrils, and tearing their way out of the

earth with a splendid golden chariot whirling at
their heels. They leaped out of the bottomless
hole, chariot and all; and there they were, tossing
their black manes, flourishing their black tails, and
curvetting with every one of their hoofs off the
ground at once, close by the spot where Proserpina stood. In the chariot sat the figure of a
man, richly dressed, with a crown on his head,
all flaming with diamonds. He was of a noble
aspect, and rather handsome, but looked sullen
and discontented; and he kept rubbing his eyes
and shading them with his hand, as if he did not
live enough in the sunshine to be very fond of its
light.

As soon as this personage saw the affrighted
Proserpina, he beckoned her to come a little
nearer.

"Do not be afraid," said he, with as cheerful
a smile as he knew how to put on. "Come.
Will not you like to ride a little way with me,
in my beautiful chariot?"

But Proserpina was so alarmed, that she wished
for nothing but to get out of his reach. And no
wonder. The stranger did not look remarkably
good natured, in spite of his smile; and as for

his voice, its tones were deep and stern, and sounded as much like the rumbling of an earthquake under ground as any thing else. As is always the case with children in trouble, Proserpina's first thought was to call for her mother.

"Mother, Mother Ceres!" cried she, all in a tremble. "Come quickly and save me."

But her voice was too faint for her mother to hear. Indeed, it is most probable that Ceres was then a thousand miles off, making the corn grow in some far distant country. Nor could it have availed her poor daughter, even had she been within hearing; for no sooner did Proserpina begin to cry out, than the stranger leaped to the ground, caught the child in his arms, and again mounting the chariot, shook the reins, and shouted to the four black horses to set off. They immediately broke into so swift a gallop, that it seemed rather like flying through the air than running along the earth. In a moment, Proserpina lost sight of the pleasant vale of Enna, in which she had always dwelt. Another instant, and even the summit of Mount Ætna had become so blue in the distance, that she could scarcely distinguish it from the smoke that gushed out of its crater But still the poor child screamed, and scattered ner apron full of flowers along the way, and left a long cry trailing behind the chariot; and many mothers, to whose ears it came, ran quickly to see if any mischief had befallen their children. But Mother Ceres was a great way off, and could not hear the cry.

As they rode on, the stranger did his best to soothe her.

" Why should you be so frightened, my pretty child?" said he, trying to soften his rough voice. " I promise not to do you any harm. What! You have been gathering flowers? Wait till we come to my palace, and I will give you a garden full of prettier flowers than those, all made of pearls, and diamonds, and rubies. Can you guess who I am? They call my name Pluto ; and I am the king of diamonds and all other precious stones. Every atom of the gold and silver that lies under the earth belongs to me, to say nothing of the copper and iron, and of the coal mines, which supply me with abundance ot fuel. Do you see this splendid crown upon my head? You may have it for a plaything. O we shall be very good friends, and you will find me more agreeable than you expect, when once we get out of this troublesome sunshine."

"Let me go home!" cried Proserpina. "Let me go home!"

"My home is better than your mother's," answered King Pluto. "It is a palace, all made of gold, with crystal windows; and because there is little or no sunshine thereabouts, the apartments are illuminated with diamond lamps. You never saw any thing half so magnificent as my throne. If you like, you may sit down on it, and be my little queen, and I will sit on the footstool."

"I don't care for golden palaces and thrones," sobbed Proserpina. "O my mother, my mother! Carry me back to my mother!"

But King Pluto, as he called himself, only shouted to his steeds to go faster.

"Pray do not be foolish, Proserpina," said he, in rather a sullen tone. "I offer you my palace and my crown, and all the riches that are under the earth; and you treat me as if I were doing you an injury. The one thing which my palace needs is a merry little maid, to run up stairs and down, and cheer up the rooms with her

smile.   And this is what you must do for King
Pluto."

"Never!" answered Proserpina, looking as miserable as she could.   "I shall never smile again
till you set me down at my mother's door."

But she might just as well have talked to the
wind that whistled past them; for Pluto urged
on his horses, and went faster than ever.   Proserpina continued to cry out, and screamed so long
and so loudly, that her poor little voice was
almost screamed away; and when it was nothing
but a whisper, she happened to cast her eyes
over a great, broad field of waving grain — and
whom do you think she saw?   Who, but Mother
Ceres, making the corn grow, and too busy to
notice the golden chariot as it went rattling
along.   The child mustered all her strength, and
gave one more scream, but was out of sight before Ceres had time to turn her head.

King Pluto had taken a road which now
began to grow excessively gloomy.   It was bordered on each side with rocks and precipices, between which the rumbling of the chariot wheels
was reverberated with a noise like rolling thunder.   The trees and bushes that grew in the

crevices of the rocks had very dismal foliage; and by and by, although it was hardly noon, the air became obscured with a gray twilight. The black horses had rushed along so swiftly, that they were already beyond the limits of the sunshine. But the duskier it grew, the more did Pluto's visage assume an air of satisfaction. After all, he was not an ill-looking person, especially when he left off twisting his features into a smile that did not belong to them. Proserpina peeped at his face through the gathering dusk, and hoped that he might not be so very wicked as she at first thought him.

"Ah, this twilight is truly refreshing," said King Pluto, "after being so tormented with that ugly and impertinent glare of the sun. How much more agreeable is lamplight or torchlight, more particularly when reflected from diamonds! It will be a magnificent sight, when we get to my palace."

"Is it much farther?" asked Proserpina. "And will you carry me back when I have seen it?"

"We will talk of that by and by," answered Pluto. "We are just entering my dominions
15

Do you see that tall gateway before us ? When we pass those gates, we are at home. And there lies my faithful mastiff at the threshold Cerberus! Cerberus! Come hither, my good dog!"

So saying, Pluto pulled at the reins, and stopped the chariot right between the tall, massive pillars of the gateway. The mastiff of which he had spoken got up from the threshold, and stood on his hinder legs, so as to put his fore paws on the chariot wheel. But, my stars, what a strange dog it was! Why, he was a big, rough, ugly-looking monster, with three separate heads, and each of them fiercer than the two others; but fierce as they were, King Pluto patted them all. He seemed as fond of his three-headed dog as if it had been a sweet little spaniel, with silken ears and curly hair. Cerberus, on the other hand, was evidently rejoiced to see his master, and expressed his attachment, as other dogs do, by wagging his tail at a great rate. Proserpina's eyes being drawn to it by its brisk motion, she saw that this tail was neither more nor less than a live dragon, with fiery eyes, and fangs that had a very poisonous aspect. And while the three-headed Cerberus was fawning so lovingly on King Pluto, there was the dragon tail wagging against its will, and looking as cross and ill natured as you can imagine, on its own separate account.

" Will the dog bite me ? " asked Proserpina, shrinking closer to Pluto. " What an ugly creature he is ! "

" O, never fear," answered her companion. " He never harms people, unless they try to enter my dominions without being sent for, or to get away when I wish to keep them here. Down, Cerberus ! Now, my pretty Proserpina, we will drive on."

On went the chariot, and King Pluto seemed greatly pleased to find himself once more in his own kingdom. He drew Proserpina's attention to the rich veins of gold that were to be seen among the rocks, and pointed to several places where one stroke of a pickaxe would loosen a bushel of diamonds. All along the road, indeed, there were sparkling gems, which would have been of inestimable value above ground, but which here were reckoned of the

meaner sort, and hardly worth a beggar's stooping for.

Not far from the gateway, they came to a
bridge, which seemed to be built of iron.   Pluto
stopped the chariot, and bade Proserpina look
at the stream which was gliding so lazily beneath it.   Never in her life had she beheld so
torpid, so black, so muddy-looking a stream : its
waters reflected no images of any thing that was
on the banks, and it moved as sluggishly as if
it had quite forgotten which way it ought to
flow, and had rather stagnate than flow either
one way or the other.

" This is the River Lethe," observed King
Pluto.   " Is it not a very pleasant stream ? "

" I think it a very dismal one," said Proserpina.

" It suits my taste, however," answered Pluto,
who was apt to be sullen when any body dis-
agreed with him.   " At all events, its water has
one very excellent quality ; for a single draught
of it makes people forget every care and sorrow
that has hitherto tormented them.   Only sip a
little of it, my dear Proserpina, and you will
instantly cease to grieve for your mother, and
will have nothing in your memory that can

prev:nt your being perfectly happy in my palace. I will send for some, in a golden goblet, the moment we arrive."

" O, no, no, no!" cried Proserpina, weeping afresh. " I had a thousand times rather be miserable with remembering my mother, than be happy in forgetting her. That dear, dear mother! I never, never will forget her."

" We shall see," said King Pluto. " You do not know what fine times we will have in my palace. Here we are just at the portal. These pillars are solid gold, I assure you."

He alighted from the chariot, and taking Proserpina in his arms, carried her up a lofty flight of steps into the great hall of the palace. It was splendidly illuminated by means of large precious stones, of various hues, which seemed to burn like so many lamps, and glowed with a hundred fold radiance all through the vast apartment. And yet there was a kind of gloom in the midst of this enchanted light; nor was there a single object in the hall that was really agreeable to behold, except the little Proserpina herself, a lovely child, with one earthly flower which she had not let fall from her hand. It is my opinion that even King Pluto had never been happy in his palace, and that this was the true reason why he had stolen away Proserpina, in order that he might have something to love, instead of cheating his heart any longer with this tiresome magnificence. And though he pretended to dislike the sunshine of the upper world, yet the effect of the child's presence, bedimmed as she was by her tears, was as if a faint and watery sunbeam had somehow or other found its way into the enchanted hall.

Pluto now summoned his domestics, and bade them lose no time in preparing a most sumptuous banquet, and above all things, not to fail of setting a golden beaker of the water of Lethe by Proserpina's plate.

" I will neither drink that nor any thing else," said Proserpina. " Nor will I taste a morsel of food, even if you keep me forever in your palace."

" I should be sorry for that," replied King Pluto, patting her cheek; for he really wished to be kind, if he had only known how. " You are a spoiled child, I perceive, my little Proserpina; but when you see the nice things which my cook will make for you, your appetite will quickly come again."

Then, sending for the head cook, he gave strict orders that all sorts of delicacies, such as young people are usually fond of, should be set before Proserpina. He had a secret motive in this; for, you are to understand, it is a fixed law, that, when persons are carried off to the land of magic, if they once taste any food there, they can never get back to their friends. Now, if King Pluto had been cunning enough to offer Proserpina some fruit, or bread and milk, (which was the simple fare to which the child had always been accustomed,) it is very probable that she would soon have been tempted to eat it. But he left the matter entirely to his cook, who, like all other cooks, considered nothing fit to eat unless it were rich pastry, or highly-seasoned meat, or spiced sweet cakes — things which Proserpina's mother had never given her, and the smell of which quite took away her appetite, instead of sharpening it.

But my story must now clamber out of King Pluto's dominions, and see what Mother Ceres has been about, since she was bereft of her daughter. We had a glimpse of her, as you remember, half hidden among the waving grain, while the four black steeds were swiftly whirling along the chariot, in which her beloved Proserpina was so unwillingly borne away. You recollect, too, the loud scream which Proserpina gave, just when the chariot was out of sight.

Of all the child's outcries, this last shriek was the only one that reached the ears of Mother Ceres. She had mistaken the rumbling of the chariot wheels for a peal of thunder, and imagined that a shower was coming up, and that it would assist her in making the corn grow. But, at the sound of Proserpina's shriek, she started, and looked about in every direction, not knowing whence it came, but feeling almost certain that it was her daughter's voice. It seemed so unaccountable, however, that the girl should have strayed over so many lands and seas, (which she herself could not have traversed without the aid of her winged dragons,) that the good Ceres tried to believe that it must be the child of some other parent, and not her own darling Proserpina, who had uttered this lamentable cry. Nevertheless, it troubled her with a vast many tender fears, such as are ready to bestir themselves in every mother's heart, when she finds it necessary to go away from her dear children without leaving them under the care of some maiden aunt, or other such faithful guardian. So she quickly left the field in which she had been so busy; and, as her work was not half done, the grain looked, next day, as if it needed both sun and rain, and as if it were blighted in the ear, and had something the matter with its roots.

The pair of dragons must have had very nimble wings; for, in less than an hour, Mother Ceres had alighted at the door of her home, and found it empty. Knowing, however, that the child was fond of sporting on the sea shore, she hastened thither as fast as she could, and there beheld the wet faces of the poor sea nymphs peeping over a wave. All this while, the good creatures had been waiting on the bank of sponge, and, once every half minute or so, had popped up their four heads above water, to see .f their playmate were yet coming back. When they saw Mother Ceres, they sat down on the crest of the surf wave, and let it toss them ashore at her feet.

"Where is Proserpina?" cried Ceres. "Where is my child? Tell me, you naughty sea nymphs, have you enticed her under the sea?"

"O, no, good Mother Ceres," said the innocent sea nymphs, tossing back their green ringlets, and looking her in the face. "We never should dream of such a thing. Proserpina has been at play with us, it is true; but she left us a long while ago, meaning only to run a little way upon the dry land, and gather some flowers for a wreath. This was early in the day, and we have seen nothing of her since."

Ceres scarcely waited to hear what the nymphs had to say, before she hurried off to make inquiries all through the neighborhood. But nobody told her any thing that could enable the poor mother to guess what had become of Proserpina. A fisherman, it is true, had noticed her little footprints in the sand, as he went homeward along the beach with a basket of fish; a rustic had seen the child stooping to gather flowers; several persons had heard either the rattling of chariot wheels, or the rumbling of distant thunder; and one old woman, while plucking vervain and catnip, had heard a scream, but sup-

posed it to be some childish nonsense, and therefore did not take the trouble to look up. The
stupid people! It took them such a tedious
while to tell the nothing that they knew, that it
was dark night before Mother Ceres found out
that she must seek her daughter elsewhere. So
she lighted a torch, and set forth, resolving never
to come back until Proserpina was discovered.

In her haste and trouble of mind, she quite
forget her car and the winged dragons; or, it
may be, she thought that she could follow up
the search more thoroughly on foot. At all
events, this was the way in which she began her
sorrowful journey, holding her torch before her,
and looking carefully at every object along the
path. And as it happened, she had not gone
far before she found one of the magnificent
flowers which grew on the shrub that Proserpina had pulled up.

"Ha!" thought Mother Ceres, examining it
by torchlight. "Here is mischief in this flower!
The earth did not produce it by any help of
mine, nor of its own accord. It is the work of
enchantment, and is therefore poisonous; and
perhaps it has poisoned my poor child."

But she put the poisonous flower in her bosom, not knowing whether she might ever find any other memorial of Proserpina.

All night long, at the door of every cottage and farm house, Ceres knocked, and called up the weary laborers to inquire if they had seen her child; and they stood, gaping and half asleep, at the threshold, and answered her pityingly, and besought her to come in and rest. At the portal of every palace, too, she made so loud a summons that the menials hurried to throw open the gate, thinking that it must be some great king or queen, who would demand a banquet for supper and a stately chamber to repose in. And when they saw only a sad and anxious woman, with a torch in her hand and a wreath of withered poppies on her head, they spoke rudely, and sometimes threatened to set the dogs upon her. But nobody had seen Proserpina, nor could give Mother Ceres the least hint which way to seek her. Thus passed the night; and still she continued her search without sitting down to rest or stopping to take food, or even remembering to put out the torch; although first the rosy dawn, and then the glad light of the morning sun made its red flame look thin and pale. But I wonder what sort of stuff this torch was made of; for it burned dimly through the day, and, at night, was as bright as ever, and never was extinguished by the rain or wind, in all the weary days and nights while Ceres was seeking for Proserpina.

It was not merely of human beings that she asked tidings of her daughter. In the woods and by the streams, she met creatures of another nature, who used, in those old times, to haunt the pleasant and solitary places, and were very sociable with persons who understood their language and customs, as Mother Ceres did. Sometimes, for instance, she tapped with her finger against the knotted trunk of a majestic oak; and immediately its rude bark would cleave asunder, and forth would step a beautiful maiden, who was the hamadryad of the oak, dwelling inside of it, and sharing its long life, and rejoicing when its green leaves sported with the breeze. But not one of these leafy damsels had seen Proserpina. Then, going a little farther, Ceres would, perhaps, come to a fountain, gushing out of a pebbly hollow in the earth, and would dabble with her hand in the water. Behold, up through its sandy and pebbly bed, along with the fountain's gush, a young woman with dripping hair would arise, and stand gazing at Mother Ceres, half out of the water, and undulating up and down with its ever-restless motion. But when the mother asked whether her poor lost child had stopped to drink out of the fountain, the naiad, with weeping eyes, (for these water nymphs had tears to spare for every body's grief,) would answer " No!" in a murmuring voice, which was just like the murmur of the stream.

" Often, likewise, she encountered fauns, who looked like sunburnt country people, except that they had hairy ears, and little horns upon their foreheads, and the hinder legs of goats, on which they gambolled merrily about the woods and fields. They were a frolicsome kind of creature, but grew as sad as their cheerful dispositions would allow, when Ceres inquired for her daughter, and they had no good news to tell. But sometimes she came suddenly upon a rude gang of satyrs, who had faces like monkeys, and horses' tails behind them, and who were gen-

erally dancing in a very boisterous manner, with
shouts of noisy laughter. When she stopped
to question them, they would only laugh the
louder, and make new merriment out of the lone
woman's distress. How unkind of those ugly
satyrs! And once, while crossing a solitary
sheep pasture, she saw a personage named Pan,
seated at the foot of a tall rock, and making
music on a shepherd's flute. He, too, had horns,
and hairy ears, and goat's feet; but, being acquainted with Mother Ceres, he answered her
question as civilly as he knew how, and invited
her to taste some milk and honey out of a wooden
bowl. But neither could Pan tell her what had
become of Proserpina, any better than the rest
of these wild people.

And thus Mother Ceres went wandering about
for nine long days and nights, finding no trace
of Proserpina, unless it were now and then a
withered flower; and these she picked up and
put in her bosom, because she fancied that they
might have fallen from her poor child's hand.
All day she travelled onward through the hot
sun; and at night, again, the flame of the torch
would redden and gleam along the pathway, and

she continued her search by its light, without ever sitting down to rest.

On the tenth day, she chanced to espy the mouth of a cavern, within which (though it was bright noon every where else) there would have been only a dusky twilight; but it so happened that a torch was burning there. It flickered, and struggled with the duskiness, but ould not half light up the gloomy cavern with all its melancholy glimmer. Ceres was resolved to leave no spot without a search; so she peeped into the entrance of the cave, and lighted it up a little more, by holding her own torch before her. In so doing, she caught a glimpse of what seemed to be a woman, sitting on the brown leaves of the last autumn, a great heap of which had been swept into the cave by the wind. This woman (if woman it were) was by no means so beautiful as many of her sex; for her head, they tell me, was shaped very much like a dog's, and, by way of ornament, she wore a wreath of snakes around it. But Mother Ceres, the moment she saw her, knew that this was an odd kind of a person, who put all her enjoyment Ir being miserable, and never would have a word to say to other people, unless they were as melancholy and wretched as she herself delighted to be.

"I am wretched enough now," thought poor Ceres, "to talk with this melancholy Hecate, were she ten times sadder than ever she was yet."

So she stepped into the cave, and sat down on the withered leaves by the dog-headed woman's side. In all the world, since her daughter's loss, she had found no other companion.

"O Hecate," said she, "if ever you lose a daughter, you will know what sorrow is. Tell me, for pity's sake, have you seen my poor child Proserpina pass by the mouth of your cavern?"

"No," answered Hecate, in a cracked voice, and sighing betwixt every word or two; "no, Mother Ceres, I have seen nothing of your daughter. But my ears, you must know, are made in such a way, that all cries of distress and affright, all over the world, are pretty sure to find their way to them; and nine days ago, as I sat in my cave, making myself very miserable, I heard the voice of a young girl, shrieking as if in great distress. Something terrible has happened to the

16

child, you may rest assured. As well as I could judge, a dragon, or some other cruel monster, was carrying her away."

"You kill me by saying so," cried Ceres, almost ready to faint. "Where was the sound, and which way did it seem to go?"

"It passed very swiftly along," said Hecate, "and, at the same time, there was a heavy rumbling of wheels towards the eastward. I can tell you nothing more, except that, in my honest opinion, you will never see your daughter again. The best advice I can give you is, to take up your abode in this cavern, where we will be the two most wretched women in the world."

"Not yet, dark Hecate," replied Ceres "But do you first come with your torch, and help me to seek for my lost child. And when there shall be no more hope of finding her, (if that black day is ordained to come,) then, if you will give me room to fling myself down, either on these withered leaves or on the naked rock, I will show you what it is to be miserable. But, until I know that she has perished from the face of the earth, I will not allow myself space even to grieve."

The dismal Hecate did not much like the idea of going abroad into the sunny world. But then she reflected that the sorrow of the disconsolate Ceres would be like a gloomy twilight round about them both, let the sun shine ever so brightly, and that therefore she might enjoy her bad spirits quite as well as she if she were to stay in the cave. So she finally consented to go, and they set out together, both carrying torches, although it was broad daylight and clear sunshine. The torchlight seemed to make a gloom; so that the people whom they met, along the road, could not very distinctly see their figures; and, indeed, if they once caught a glimpse of Hecate, with the wreath of snakes round her forehead, they generally thought it prudent to run away, without waiting for a second glance.

As the pair travelled along in this woe-begone manner, a thought struck Ceres.

"There is one person," she exclaimed, "who must have seen my poor child, and can doubtless tell what has become of her. Why did not I think of him before? It is Phœbus."

"What," said Hecate, "the young man that

always sits in the sunshine? O, pray do not think of going near him. He is a gay, light, frivolous young fellow, and will only smile in your face. And besides, there is such a glare of the sun about him, that he will quite blind my poor eyes, which I have almost wept away already."

" You have promised to be my companion," answered Ceres. " Come, let us make haste, or the sunshine will be gone, and Phœbus along with it."

Accordingly, they went along in quest of Phœbus, both of them sighing grievously, and Hecate, to say the truth, making a great deal worse lamentation than Ceres; for all the pleasure she had, you know, lay in being. miserable, and therefore she made the most of it. By and by, after a pretty long journey, they arrived at the sunniest spot in the whole world. There they beheld a beautiful young man, with long, curling ringlets, which seemed to be made of golden sunbeams; his garments were like light summer clouds; and the expression of his face was so exceedingly vivid, that Hecate held her hands before her eyes, muttering that he ought to wear a black veil. Phœbus (for this was the very person whom they were seeking) had a lyre in his hands, and was making its chords tremble with sweet music; at the same time singing a most exquisite song, which he had recently composed. For, besides a great many other accomplishments, this young man was renowned for his admirable poetry.

As Ceres and her dismal companion approached him, Phœbus smiled on them so cheerfully that Hecate's wreath of snakes gave a spiteful hiss, and Hecate heartily wished herself back in her cave. But as for Ceres, she was too earnest in her grief either to know or care whether Phœbus smiled or frowned.

" Phœbus!" exclaimed she, " I am in great trouble, and have come to you for assistance. Can you tell me what has become of my dear child Proserpina ? "

" Proserpina! Proserpina, did you call her name?" answered Phœbus, endeavoring to recollect; for there was such a continual flow of pleasant ideas in his mind, that he was apt to forget what had happened no longer ago than yesterday. " Ah, yes, I remember her now. A

very lovely child, indeed. I am happy to tell
you, my dear madam, that I did see the little
Proserpina not many days ago. You may
make yourself perfectly easy about her. She is
safe, and in excellent hands."

"O, where is my dear child?" cried Ceres,
clasping her hands and flinging herself at his
feet.

"Why," said Phœbus, — and as he spoke, he
kept touching his lyre so as to make a thread
of music run in and out among his words, —
"as the little damsel was gathering flowers, (and
she has really a very exquisite taste for flowers,)
she was suddenly snatched up by King Pluto,
and carried off to his dominions. I have never
been in that part of the universe; but the royal
palace, I am told, is built in a very noble style
of architecture, and of the most splendid and
costly materials. Gold, diamonds, pearls, and
all manner of precious stones, will be your
daughter's ordinary playthings. I recommend
to you, my dear lady, to give yourself no un-
easiness. Proserpina's sense of beauty will be
duly gratified, and, even in spite of the lack of
sunshine, she will lead a very enviable life."

"Hush! Say not such a word!" answered Ceres, indignantly. "What is there to gratify her heart? What are all the splendors you speak of, without affection? 1 must have her back again Will you go with me, Phœbus, to demand my daughter of this wicked Pluto?"

"Pray excuse me," replied Phœbus, with an elegant obeisance. "I certainly wish you success, and regret that my own affairs are so immediately pressing that I cannot have the pleasure of attending you. Besides, I am not upon the best of terms with King Pluto. To tell you the truth, his three-headed mastiff would never let me pass the gateway; for I should be compelled to take a sheaf of sunbeams along with me, and those, you know, are forbidden things in Pluto's kingdom."

"Ah, Phœbus," said Ceres, with bitter meaning in her words, "you have a harp instead of a heart. Farewell."

"Will not you stay a moment," asked Phœbus, "and hear me turn the pretty and touching story of Proserpina into extemporary verses?"

But Ceres shook her head, and hastened away, along with Hecate. Phœbus (who, as I have

told you, was an exquisite poet) forthwith began
to make an ode about the poor mother's grief;
and, if we were to judge of his sensibility by
this beautiful production, he must have been
endowed with a very tender heart. But when a
poet gets into the habit of using his heartstrings
to make chords for his lyre, he may thrum upon
them as much as he will, without any great pain
to himself. Accordingly, though Phœbus sang
a very sad song, he was as merry all the while
as were the sunbeams amid which he dwelt.

Poor Mother Ceres had now found out what
had become of her daughter, but was not a whit
happier than before. Her case, on the contrary,
looked more desperate than ever. As long as
Proserpina was above ground, there might have
been hopes of regaining her. But now that the
poor child was shut up within the iron gates of
the king of the mines, at the threshold of which
lay the three-headed Cerberus, there seemed no
possibility of her ever making her escape. The
dismal Hecate, who loved to take the darkest
view of things, told Ceres that she had better
come with her to the cavern, and spend the rest
of her life in being miserable. Ceres answered.

that Hecate was welcome to go back thither herself, but that, for her part, she would wander
about the earth in quest of the entrance to King
Pluto's dominions. And Hecate took her at her
word, and hurried back to her beloved cave,
frightening a great many little children with a
glimpse of her dog's face, as she went.

Poor Mother Ceres! It is melancholy to think
of her, pursuing her toilsome way, all alone, and
holding up that never-dying torch, the flame of
which seemed an emblem of the grief and hope
that burned together in her heart. So much did
she suffer, that, though her aspect had been quite
youthful when her troubles began, she grew to
look like an elderly person in a very brief time.
She cared not how she was dressed, nor had she
ever thought of flinging away the wreath of
withered poppies, which she put on the very
morning of Proserpina's disappearance. She
roamed about in so wild a way, and with her
hair so dishevelled, that people took her for some
distracted creature, and never dreamed that this
was Mother Ceres, who had the oversight of every
seed which the husbandman planted. Nowadays, however, she gave herself no trouble about

seed time nor harvest, but left the farmers to
take care of their own affairs, and the crops to
fade or flourish, as the case might be. There
was nothing, now, in which Ceres seemed to feel
an interest, unless when she saw children at
play, or gathering flowers along the wayside.
Then, indeed, she would stand and gaze at them
with tears in her eyes. The children, too, appeared to have a sympathy with her grief, and
would cluster themselves in a little group about
her knees, and look up wistfully in her face; and
Ceres, after giving them a kiss all round, would
lead them to their homes, and advise their mothers never to let them stray out of sight.

"For if they do," said she, "it may happen to
you, as it has to me, that the iron-hearted King
Pluto will take a liking to your darlings, and
snatch them up in his chariot, and carry them
away."

One day, during her pilgrimage in quest of
the entrance to Pluto's kingdom, she came to
the palace of King Celeus, who reigned at Eleu-
sis. Ascending a lofty flight of steps, she entered the portal, and found the royal household
in very great alarm about the queen's baby.

The infant, it seems, was sickly, (being trouoled with its teeth, I suppose,) and would take no food, and was all the time moaning with pain. The queen — her name was Metanira — was de- sirous of finding a nurse ; and when she beheld a woman of matronly aspect coming up the palace steps, she thought, in her own mind, that here was the very person whom she needed. So Queen Metanira ran to the door, with the poor wailing baby in her arms, and besought Ceres to take charge of it, or, at least, to tell her what would do it good.

" Will you trust the child entirely to me ? " asked Ceres.

" Yes, and gladly too," answered the queen, "if you will devote all your time to him. For I can see that you have been a mother."

" You are right," said Ceres. " I once had a child of my own. Well; I will be the nurse of this poor, sickly boy. But beware, I warn you, that you do not interfere with any kind of treat- ment which I may judge proper for him. If you do so, the poor infant must suffer for his mother's folly."

Then she kissed the child, and it seemed to do

him good, for he smiled and nestled closely into her bosom.

So Mother Ceres set her torch in a corner, (where it kept burning all the while,) and took up her abode in the palace of King Celeus, as nurse to the little Prince Demophoön. She treated him as if he were her own child, and allowed neither the king nor the queen to say whether he should be bathed in warm or cold water, or what he should eat, or how often he should take the air, or when he should be put to bed. You would hardly believe me, if I were to tell how quickly the baby prince got rid of his ailments, and grew fat, and rosy, and strong, and how he had two rows of ivory teeth in less time than any other little fellow, before or since. Instead of the palest, and wretchedest, and puniest imp in the world, (as his own mother confessed him to be, when Ceres first took him in charge,) he was now a strapping baby, crowing, laughing, kicking up his heels, and rolling from one end of the room to the other. All the good women of the neighborhood crowded to the palace, and held up their hands, in unutterable amazement, at the beauty and wholesomeness of this darling

little prince. Their wonder was the greater, because he was never seen to taste any food; not
even so much as a cup of milk.

"Pray, nurse," the queen kept saying, "how
is it that you make the child thrive so?"

"I was a mother once," Ceres always replied;
"and having nursed my own child, I know what
other children need."

But Queen Metanira, as was very natural, had
a great curiosity to know precisely what the
nurse did to her child. One night, therefore, she
hid herself in the chamber where Ceres and the
little prince were accustomed to sleep. There
was a fire in the chimney, and it had now
crumbled into great coals and embers, which lay
glowing on the hearth, with a blaze flickering
up now and then, and flinging a warm and rud-
dy light upon the walls. Ceres sat before the
hearth with the child in her lap, and the firelight making her shadow dance upon the ceiling
overhead. She undressed the little prince, and
bathed him all over with some fragrant liquid
out of a vase. The next thing she did was to
rake back the red embers, and make a hollow
place among them, just where the backlog had

oeen.   At last, while the baby was crowing, and clapping its fat little hands, and laughing in the nurse's face, (just as you may have seen your little brother or sister do before going into its warm bath,) Ceres suddenly laid him, all naked as he was, in the hollow among the red-hot err - bers.   She then raked the ashes over him, and turned quietly away.

You may imagine, if you can, how Queen Metanira shrieked, thinking nothing less than that her dear child would be burned to a cinder. She burst forth from her hiding-place, and running to the hearth, raked open the fire, and snatched up poor little Prince Demophoön out of his bed of live coals, one of which he was griping in each of his fists.   He immediately set up a grievous cry, as babies are apt to do, when rudely startled out of a sound sleep.   To the queen's astonishment and joy, she could perceive no token of the child's being injured by the hot fire in which he had lain.   She now turned to Mother Ceres, and asked her to explain the mystery.

" Foolish woman," answered Ceres, " did you not promise to intrust this poor infant entirely to me? You little know the mischief you have done him. Had you left him to my care, he would have grown up like a child of celestial birth, endowed with superhuman strength and intelligence, and would have lived forever. Do you imagine that earthly children are to become immortal without being tempered to it in the fiercest heat of the fire? But you have ruined your own son. For though he will be a strong man and a hero in his day, yet, on account of your folly, he will grow old, and finally die, like the sons of other women. The weak tenderness of his mother has cost the poor boy an immortality. Farewell."

Saying these words, she kissed the little Prince Demophoön, and sighed to think what he had lost, and took her departure without heeding Queen Metanira, who entreated her to remain, and cover up the child among the hot embers as often as she pleased. Poor baby! He never slept so warmly again.

While she dwelt in the king's palace, Mother Ceres had been so continually occupied with taking care of the young prince, that her heart was a little lightened of its grief for Proserpina

But now, having nothing else to busy herself about, she became just as wretched as before. At length, in her despair, she came to the dreadful resolution that not a stalk of grain, nor a blade of grass, not a potato, nor a turnip, nor any other vegetable that was good for man or beast to eat, should be suffered to grow until her daughter were restored. She even forbade the flowers to bloom, lest somebody's heart should be cheered by their beauty.

Now, as not so much as a head of asparagus ever presumed to poke itself out of the ground, without the especial permission of Ceres, you may conceive what a terrible calamity had here fallen upon the earth. The husbandmen ploughed and planted as usual; but there lay the rich black furrows, all as barren as a desert of sand. The pastures looked as brown in the sweet month of June as ever they did in chill November. The rich man's broad acres and the cottager's small garden patch were equally blighted. Every little girl's flower bed showed nothing but dry stalks. The old people shook their white heads, and said that the earth had grown aged like themselves, and was no longer capable of wearing the warm smile of summer on its face. It was really piteous to see the poor, starving cattle and sheep, how they followed behind Ceres, lowing and bleating, as if their instinct taught them to expect help from her; and every body that was acquainted with her power besought her to have mercy on the human race, and, at all events, to let the grass grow. But Mother Ceres, though naturally of an affectionate disposition, was now inexorable.

"Never," said she. "If the earth is ever again to see any verdure, it must first grow along the path which my daughter will tread in coming back to me."

Finally, as there seemed to be no other remedy, our old friend Quicksilver was sent post haste to King Pluto, in hopes that he might be persuaded to undo the mischief he had done, and to set every thing right again, by giving up Proserpina. Quicksilver accordingly made the best of his way to the great gate, took a flying leap right over the three-headed mastiff, and stood at the door of the palace in an inconceivably short time. The servants knew him both by his face and garb; for his short cloak, and his

17

winged cap and shoes, and his snaky staff had often been seen thereabouts in times gone by He requested to be shown immediately into the king's presence; and Pluto, who heard his voice from the top of the stairs, and who loved to rec· reate himself with Quicksilver's merry talk called out to him to come up. And while they settle their business together, we must inquire what Proserpina has been doing ever since we saw her last.

The child had declared, as you may remember that she would not taste a mouthful of food as long as she should be compelled to remain in King Pluto's palace. How she contrived to maintain her resolution, and at the same time to keep herself tolerably plump and rosy, is more than I can explain; but some young ladies, I am given to understand, possess the faculty of living on air, and Proserpina seems to have possessed it too. At any rate, it was now six months since she left the outside of the earth; and not a morsel, so far as the attendants were able to testify, had yet passed between her teeth. This was the more creditable to Proserpina, inasmuch as King Pluto had caused her to be tempted lay after day, with all manner of sweetmeats, and richly-preserved fruits, and delicacies of every sort, such as young people are generally most fond of. But her good mother had often told her of the hurtfulness of these things; and for that reason alone, if there had been no other, she would have resolutely refused to taste them.

All this time, being of a cheerful and active disposition, the little damsel was not quite so unhappy as you may have supposed. The immense palace had a thousand rooms, and was full of beautiful and wonderful objects. There was a never-ceasing gloom, it is true, which half hid itself among the innumerable pillars, gliding before the child as she wandered among them, and treading stealthily behind her in the echo of her footsteps. Neither was all the dazzle of the precious stones, which flamed with their own light, worth one gleam of natural sunshine; nor could the most brilliant of the many-colored gems, which Proserpina had for playthings, vie with the simple beauty of the flowers she used to gather. But still, wherever the girl went, among those gilded halls and chambers, it seemed as if she carried nature and sunshine along with her, and as if she scattered dewy blossoms on her right hand and on her left. After Proserpina came, the palace was no longer the same abode of stately artifice and dismal magnificence that it had before been. The inhabitants all felt this, and King Pluto more than any of them.

"My own little Proserpina," he used to say, "I wish you could like me a little better. We gloomy and cloudy-natured persons have often as warm hearts, at bottom, as those of a more cheerful character. If you would only stay with me of your own accord, it would make me happier than the possession of a hundred such palaces as this."

"Ah," said Proserpina, "you should have tried to make me like you before carrying me off. And the best thing you can now do is, to let me go again. Then I might remember you sometimes, and think that you were as kind as you knew how to be. Perhaps, too, one day or other, I might come back, and pay you a visit."

"No, no," answered Pluto, with his gloomy smile, "I will not trust you for that. You are too fond of living in the broad daylight, and gathering flowers. What an idle and childish taste that is! Are not these gems, which 1 have ordered to be dug for you, and which are richer than any in my crown — are they not prettier than a violet?"

" Not half so pretty," said Proserpina, snatching the gems from Pluto's hand, and flinging them to the other end of the hall. " O my sweet violets, shall I never see you again?"

And then she burst into tears. But young people's tears have very little saltness or acidity in them, and do not inflame the eyes so much as those of grown persons; so that it is not to be wondered at, if, a few moments afterwards, Proserpina was sporting through the hall almost as merrily as she and the four sea nymphs had sported along the edge of the surf wave. King Pluto gazed after her, and wished that he, too, was a child. And little Proserpina, when she turned about, and beheld this great king standing in his splendid hall, and looking so grand, and so melancholy, and so lonesome, was smitten with a kind of pity. She ran back to him, and, for the first time in all her life, put her small, soft hand in his.

' 1 love you a little," whispered she, looking up in his face.

"Do you, indeed, my dear child?" cried **Pluto**, bending his dark face down to kiss her; but Proserpina shrank away from the kiss, for though his features were noble, they were very dusky and grim.   "Well, I have not deserved it of you, after keeping you a prisoner for so many months, and starving you, besides.   Are you not terribly hungry?   Is there nothing which I can get you to eat?"

In asking this question, the king of the mines had a very cunning purpose; for, you will recollect, if Proserpina tasted a morsel of food in his dominions, she would never afterwards be at liberty to quit them.

"No, indeed," said Proserpina.   "Your head cook is always baking, and stewing, and roasting, and rolling out paste, and contriving one dish or another, which he imagines may be to my liking.   But he might just as well save himself the trouble, poor, fat little man that he is.   I have no appetite for any thing in the world, unless it were a slice of bread, of my mother's own baking, or a little fruit out of her garden."

When Pluto heard this, he began to see that he had mistaken the best method of tempting

Proserpina to eat. The cook's made dishes and artificial dainties were not half so delicious, in the good child's opinion, as the simple fare to which Mother Ceres had accustomed her. Wondering that he had never thought of it before, the king now sent one of his trusty attendants, with a large basket, to get some of the finest and juiciest pears, peaches, and plums which could any where be found in the upper world. Unfortunately, however, this was during the time when Ceres had forbidden any fruits or vegetables to grow; and, after seeking all over the earth, King Pluto's servant found only a single pomegranate, and that so dried up as to be not worth eating. Nevertheless, since there was no better to be had, he brought this dry, old, withered pomegranate home to the palace, put it on a magnificent golden salver, and carried it up to Proserpina. Now, it happened, curiously enough, that, just as the servant was bringing the pomegranate into the back door of the palace, our friend Quicksilver had gone up the front steps, on his errand to get Proserpina away from King Pluto.

As soon as Proserpina saw the pomegranate

on the golden salver, she told the servant he
had better take it away again.

"I shall not touch it, I assure you," said she.
"If I were ever so hungry, I should never think
of eating such a miserable, dry pomegranate as
that."

"It is the only one in the world," said the
servant.

He set down the golden salver, with the wizened
pomegranate upon it, and left the room.   When
he was gone, Proserpina could not help coming
close to the table, and looking at this poor specimen of dried fruit with a great deal of eagerness;
for, to say the truth, on seeing something that
suited her taste, she felt all the six months' appetite taking possession of her at once.   To be
sure, it was a very wretched-looking pomegranate, and seemed to have no more juice in it than
an oyster shell.   But there was no choice of
such things in King Pluto's palace.   This was
the first fruit she had seen there, and the last she
was ever likely to see ; and unless she ate it up
immediately, it would grow drier than it already
was, and be wholly unfit to eat.

"At least, I may smell it," thought Proserpina

So she took up the pomegranate, and applied it to her nose; and, somehow or other, being in such close neighborhood to her mouth, the fruit found its way into that little red cave. Dear me! what an everlasting pity! Before Proserpina knew what she was about, her teeth had actually bitten it, of their own accord. Just as this fatal deed was done, the door of the apartment opened, and in came King Pluto, followed by Quicksilver, who had been urging him to let his little prisoner go. At the first noise of their entrance, Proserpina withdrew the pomegranate from her mouth. But Quicksilver (whose eyes were very keen, and his wits the sharpest that ever any body had) perceived that the child was a little confused; and seeing the empty salver, he suspected that she had been taking a sly nibble of something or other. As for honest Pluto, he never guessed at the secret.

"My little Proserpina," said the king, sitting down, and affectionately drawing her between his knees, "here is Quicksilver, who tells me that a great many misfortunes have befallen innocent people on account of my detaining you in my dominions. To confess the truth, I my-

self had already reflected that it was an unjusti-
fiable act to take you away from your good
mother. But, then, you must consider, my dear
child, that this vast palace is apt to be gloomy,
(although the precious stones certainly shine very
bright,) and that I am not of the most cheerful
disposition, and that therefore it was a natural
thing enough to seek for the society of some
merrier creature than myself. I hoped you
would take my crown for a plaything, and me —
ah, you laugh, naughty Proserpina — me, grim
as I am, for a playmate. It was a silly ex-
pectation."

"Not so extremely silly," whispered Proserpina. "You have really amused me very much,
sometimes."

"Thank you," said King Pluto, rather dryly.
"But I can see, plainly enough, that you think
my palace a dusky prison, and me the iron-
hearted keeper of it. And an iron heart I should
surely have, if I could detain you here any
longer, my poor child, when it is now six months
since you tasted food. I give you your liberty.
Go with Quicksilver. Hasten home to your
dear mother"

Now, although you may not have supposed it, Proserpina found it impossible to take leave of poor King Pluto without some regrets, and a good deal of compunction for not telling him about the pomegranate She even shed a tear or two, thinking how lonely and cheerless the great palace would seem to him, with all its ugly glare of artificial light, after she herself — his one little ray of natural sunshine, whom he had stolen, to be sure, but only because he valued her so much — after she should have departed. I know not how many kind things she might have said to the disconsolate king of the mines, had not Quicksilver hurried her away.

" Come along quickly," whispered he in her ear, " or his majesty may change his royal mind. And take care, above all things, that you say nothing of what was brought you on the golden salver."

In a very short time, they had passed the great gateway, (leaving the three-headed Cerberus, barking, and yelping, and growling, with three fold din, behind them,) and emerged upon the surface of the earth. It was delightful to behold, as Proserpina hastened along, how the path grew

verdant behind and on either side of her.   Wher
ever she set her blessed foot, there was at once
a dewy flower.   The violets gushed up along
the wayside.   The grass and the grain began to
sprout with tenfold vigor and luxuriance, to
make up for the dreary months that had been
wasted in barrenness.   The starved cattle imme
diately set to work grazing, after their long fast,
and ate enormously, all day, and got up at midnight to eat more.   But I can assure you it was
a busy time of year with the farmers, when they
found the summer coming upon them with such
a rush.   Nor must I forget to say, that all the
birds in the whole world hopped about upon the
newly-blossoming trees, and sang together, in a
prodigious ecstasy of joy.

Mother Ceres had returned to her deserted
home, and was sitting disconsolately on the door-
step, with her torch burning in her hand.   She
had been idly watching the flame for some moments past, when, all at once, it flickered and
went out.

"What does this mean?" thought she.   "It
was an enchanted torch, and should have kept
burning till my child came back."

Lifting her eyes, she was surprised to see a sudden verdure flashing over the brown and barren fields, exactly as you may have observed a golden hue gleaming far and wide across the landscape, from the just risen sun.

"Does the earth disobey me?" exclaimed Mother Ceres, indignantly. "Does it presume to be green, when I have bidden it be barren, until my daughter shall be restored to my arms?"

"Then open your arms, dear mother," cried a well-known voice, "and take your little daughter into them."

And Proserpina came running, and flung herself upon her mother's bosom. Their mutual transport is not to be described. The grief of their separation had caused both of them to shed a great many tears; and now they shed a great many more, because their joy could not so well express itself in any other way.

When their hearts had grown a little more quiet, Mother Ceres looked anxiously at Proserpina.

"My child," said she, 'did you taste any food while you were in King Pluto's palace?"

"Dearest mother," answered Proserpina, "I will tell you the whole truth. Until this very morning, not a morsel of food had passed my lips. But to-day, they brought me a pomegranate, (a very dry one it was, and all shrivelled up, till there was little left of it but seeds and skin,) and having seen no fruit for so long a time, and being faint with hunger, I was tempted just to bite it. The instant I tasted it, King Pluto and Quicksilver came into the room. I had not swallowed a morsel; but — dear mother, I hope it was no harm — but six of the pomegranate seeds, I am afraid, remained in my mouth."

"Ah, unfortunate child, and miserable me!" exclaimed Ceres. "For each of those six pomegranate seeds you must spend one month of every year in King Pluto's palace. You are but half restored to your mother. Only six months with me, and six with that good-for-nothing King of Darkness!"

"Do not speak so harshly of poor King Pluto," said Proserpina, kissing her mother. "He has some very good qualities; and I really think I can bear to spend six months in his palace, if he will only let me spend the other six with you He certainly did very wrong to carry me off; but then, as he says, it was but a dismal sort of life for him, to live in that great gloomy place, all alone; and it has made a wonderful change in his spirits to have a little girl to run up stairs and down. There is some comfort in making him so happy; and so, upon the whole, dearest mother, let us be thankful that he is not to keep me the whole year round."

THE GOLDEN FLEECE.

WHEN Jason, the son of the dethroned King
of Iolchos, was a little boy, he was sent away
from his parents, and placed under the queerest
schoolmaster that ever you heard of. This
learned person was one of the people, or quadru-
peds, called Centaurs. He lived in a cavern,
and had the body and legs of a white horse,
with the head and shoulders of a man. His
name was Chiron ; and, in spite of his odd appearance, he was a very excellent teacher, and
had several scholars, who afterwards did him
credit by making a great figure in the world.
The famous Hercules was one, and so was
Achilles, and Philoctetes, likewise, and Æscula-
pius, who acquired immense repute as a doctor
The good Chiron taught his pupils how to play
upon the harp, and how to cure diseases, and

how to use the sword and shield, together with various other branches of education, in which the lads of those days used to be instructed, instead of writing and arithmetic.

I have sometimes suspected that Master Chiron was not really very different from other people, but that, being a kind-hearted and merry old fellow, he was in the habit of making believe that he was a horse, and scrambling about the school room on all fours, and letting the little boys ride upon his back. And so, when his scholars had grown up, and grown old, and were trotting their grandchildren on their knees, they told them about the sports of their school days ; and these young folks took the idea that their grandfathers had been taught their letters by a Centaur, half man and half horse. Little children, not quite understanding what is said to them, often get such absurd notions into their heads, you know.

Be that as it may, it has always been told for a fact, (and always will be told, as long as the world lasts,) that Chiron, with the head of a schoolmaster, had the body and legs of a horse. Just imagine the grave old gentleman clattering

18

and stamping into the school room on his four hoofs, perhaps treading on some little fellow's toes, flourishing his switch tail instead of a rod, and, now and then, trotting out of doors to eat a mouthful of grass! I wonder what the black-smith charged him for a set of iron shoes.

So Jason dwelt in the cave, with this four-footed Chiron, from the time that he was an infant, only a few months old, until he had grown to the full height of a man. He became a very good harper, I suppose, and skilful in the use of weapons, and tolerably acquainted with herbs and other doctor's stuff, and, above all, an admirable horseman; for, in teaching young people to ride, the good Chiron must have been without a rival among schoolmasters. At length, being now a tall and athletic youth, Jason re-solved to seek his fortune in the world, without asking Chiron's advice, or telling him any thing about the matter. This was very unwise, to be sure; and I hope none of you, my little hearers, will ever follow Jason's example. But, you are to understand, he had heard how that he himself was a prince royal, and how his father, King Æson, had been deprived of the kingdom of

Iolchos by a certain Pelias, who would also have killed Jason, had he not been hidden in the Centaur's cave. And, being come to the strength of a man, Jason determined to set all this business to rights, and to punish the wicked Pelias for wronging his dear father, and to cast him down from the throne, and seat himself there instead.

With this intention, he took a spear in each hand, and threw a leopard's skin over his shoulders, to keep off the rain, and set forth on his travels, with his long yellow ringlets waving in the wind. The part of his dress on which he most prided himself was a pair of sandals, that had been his father's. They were handsomely embroidered, and were tied upon his feet with strings of gold. But his whole attire was such as people did not very often see; and as he passed along, the women and children ran to the doors and windows, wondering whither this beautiful youth was journeying, with his leopard's skin and his golden-tied sandals, and what heroic deeds he meant to perform, with a spear in his right hand and another in his left.

I know not how far Jason had travelled when he came to a turbulent river, which rushed right across his pathway, with specks of white foam among its black eddies, hurrying tumultuously onward, and roaring angrily as it went. Though not a very broad river in the dry seasons of the year, it was now swollen by heavy rains and by the melting of the snow on the sides of Mount Olympus; and it thundered so loudly, and looked so wild and dangerous, that Jason, bold as he was, thought it prudent to pause upon the brink. The bed of the stream seemed to be strewn with sharp and rugged rocks, some of which thrust themselves above the water. By and by, an up-rooted tree, with shattered branches, came drift-ing along the current, and got entangled among the rocks. Now and then, a drowned sheep, and once the carcass of a cow, floated past.

In short, the swollen river had already done a great deal of mischief. It was evidently too deep for Jason to wade, and too boisterous for him to swim; he could see no bridge; and as for a boat, had there been any, the rocks would have broken it to pieces in an instant.

"See the poor lad," said a cracked voice close to his side. "He must have had but a poor ed-ucation, since he does not know how to cross a little stream like this. Or is he afraid of wetting his fine golden-stringed sandals ? It is a pity his four footed schoolmaster is not here to carry him safely across on his back!"

Jason looked round greatly surprised, for he did not know that any body was near. But beside him stood an old woman, with a ragged mantle over her head, leaning on a staff, the top of which was carved into the shape of a cuckoo. She looked very aged, and wrinkled, and infirm ; and yet her eyes, which were as brown as those of an ox, were so extremely large and beautiful, that, when they were fixed on Jason's eyes, he could see nothing else but them. The old woman had a pomegranate in her hand, although the fruit was then quite out of season.

" Whither are you going, Jason ?" she now asked.

She seemed to know his name, you will observe ; and, indeed, those great brown eyes looked as if they had a knowledge of every thing, whether past or to come. While Jason was gazing at her, a peacock strutted forward, and took his stand at the old woman's side.

" I am going to Iolchos," answered the young

man, "to bid the wicked King Pelias come
down from my father's throne, and let me reign
n his stead."

" Ah, well, then," said the old woman, still
with the same cracked voice, "if that is all your
business, you need not be in a very great hurry
Just take me on your back, there's a good
youth, and carry me across the river. I and
my peacock have something to do on the other
side, as well as yourself."

" Good mother," replied Jason, "your business
can hardly be so important as the pulling down
a king from his throne. Besides, as you may
see for yourself, the river is very boisterous ; and
if I should chance to stumble, it would sweep
both of us away more easily than it has carried
off yonder uprooted tree. I would gladly help
you if I could; but I doubt whether I am strong
enough to carry you across."

" Then," said she, very scornfully, "neither are
you strong enough to pull King Pelias off his
throne. And, Jason, unless you will he_p an
old woman at her need, you ought not to be a
king. What are kings made for, save to succor
the feeble and distressed? But do as you please

'Either take me on your back, or with my poor old limbs I shall try my best to struggle across the stream."

Saying this, the old woman poked with her staff in the river, as if to find the safest place in its rocky bed where she might make the first step. But Jason, by this time, had grown ashamed of his reluctance to help her. He felt that he could never forgive himself, if this poor feeble creature should come to any harm in attempting to wrestle against the headlong current. The good Chiron, whether half horse or no, had taught him that the noblest use of his strength was to assist the weak; and also that he must treat every young woman as if she were his sister, and every old one like a mother. Remembering these maxims, the vigorous and beautiful young man knelt down, and requested the good dame to mount upon his back.

" The passage seems to me not very safe," he remarked. " But as your business is so urgent, I will try to carry you across. If the river sweeps you away, it shall take me too."

" That, no doubt, will be a great comfort to both of us," quoth the old woman. " But never fear. We shall get safely across."

So she threw her arms around Jason's neck; and lifting her from the ground, he stepped bold ly into the raging and foamy current, and began to stagger away from the shore. As for the pea- cock, it alighted on the old dame's shoulder. Jason's two spears, one in each hand, kept him from stumbling, and enabled him to feel his way among the hidden rocks; although, every in- stant, he expected that his companion and him- self would go down the stream, together with the driftwood of shattered trees, and the car- casses of the sheep and cow. Down came the cold, snowy torrent from the steep side of Olympus, raging and thundering as if it had a real spite against Jason, or, at all events, were determined to snatch off his living burden from his shoulders. When he was half way across, the uprooted tree (which I have already told you about) broke loose from among the rocks, and bore down upon him, with all its splintered branches sticking out like the hundred arms of the giant Briareus. It rushed past, however, without touching him. But the next moment, his foot was caught in a crevice between two rocks, and stuck there so fast, that, in the effort to get free, he lost one of his gold n-stringed sandals.

At this accident Jason could not help uttering a cry of vexation.

"What is the matter, Jason?" asked the old woman.

"Matter enough," said the young man. "I have lost a sandal here among the rocks. And what sort of a figure shall I cut, at the court of King Pelias, with a golden-stringed sandal on one foot, and the other foot bare!"

"Do not take it to heart," answered his companion, cheerily. "You never met with better fortune than in losing that sandal. It satisfies me that you are the very person whom the Speaking Oak has been talking about."

There was no time, just then, to inquire what the Speaking Oak had said. But the briskness of her tone encouraged the young man; and besides, he had never in his life felt so vigorous and mighty as since taking this old woman on his back. Instead of being exhausted, he gathered strength as he went on; and, struggling up against the torrent, he at last gained the opposite shore, clambered up the bank, and set down the old dame and her peacock safely on the grass. As soon as this was done, however, he

could not help looking rather despondently at
his bare foot, with only a remnant of the golden
string of the sandal clinging round his ankle.

"You will get a handsomer pair of sandals
by and by," said the old woman, with a kindly
look out of her beautiful brown eyes. "Only
let King Pelias get a glimpse of that bare foot,
and you shall see him turn as pale as ashes, I
promise you. There is your path. Go along,
my good Jason, and my blessing go with you.
And when you sit on your throne, remember the
old woman whom you helped over the river."

With these words, she hobbled away, giving
him a smile over her shoulder as she departed.
Whether the light of her beautiful brown eyes
threw a glory round about her, or whatever the
cause might be, Jason fancied that there was
something very noble and majestic in her figure,
after all, and that, though her gait seemed to be
a rheumatic hobble, yet she moved with as much
grace and dignity as any queen on earth. Her
peacock, which had now fluttered down from her
shoulder, strutted behind her in prodigious pomp,
and spread out its magnificent tail on purpose
for Jason to admire it.

When the old dame and her peacock were out of sight, Jason set forward on his journey. After travelling a pretty long distance, he came to a town situated at the foot of a mountain, and not a great way from the shore of the sea. On the outside of the town there was an immense crowd of people, not only men and women, but children too, all in their best clothes, and evidently enjoying a holiday. The crowd was thickest towards the sea shore; and in that direction, over the people's heads, Jason saw a wreath of smoke curling upward to the blue sky. He inquired of one of the multitude what town it was, near by, and why so many persons were here assembled togther.

"This is the kingdom of Iolchos," answered the man, "and we are the subjects of King Pelias. Our monarch has summoned us together, that we may see him sacrifice a black bull to Neptune, who, they say, is his majesty's father. Yonder is the king, where you see the smoke going up from the altar."

While the man spoke he eyed Jason with great curiosity; for his garb was quite unlike that of the Iolchians, and it looked very odd to see a youth with a leopard's skin over his shoulders, and each hand grasping a spear. Jason perceived, too, that the man stared particularly at his feet, one of which, you remember, was bare, while the other was decorated with his father's golden-stringed sandal.

"Look at him! only look at him!" said the man to his next neighbor. "Do you see? He wears but one sandal!"

Upon this, first one person, and then another, began to stare at Jason, and every body seemed to be greatly struck with something in his aspect; though they turned their eyes much oftener towards his feet than to any other part of his figure. Besides, he could hear them whispering to one another.

"One sandal! One sandal!" they kept saying. "The man with one sandal! Here he is at last! Whence has he come? What does he mean to do? What will the king say to the one-sandalled man?"

Poor Jason was greatly abashed, and made up his mind that the people of Iolchos were exceedingly ill bred, to take such public notice of an accidental deficiency in his dress. Meanwhile, whether it were that they hustled him forward, or that Jason, of his own accord, thrust a passage through the crowd, it so happened that he soon found himself close to the smoking altar where King Pelias was sacrificing the black bull. The murmur and hum of the multitude, in their surprise at the spectacle of Jason with his one bare foot, grew so loud that it disturbed the ceremonies; and the king, holding the great knife with which he was just going to cut the bull's throat, turned angrily about, and fixed his eyes on Jason. The people had now withdrawn from around him, so that the youth stood in an open space, near the smoking altar, front to front with the angry King Pelias.

" Who are you? " cried the king, with a terrible frown. " And how dare you make this disturbance, while I am sacrificing a black bull to my father Neptune ? "

" It is no fault of mine," answered Jason. " Your majesty must blame the rudeness of your subjects, who have raised all this tumult because one of my feet happens to be bare."

When Jason said this, the king gave a quick, startled glance down at his feet.

" Ha!" muttered he, " here is the one-san·
dalled fellow, sure enough! What can I do
with him ? "

And he clutched more closely the great knife
in his hand, as if he were half a mind to slay
Jason, instead of the black bull. The people
round about caught up the king's words, indistinctly as they were uttered; and first there was
a murmur among them, and then a loud shout.

" The one-sandalled man has come! The
prophecy must be fulfilled! "

For you are to know, that, many years before,
King Pelias had been told by the Speaking Oak
of Dodona, that a man with one sandal should
cast him down from his throne. On this account, he had given strict orders that nobody
should ever come into his presence, unless both
sandals were securely tied upon his feet; and
he kept an officer in his palace, whose sole business it was to examine people's sandals, and to
supply them with a new pair, at the expense of
the royal treasury, as soon as the old ones began
to wear out. In the whole course of the king's
reign, he had never been thrown into such a
fright and agitation as by the spectacle of poor

Jason's bare foot. But, as he was naturally a bold and hard-hearted man, he soon took courage, and began to consider in what way he might rid himself of this terrible one-sandalled stranger.

" My good young man," said King Pelias, taking the softest tone imaginable, in order to throw Jason off his guard, "you are excessively welcome to my kingdom. Judging by your dress, you must have travelled a long distance; for it is not the fashion to wear leopard skins in this part of the world. Pray what may I call your name? and where did you receive your education ? "

" My name is Jason," answered the young stranger. " Ever since my infancy, I have dwelt in the cave of Chiron the Centaur. He was my instructor, and taught me music, and horsemanship, and how to cure wounds, and likewise how to inflict wounds with my weapons ! "

" I have heard of Chiron the schoolmaster," replied King Pelias, " and how that there is an immense deal of learning and wisdom in his head, although it happens to be set on a horse's body. It gives me great delight to see one of his scholars at my court. But, to test how much

you have profited under so excellent a teacher.
will you allow me to ask you a single question?"

"I do not pretend to be very wise," said Jason.
"But ask me what you please, and I will answer
to the best of my ability."

Now King Pelias meant cunningly to entrap
the young man, and to make him say something
that should be the cause of mischief and destruction to himself. So, with a crafty and evil smile
upon his face, he spoke as follows: —

"What would you do, brave Jason," asked he,
"if there were a man in the world, by whom, as
you had reason to believe, you were doomed to
be ruined and slain — what would you do, I say,
if that man stood before you, and in your
power?"

When Jason saw the malice and wickedness
which King Pelias could not prevent from gleaming out of his eyes, he probably guessed that the
king had discovered what he came for, and that
he intended to turn his own words against himself. Still he scorned to tell a falsehood. Like
an upright and honorable prince, as he was, he
determined to speak out the real truth. Since
the king had chosen to ask him the question,

and since Jason had promised him an answer, there was no right way, save to tell him precisely what would be the most prudent thing to do, if he had his worst enemy in his power.

Therefore, after a moment's consideration, he spoke up, with a firm and manly voice.

" I would send such a man," said he, " in quest of the Golden Fleece ! "

This enterprise, you will understand, was, of all others, the most difficult and dangerous in the world. In the first place, it would be necessary to make a long voyage through unknown seas. There was hardly a hope, or a possibility, that any young man who should undertake this voyage would either succeed in obtaining the Golden Fleece, or would survive to return home, and tell of the perils he had run. The eyes of King Pelias sparkled with joy, therefore, when he heard Jason's reply.

" Well said, wise man with the one sandal!" cried he. " Go, then, and at the peril of your life, bring me back the Golden Fleece."

" I go," answered Jason, composedly. " If I fail, you need not fear that I will ever come back to trouble you again. But if I return to Iolchos with the prize, then, King Pelias, you must hasten down from your lofty throne, and give me your crown and sceptre."

" That I will," said the king, with a sneer. " Meantime, I will keep them very safely for you."

The first thing that Jason thought of doing, after he left the king's presence, was to go to Dodona, and inquire of the Talking Oak what course it was best to pursue. This wonderful tree stood in the centre of an ancient wood. Its stately trunk rose up a hundred feet into the air, and threw a broad and dense shadow over more than an acre of ground. Standing beneath it, Jason looked up among the knotted branches and green leaves, and into the mysterious heart of the old tree, and spoke aloud, as if he were addressing some person who was hidden in the depths of the foliage.

" What shall I do," said he, " in order to win the Golden Fleece ? "

At first there was a deep silence, not only within the shadow of the Talking Oak, but all through the solitary wood. In a moment or two however, the leaves of the oak began to stir and rustle, as if a gentle breeze were wandering amongst them, although the other trees of the wood were perfectly still. The sound grew louder, and became like the roar of a high wind. By and by, Jason imagined that he could distinguish words, but very confusedly, because each separate leaf of the tree seemed to be a tongue, and the whole myriad of tongues were babbling at once. But the noise waxed broader and deeper, until it resembled a tornado sweeping through the oak, and making one great utterance out of the thousand and thousand of little murmurs which each leafy tongue had caused by its rustling. And now, though it still had the tone of a mighty wind roaring among the branches, it was also like a deep bass voice, speaking, as distinctly as a tree could be expected to speak, the following words: —

" Go to Argus, the ship builder, and bid him build a galley with fifty oars."

Then the voice melted again into the indistinct murmur of the rustling leaves, and died gradually away. When it was quite gone, Jason felt inclined to doubt whether he had actually heard the words, or whether his fancy had not shaped them out of the ordinary sound made by a breeze, while passing through the thick foliage of the tree.

But on inquiry among the people of Iolchos, he found that there was really a man in the city, by the name of Argus, who was a very skilful builder of vessels. This showed some intelligence in the oak; else how should it have known that any such person existed? At Jason's request, Argus readily consented to build him a galley so big that it should require fifty strong men to row it; although no vessel of such a size and burden had heretofore been seen in the world. So the head carpenter, and all his journeymen and apprentices, began their work; and for a good while afterwards, there they were, busily employed, hewing out the timbers, and making a great clatter with their hammers; until the new ship, which was called the Argo, seemed to be quite ready for sea. And, as the Talking Oak had already given him such good advice, Jason thought that it would not be amiss to ask for a little more. He visited it again, therefore, and standing beside its huge, rough trunk, inquired what he should do next.

This time, there was no such universal quivering of the leaves, throughout the whole tree, as there had been before. But after a while, Jason observed that the foliage of a great branch which stretched above his head had begun to rustle, as if the wind were stirring that one bough, while all the other boughs of the oak were at rest.

"Cut me off!" said the branch, as soon as it could speak distinctly; "cut me off! cut me off! and carve me into a figure head for your galley."

Accordingly, Jason took the branch at its word, and lopped it off the tree. A carver in the neighborhood engaged to make the figure head. He was a tolerably good workman, and had already carved several figure heads, in what he intended for feminine shapes, and looking pretty much like those which we see nowadays stuck up under a vessel's bowsprit, with great staring eyes, that never wink at the dash of the spray. But (what was very strange) the carver found that his hand was guided by some unseen power, and by a skill beyond his own, and that his tools shaped out an image which he had never dreamed of. When the work was finished, it turned out to be the figure of a beautiful woman, with a helmet on her head, from beneath which the long ringlets fell down upon her shoulders. On the left arm was a shield, and in its centre appeared a lifelike representation of the head of Medusa with the snaky locks. The right arm was extended, as if pointing onward. The face of this wonderful statue, though not angry or forbidding, was so grave and majestic, that perhaps you might call it severe ; and as for the mouth, it seemed just ready to unclose its lips, and utter words of the deepest wisdom.

Jason was delighted with the oaken image, and gave the carver no rest until it was com· pleted, and set up where a figure head has always stood, from that time to this, in the ves· sel's prow.

" And now," cried he, as he stood gazing at the calm, majestic face of the statue, " I must go to the Talking Oak, and inquire what next to do."

" There is no need of that, Jason," said a voice which, though it was far lower, reminded him of the mighty tones of the great oak. " When you desire good advice, you can seek it of me."

Jason had been looking straight into the face of the image when these words were spoken. But he could hardly believe either his ears or his eyes. The truth was, however, that the oaken lips had moved, and, to all appearance, the voice had proceeded from the statue's mouth. Recovering a little from· his surprise, Jason bethought himself that the image had been carved out of the wood of the Talking Oak, and that, therefore, it was really no great wonder, but, on the contrary, the most natural thing in the world, that it should possess the faculty of speech. It would have been very odd, indeed, if it had not. But certainly it was a great piece of good fortune that he should be able to carry so wise a block of wood along with him in his perilous voyage.

" Tell me, wondrous image," exclaimed Jason, —"since you inherit the wisdom of the Speaking Oak of Dodona, whose daughter you are, — tell me, where shall I find fifty bold youths, who will take each of them an oar of my galley? They must have sturdy arms to row, and brave hearts to encounter perils, or we shall never win the Golden Fleece."

"Go," replied the oaken image, "go, sum·
mon all the heroes of Greece."

And, in fact, considering what a great deed
was to be done, could any advice be wiser than
this which Jason received from the figure head
of his vessel?   He lost no time in sending mes·
sengers to all the cities, and making known to
the whole people of Greece, that Prince Jason,
the son of King Æson, was going in quest of
the Fleece of Gold, and that he desired the help
of forty-nine of the bravest and strongest young
men alive, to row his vessel and share his dangers.   And Jason himself would be the fiftieth.

At this news, the adventurous youths, all over
the country, began to bestir themselves.   Some
of them had already fought with giants, and
slain dragons; and the younger ones, who had
not yet met with such good fortune, thought
it a shame to have lived so long without getting
astride of a flying serpent, or sticking their
spears into a Chimæra, or, at least, thrusting their
right arms down a monstrous lion's throat.
There was a fair prospect that they would meet
with plenty of such adventures before finding
the Golden Fleece.   As soon as they could fur-

bish up their helmets and shields, therefore, and gird on their trusty swords, they came thronging to Iolchos, and clambered on board the new galley. Shaking hands with Jason, they assured him that they did not care a pin for their lives, but would help row the vessel to the remotest edge of the world, and as much farther as he might think it best to go.

Many of these brave fellows had been educated by Chiron, the four-footed pedagogue, and were therefore old schoolmates of Jason, and knew him to be a lad of spirit. The mighty Hercules, whose shoulders afterwards held up the sky, was one of them. And there were Castor and Pollux, the twin brothers, who were never accused of being chicken-hearted, although they had been hatched out of an egg; and Theseus, who was so renowned for killing the Minotaur; and Lynceus, with his wonderfully sharp eyes, which could see through a millstone, or look right down into the depths of the earth, and discover the treasures that were there; and Orpheus, the very best of harpers, who sang and played upon his lyre so sweetly, that the brute beasts stood upon their hind legs, and

capered merrily to the music. Yes, and at some
of his more moving tunes, the rocks bestirred
their moss-grown bulk out of the ground, and a
grove of forest trees uprooted themselves, and,
nodding their tops to one another, performed a
country dance.

One of the rowers was a beautiful young
woman, named Atalanta, who had been nursed
among the mountains by a bear. So light of
foot was this fair damsel, that she could step
from one foamy crest of a wave to the foamy
crest of another, without wetting more than
the sole of her sandal. She had grown up
in a very wild way, and talked much about
the rights of women, and loved hunting and
war far better than her needle. But, in my
opinion, the most remarkable of this famous
company were two sons of the North Wind
(airy youngsters, and of rather a blustering disposition,) who had wings on their shoulders,
and, in case of a calm, could puff out their
cheeks, and blow almost as fresh a breeze as
their father. I ought not to forget the prophets
and conjurers, of whom there were several in
the crew, and who could foretell what would

happen to-morrow, or the next day, or a hundred
years hence, but were generally quite unconscious of what was passing at the moment.

Jason appointed Tiphys to be helmsman, because he was a star-gazer, and knew the points
of the compass. Lynceus, on account of his
sharp sight, was stationed as a lookout in the
prow, where he saw a whole day's sail ahead,
but was rather apt to overlook things that lay
directly under his nose. If the sea only happened to be deep enough, however, Lynceus
could tell you exactly what kind of rocks or
sands were at the bottom of it; and he often
cried out to his companions, that they were
sailing over heaps of sunken treasure, which
yet he was none the richer for beholding. To
confess the truth, few people believed him when
he said it.

Well! But when the Argonauts, as these
fifty brave adventurers were called, had prepared
every thing for the voyage, an unforeseen diffi-
culty threatened to end it before it was begun.
The vessel, you must understand, was so long,
and broad, and ponderous, that the united force
of all the fifty was insufficient to shove her into

the water. Hercules, I suppose, had not grown to his full strength, else he might have set her afloat as easily as a little boy launches his boat upon a puddle. But here were these fifty heroes, pushing, and straining, and growing red in the face, without making the Argo start an inch. At last, quite wearied out, they sat themselves down on the shore, exceedingly disconsolate, and thinking that the vessel must be left to rot and fall in pieces, and that they must either swim across the sea or lose the Golden Fleece.

All at once, Jason bethought himself of the galley's miraculous figure head.

" O, daughter of the Talking Oak," cried he, " how shall we set to work to get our vessel into the water ? "

" Seat yourselves," answered the image, (for it had known what had ought to be done from the very first, and was only waiting for the question to be put,) — " seat yourselves, and handle your oars, and let Orpheus play upon his harp."

Immediately the fifty heroes got on board, and seizing their oars, held them perpendicularly in the air, while Orpheus (who liked such a task far better than rowing) swept his fingers across the harp. At the first ringing note of the music, they felt the vessel stir. Orpheus thrummed away briskly, and the galley slid at once into the sea, dipping her prow so deeply that the figure head drank the wave with its marvellous lips, and rising again as buoyant as a swan. The rowers plied their fifty oars; the white foam boiled up before the prow; the water gurgled and bubbled in their wake; while Orpheus continued to play so lively a strain of music, that the vessel seemed to dance over the billows by way of keeping time to it. Thus triumphantly did the Argo sail out of the harbor, amidst the huzzas and good wishes of every body except the wicked old Pelias, who stood on a promontory, scowling at her, and wishing that he could blow out of his lungs the tempest of wrath that was in his heart, and so sink the galley with all on board. When they had sailed above fifty miles over the sea, Lynceus happened to cast his sharp eyes behind, and said that there was this bad-hearted king, still perched upon the promontory, and scowling so gloomily that it looked like a black thunder cloud in that quarter of the horizon

In order to make the time pass away more
pleasantly during the voyage, the heroes talked
about the Golden Fleece.   It originally belonged,
it appears, to a Bœotian ram, who had taken on
his back two children, when in danger of their
lives, and fled with them over land and sea, as far
as Colchis.   One of the children, whose name
was Helle, fell into the sea and was drowned.
But the other, (a little boy, named Phrixus) was
brought safe ashore by the faithful ram, who
however, was so exhausted that he immediately
lay down and died.   In memory of this good
deed, and as a token of his true heart, the fleece
of the poor dead ram was miraculously changed
to gold, and became one of the most beautiful
objects ever seen on earth.   It was hung upon a
tree in a sacred grove, where it had now been
kept I know not how many years, and was the
envy of mighty kings, who had nothing so magnificent in any of their palaces.

If I were to tell you all the adventures of the
Argonauts, it would take me till nightfall, and
perhaps a great deal longer.   There was no ack
of wonderful events, as you may judge from what
you have already heard.   At a certain island

they were hospitably received by King Cyzicus, its sovereign, who made a feast for them, and treated them like brothers. But the Argonauts saw that this good king looked downcast and very much troubled, and they therefore inquired of him what was the matter. King Cyzicus hereupon informed them that he and his subjects were greatly abused and incommoded by the inhabitants of a neighboring mountain, who made war upon them, and killed many people, and ravaged the country. And while they were talking about it, Cyzicus pointed to the mountain, and asked Jason and his companions what they saw there.

"I see some very tall objects," answered Jason; "but they are at such a distance that I cannot distinctly make out what they are. To tell your majesty the truth, they look so very strangely that I am inclined to think them clouds, which have chanced to take something like human shapes."

"I see them very plainly," remarked Lynceus, whose eyes, you know, were as far sighted as a telescope. "They are a band of enormous giants, all of whom have six arms apiece, and a

club, a sword, or some other weapon in each
of their hands."

" You have excellent eyes," said King Cyzicus.
" Yes; they are six armed giants, as you say,
and these are the enemies whom I and my
subjects have to contend with."

The next day, when the Argonauts were about
setting sail, down came these terrible giants,
stepping a hundred yards at a stride, brandishing their six arms apiece, and looking very formidable, so far aloft in the air. Each of these
monsters was able to carry on a whole war by
himself, for with one of his arms he could fling
immense stones, and wield a club with another,
and a sword with a third, while the fourth was
poking a long spear at the enemy, and the fifth
and sixth were shooting him with a bow and
arrow. But, luckily, though the giants were so
huge, and had so many arms, they had each
but one heart, and that no bigger nor braver
than the heart of an ordinary man. Besides, if
they had been like the hundred-armed Briareus,
the brave Argonauts would have given them their
hands full of fight. Jason and his friends went
boldly to meet them, slew a great many, and

made the rest take to their heels, so that, if the giants had had six legs apiece instead of six arms, it would have served them better to run away with.

Another strange adventure happened when the voyagers came to Thrace, where they found a poor blind king, named Phineus, deserted by his subjects, and living in a very sorrowful way, all by himself. On Jason's inquiring whether they could do him any service, the king answered that he was terribly tormented by three great winged creatures, called Harpies, which had the faces of women, and the wings, bodies, and claws of vultures. These ugly wretches were in the habit of snatching away his dinner, and allowed him no peace of his life. Upon hearing this, the Argonauts spread a plentiful feast on the sea shore, well knowing, from what the blind king said of their greediness, that the Harpies would snuff up the scent of the victuals, and quickly come to steal them away. And so it turned out; for, hardly was the table set, before the three hideous vulture women came flapping their wings, seized the food in their talons, and flew off as fast as they could. But the two sons

of the North Wind drew their swords, spread
their pinions, and set off through the air in pursuit of the thieves, whom they at last overtook
among some islands, after a chase of hundreds
of miles.   The two winged youths blustered
terribly at the Harpies, (for they had the rough
temper of their father,) and so frightened them
with their drawn swords, that they solemnly
promised never to trouble King Phineus again.

Then the Argonauts sailed onward, and met
with many other marvellous incidents, any one
of which would make a story by itself.   At one
time, they landed on an island, and were reposing
on the grass, when they suddenly found themselves assailed by what seemed a shower of
steel-headed arrows.   Some of them stuck in
the ground, while others hit against their shields,
and several penetrated their flesh.   The fifty
heroes started up, and looked about them for the
hidden enemy, but could find none, nor see any
spot, on the whole island, where even a single
archer could lie concealed.   Still, however, the
steel-headed arrows came whizzing among them ·
and, at last, happening to look upward, they
beheld a large flock of birds, hovering and wheel-

ing aloft, and shooting their feathers down upon the Argonauts. These feathers were the steel-headed arrows that had so tormented them. There was no possibility of making any resistance; and the fifty heroic Argonauts might all have been killed or wounded by a flock of troublesome birds, without ever setting eyes on the Golden Fleece, if Jason had not thought of asking the advice of the oaken image.

So he ran to the galley as fast as his legs would carry him.

" O, daughter of the Speaking Oak," cried he, all out of breath, " we need your wisdom more than ever before! We are in great peril from a flock of birds, who are shooting us with their steel-pointed feathers. What can we do to drive them away? "

" Make a clatter on your shields," said the image.

On receiving this excellent counsel, Jason hurried back to his companions, (who were far more dismayed than when they fought with the six-armed giants,) and bade them strike with their swords upon their brazen shields. Forth-with the fifty heroes set heartily to work, bang-

ing with might and main, and raised such a
terrible clatter, that the birds made what haste
they could to get away; and though they
had shot half the feathers out of their wings,
they were soon seen skimming among the
clouds, a long distance off, and looking like a
flock of wild geese. Orpheus celebrated this
victory by playing a triumphant anthem on his
harp, and sang so melodiously that Jason begged
him to desist, lest, as the steel-feathered birds
had been driven away by an ugly sound, they
might be enticed back again by a sweet one.

While the Argonauts remained on this island,
they saw a small vessel approaching the shore,
in which were two young men of princely demeanor, and exceedingly handsome, as young
princes generally were, in those days. Now,
who do you imagine these two voyagers turned
out to be? Why, if you will believe me, they
were the sons of that very Phrixus, who, in his
childhood, had been carried to Colchis on the
back of the golden-fleeced ram. Since that
time, Phrixus had married the king's daughter;
and the two young princes had been born and
brought up at Colchis, and had spent their play

days in the outskirts of the grove, in the centre of which the Golden Fleece was hanging upon a tree. They were now on their way to Greece, in hopes of getting back a kingdom that had been wrongfully taken from their father.

When the princes understood whither the Argonauts were going, they offered to turn back, and guide them to Colchis. At the same time, however, they spoke as if it were very doubtful whether Jason would succeed in getting the Golden Fleece. According to their account, the tree on which it hung was guarded by a terrible dragon, who never failed to devour, at one mouthful, every person who might venture within his reach.

" There are other difficulties in the way," continued the young princes. " But is not this enough? Ah, brave Jason, turn back before it is too late. It would grieve us to the heart, if you and your nine and forty brave companions should be eaten up, at fifty mouthfuls, by this execrable dragon."

" My young friends," quietly replied Jason, " I do not wonder that you think the dragon very terrible. You have grown up from infancy

in the fear of this monster, and therefore still regard him with the awe that children feel for the
bugbears and hobgoblins which their nurses
have talked to them about.   But, in my view
of the matter, the dragon is merely a pretty large
serpent, who is not half so likely to snap me up
at one mouthful as I am to cut off his ugly
head, and strip the skin from his body.   At all
events, turn back who may, I will never see
Greece again, unless I carry with me the Golden
Fleece."

"We will none of us turn back!" cried his
nine and forty brave comrades.   "Let us get on
board the galley this instant; and if the dragon
is to make a breakfast of us, much good may it
do him."

And Orpheus (whose custom it was to set
every thing to music) began to harp and sing
most gloriously, and made every mother's son of
them feel as if nothing in this world were so de-
lectable as to fight dragons, and nothing so truly
honorable as to be eaten up at one mouthful, in
case of the worst.

After this, (being now under the guidance of
the two princes, who were well acquainted with

the way,) they quickly sailed to Colchis. When
the king of the country, whose name was Æetes,
heard of their arrival, he instantly summoned
Jason to court. The king was a stern and cruel-
looking potentate; and though he put on as
polite and hospitable an expression as he could,
Jason did not like his face a whit better tha
that of the wicked King Pelias, who dethroned
his father.

"You are welcome, brave Jason," said King
Æetes. "Pray, are you on a pleasure voyage?
— or do you meditate the discovery of unknown
islands? — or what other cause has procured me
the happiness of seeing you at my court?"

"Great sir," replied Jason, with an obeisance,
— for Chiron had taught him how to behave
with propriety, whether to kings or beggars, —
"I have come hither with a purpose which I
now beg your majesty's permission to execute.
King Pelias, who sits on my father's throne, (to
which he has no more right than to the one on
which your excellent majesty is now seated,) has
engaged to come down from it, and to give me
his crown and sceptre, provided I bring him the
Golden Fleece This, as your majesty is aware,

is now hanging on a tree here at Colchis; and
I humbly solicit your gracious leave to take it
away."

In spite of himself, the king's face twisted itself into an angry frown; for, above all things
else in the world, he prized the Golden Fleece,
and was even suspected of having done a very
wicked act, in order to get it into his own possession. It put him into the worst possible humor, therefore, to hear that the gallant Prince
Jason, and forty-nine of the bravest young warriors of Greece, had come to Colchis with the
sole purpose of taking away his chief treasure.

"Do you know," asked King Æetes, eying
Jason very sternly, "what are the conditions
which you must fulfil before getting possession
of the Golden Fleece?"

"I have heard," rejoined the youth, "that a
dragon lies beneath the tree on which the prize
hangs, and that whoever approaches him runs
the risk of being devoured at a mouthful."

"True," said the king, with a smile that did
not look particularly good natured. "Very true,
young man. But there are other things as
hard, or perhaps a little harder, to be done,

before you can even have the privilege of being devoured by the dragon. For example, you must first tame my two brazen-footed and brazen-lunged bulls, which Vulcan, the wonderful blacksmith, made for me. There is a furnace in each of their stomachs; and they breathe such hot fire out of their mouths and nostrils, that nobody has hitherto gone nigh them without being instantly burned to a small, black cinder. What do you think of this, my brave Jason?"

" I must encounter the peril," answered Jason, composedly, " since it stands in the way of my purpose."

" After taming the fiery bulls," continued King Æetes, who was determined to scare Jason if possible, " you must yoke them to a plough, and must plough the sacred earth in the grove of Mars, and sow some of the same dragon's teeth from which Cadmus raised a crop of armed men. They are an unruly set of reprobates, those sons of the dragon's teeth; and unless you treat them suitably, they will fall upon you sword in hand. You and your nine and forty Argonauts, my bold Jason, are hardly numerous or strong enough to fight with such a host as will spring up."

" My master Chiron," replied Jason, " taught
me, long ago, the story of Cadmus. Perhaps I
can manage the quarrelsome sons of the dragon's teeth as well as Cadmus did."

" I wish the dragon had him," muttered King
Æetes to himself, "and the four-footed pedant,
his schoolmaster, into the bargain. Why, what a
foolhardy, self-conceited coxcomb he is! We'll
see what my fire-breathing bulls will do for him.
Well, Prince Jason," he continued, aloud, and as
complaisantly as he could, " make yourself comfortable for to-day, and to-morrow morning, since
you insist upon it, you shall try your skill at
the plough."

While the king talked with Jason, a beautiful
young woman was standing behind the throne.
She fixed her eyes earnestly upon the youthful
stranger, and listened attentively to every word
that was spoken; and when Jason withdrew
from the king's presence, this young woman
followed him out of the room.

" I am the king's daughter," she said to him,
" and my name is Medea. I know a great deal
of which other young princesses are ignorant,
and can do many things which they would be

afraid so much as to dream of. If you will trust to me, I can instruct you how to tame the fiery bulls, and sow the dragon's teeth, and get the Golden Fleece."

" Indeed, beautiful princess," answered Jason, "it you will do me this service, I promise to be grateful to you my whole life long."

Gazing at Medea, he beheld a wonderful intelligence in her face. She was one of those persons whose eyes are full of mystery; so that, while looking into them, you seem to see a very great way, as into a deep well, yet can never be certain whether you see into the farthest depths, or whether there be not something else hidden at the bottom. If Jason had been capable of fearing any thing, he would have been afraid of making this young princess his enemy; for, beautiful as she now looked, she might, the very next instant, become as terrible as the dragon that kept watch over the Golden Fleece.

" Princess," he exclaimed, " you seem indeed very wise and very powerful. But how can you help me to do the things of which you speak? Are you an enchantress?"

" Yes, Prince Jason," answered Medea with a

smile, " you have hit upon the truth. I am an enchantress. Circe, my father's sister, taught me to be one, and I could tell you, if I pleased, who was the old woman with the peacock, the pomegranate, and the cuckoo staff, whom you carried over the river; and, likewise, who it is that speaks through the lips of the oaken image, that stands in the prow of your galley. I am acquainted with some of your secrets, you perceive. It is well for you that I am favorably inclined; for, otherwise, you would hardly escape being snapped up by the dragon."

" I should not so much care for the dragon," replied Jason, " if I only knew how to manage the brazen-footed and fiery-lunged bulls."

" If you are as brave as I think you, and as you have need to be," said Medea, " your own bold heart will teach you that there is but one way of dealing with a mad bull. What it is I leave you to find out in the moment of peril. As for the fiery breath of these animals, I have a charmed ointment here, which will prevent you from being burned up, and cure you if you chance to be a little scorched."

So she put a golden box into his hand, and

directed him how to apply the perfumed **unguent** which it contained, and where to meet **her** at midnight

"Only be brave," added she, "and before daybreak the brazen bulls shall be tamed."

The young man assured her that his **heart** would not fail him. He then rejoined his **comrades**, and told them what had passed between the princess and himself, and warned them **to** be in readiness in case there might be need of their help.

At the appointed hour he met the beautiful Medea on the marble steps of the king's palace. She gave him a basket, in which were the **dragon's** teeth, just as they had been pulled out of the monster's jaws by Cadmus, long ago. Medea then led Jason down the palace steps, and through the silent streets of the city, and into the royal pasture ground, where the two brazen footed bulls were kept. It was a starry night, with a bright gleam along the eastern edge of the sky, where the moon was soon going to show herself. After entering the pasture, the princess paused and looked around.

"There they are," said she, "reposing themselves and chewing their fiery cuds in that farthest corner of the field. It will be excellent sport, I assure you, when they catch a glimpse of your figure. My father and all his court delight in nothing so much as to see a stranger trying to yoke them, in order to come at the Golden Fleece. It makes a holiday in Colchis whenever such a thing happens. For my part, I enjoy it immensely. You cannot imagine in what a mere twinkling of an eye their hot breath shrivels a young man into a black cinder."

"Are you sure, beautiful Medea," asked Jason, "quite sure, that the unguent in the gold box will prove a remedy against those terrible burns?"

"If you doubt, if you are in the least afraid," said the princess, looking him in the face by the dim starlight, "you had better never have been born than go a step nigher to the bulls."

But Jason had set his heart steadfastly on getting the Golden Fleece; and I positively doubt whether he would have gone back without it, even had he been certain of finding himself turned into a red-hot cinder, or a handful of white ashes, the instant he made a step farther

He therefore let go Medea's hand, and walked boldly forward in the direction whither she had pointed. At some distance before him he perceived four streams of fiery vapor, regularly appearing, and again vanishing, after dimly lighting up the surrounding obscurity. These, you will understand, were caused by the breath of the brazen bulls, which was quietly stealing out of their four nostrils, as they lay chewing their cuds.

At the first two or three steps which Jason made, the four fiery streams appeared to gush out somewhat more plentifully; for the two brazen bulls had heard his foot tramp, and were lifting up their hot noses to snuff the air. He went a little farther, and by the way in which the red vapor now spouted forth, he judged that the creatures had got upon their feet. Now he could see glowing sparks, and vivid jets of flame At the next step, each of the bulls made the pasture echo with a terrible roar, while the burning breath, which they thus belched forth, lit up the whole field with a momentary flash. One other stride did bold Jason make; and, suddenly, as a streak of lightning, on came these fiery

animals, roaring like thunder, and sending ou
sheets of white flame, which so kindled up the
scene that the young man could discern every
object more distinctly than by daylight. Most
distinctly of all he saw the two horrible creatures
galloping right down upon him, their brazen
hoofs rattling and ringing over the ground, and
their tails sticking up stiffly into the air, as has
always been the fashion with angry bulls. Their
breath scorched the herbage before them. So
intensely hot it was, indeed, that. it caught a dry
tree, under which Jason was now standing, and
set it all in a light blaze. But as for Jason himself, (thanks to Medea's enchanted ointment,)
the white flame curled around his body, without
injuring him a jot more than if he had been
made of asbestos.

Greatly encouraged at finding himself not yet
turned into a cinder, the young man awaited the
attack of the bulls. Just as the brazen brutes
fancied themselves sure of tossing him into the
air, he caught one of them by the horn, and the
other by his screwed-up tail, and held them in a
gripe like that of an iron vice, one with his right
hand, the other with his left. Well, he must

have been wonderfully strong in his arms, to be sure. But the secret of the matter was, that the brazen bulls were enchanted creatures, and that Jason had broken the spell of their fiery fierceness by his bold way of handling them. And, ever since that time, it has been the favorite method of brave men, when danger assails them, to do what they call "taking the bull by the horns;" and to gripe him by the tail is pretty much the same thing — that is, to throw aside fear, and overcome the peril by despising it.

It was now easy to yoke the bulls, and to harness them to the plough, which had lain rusting on the ground for a great many years gone by; so long was it before any body could be found capable of ploughing that piece of land. Jason, I suppose, had been taught how to draw a furrow by the good old Chiron, who, perhaps, used to allow himself to be harnessed to the plough. At any rate, our hero succeeded perfectly well in breaking up the greensward; and, by the time that the moon was a quarter of her journey up the sky, the ploughed field lay before him, a large tract of black earth, ready to be sown with the dragon's teeth. So Jason scattered them broadcast, and harrowed them into the soil with a brush-harrow, and took his stand on the edge of the field, anxious to see what would happen next.

"Must we wait long for harvest time," he inquired of Medea, who was now standing by his side.

"Whether sooner or later, it will be sure to come," answered the princess. "A crop of armed men never fails to spring up, when the dragon's teeth have been sown."

The moon was now high aloft in the heavens, and threw its bright beams over the ploughed field, where as yet there was nothing to be seen. Any farmer, on viewing it, would have said that Jason must wait weeks before the green blades would peep from among the clods, and whole months before the yellow grain would be ripened for the sickle. But by and by, all over the field, there was something that glistened in the moon-beams, like sparkling drops of dew. These bright objects sprouted higher, and proved to be the steel heads of spears. Then there was a dazzling gleam from a vast number of polished brass helmets, beneath which, as they grew farther out of the soil, appeared the dark and bearded visages of warriors, struggling to free themselves from the imprisoning earth. The first look that they gave at the upper world was a glare of wrath and defiance. Next were seen their bright breastplates; in every right hand there was a sword or a spear, and on each left arm a shield; and when this strange crop of warriors had but half grown out of the earth, they struggled, — such was their impatience of restraint, — and, as it were, tore themselves up by the roots. Wherever a dragon's tooth had fallen, there stood a man armed for battle. They made a clangor with their swords against their shields, and eyed one another fiercely; for they had come into this beautiful world, and into the peaceful moonlight, full of rage and stormy passions, and ready to take the life of every human brother, in recompense of the boon of their own existence.

There have been many other armies in the world that seemed to possess the same fierce nature with the one which had now sprouted from the dragon's teeth · but these, in the moonlit field, were the more excusable, because they never had women for their mothers. And how it would have rejoiced any great captain, who was bent on conquering the world, like Alexander or Napoleon, to raise a crop of armed soldiers as easily as Jason did!

For a while, the warriors stood flourishing their weapons, clashing their swords against their shields, and boiling over with the red-hot thirst for battle. Then they began to shout — "Show us the enemy! Lead us to the charge! Death or victory! Come on, brave comrades! Conquer or die!" and a hundred other outcries, such as men always bellow forth on a battle field, and which these dragon people seemed to have at their tongues' ends. At last, the front rank caught sight of Jason, who, beholding the flash of so many weapons in the moonlight, had thought it best to draw his sword. In a moment all the sons of the dragon's teeth appeared to take Jason for an enemy; and crying with one voice, "Guard the Golden Fleece!" they ran at him with uplifted swords and protruded spears. Jason knew that it would be impossible to withstand this bloodthirsty battalion with his single arm, but determined, since there was nothing better to be done, to die as valiantly as if he himself had sprung from a dragon's tooth.

Medea, however, made him snatch up a stone from the ground.

"Throw it among them quickly!" cried she. "It is the only way to save yourself."

The armed men were now so nigh that Jason could discern the fire flashing out of their enraged eyes, when he let fly the stone, and saw it strike the helmet of a tall warrior, who was rushing upon him with his blade aloft. The stone glanced from this man's helmet to the shield of his nearest comrade, and thence flew right into the angry face of another, hitting him smartly between the eyes. Each of the three who had been struck by the stone took it for granted that his next neighbor had given him a blow; and instead of running any farther towards Jason, they began a fight among themselves. The confusion spread through the host, so that it seemed scarcely a moment before they were all hacking, hewing, and stabbing at one another, lopping off arms, heads, and legs, and doing such memorable deeds that Jason was filled with immense admiration; although, at the same time, he could not help laughing to behold these mighty men punishing each other for an offence which he himself had committed. In an incredibly short space of time, (almost as short, indeed, as it had taken them to grow up,) all but one of the heroes of the dragon's teeth were stretched lifeless on the field. The last survivor, the bravest and strongest of the whole, had just force enough to wave his crimson sword over his head, and give a shout of exultation, crying, "Victory! Victory! Immortal fame!" when he himself fell down, and lay quietly among his slain brethren.

And there was the end of the army that had sprouted from the dragon's teeth. That fierce and feverish fight was the only enjoyment which they had tasted on this beautiful earth.

"Let them sleep in the bed of honor," said the Princess Medea, with a sly smile at Jason. "The world will always have simpletons enough, just like them, fighting and dying for they know not what, and fancying that posterity will take the trouble to put laurel wreaths on their rusty and battered helmets. Could you help smiling, Prince Jason, to see the self-conceit of that last fellow, just as he tumbled down?"

"It made me very sad," answered Jason, gravely. "And, to tell you the truth, princess, the Golden Fleece does not appear so well worth the winning, after what I have here beheld."

"You will think differently in the morning," said Medea. "True, the Golden Fleece may not be so valuable as you have thought it; but then there is nothing better in the world; and one must needs have an object, you know. Come! Your night's work has been well performed; and to-morrow you can inform King Æetes that the first part of your allotted task is fulfilled."

Agreeably to Medea's advice, Jason went betimes in the morning to the palace of King Æetes. Entering the presence chamber, he stood at the foot of the throne, and made a low obeisance.

"Your eyes look heavy, Prince Jason," observed the king; "you appear to have spent a sleepless night. I hope you have been considering the matter a little more wisely, and have concluded not to get yourself scorched to a cinder, in attempting to tame my brazen-lunged bulls."

" That is already accomplished, may it please your majesty," replied Jason. " The bulls have been tamed and yoked; the field has been ploughed; the dragon's teeth have been sown broadcast, and harrowed into the soil; the crop of armed warriors have sprung up, and they have slain one another, to the last man. And now I solicit your majesty's permission to encounter the dragon, that I may take down the Golden Fleece from the tree, and depart, with my nine and forty comrades."

King Æetes scowled, and looked very angry and excessively disturbed; for he knew that, in accordance with his kingly promise, he ought now to permit Jason to win the fleece, if his courage and skill should enable him to do so But, since the young man had met with such good luck in the matter of the brazen bulls and the dragon's teeth, the king feared that he would be equally successful in slaying the dragon And therefore, though he would gladly have seen Jason snapped up at a mouthful, he was resolved (and it was a very wrong thing of this wicked potentate) not to run any further risk of losing his beloved fleece.

" You never would have succeeded in this business, young man," said he, "if my undutiful daughter Medea had not helped you with her enchantments. Had you acted fairly, you would have been, at this instant, a black cinder, or a handful of white ashes. I forbid you, on pain of death, to make any more attempts to get the Golden Fleece. To speak my mind plainly, you shall never set eyes on so much as one of its glistening locks."

Jason left the king's presence in great sorrow and anger. He could think of nothing better to be done than to summon together his forty-nine brave Argonauts, march at once to the grove of Mars, slay the dragon, take possession of the Golden Fleece, get on board the Argo, and spread all sail for Iolchos. The success of this scheme depended, it is true, on the doubtful point whether all the fifty heroes might not be snapped up, at so many mouthfuls, by the dragon. But, as Jason was hastening down the palace steps, the Princess Medea called after him, and beckoned him to return. Her black eyes shone upon him with such a keen intelligence, that he felt as if there were a serpent peeping out of them; and,

although she had done him so much service only
the night before, he was by no means very certain
that she would not do him an equally great mischief before sunset. These enchantresses, you
must know, are never to be depended upon.

"What says King Æetes, my royal and upright father?" inquired Medea, slighty smiling.
"Will he give you the Golden Fleece, without
any further risk or trouble?"

"On the contrary," answered Jason, "he is
very angry with me for taming the brazen bulls
and sowing the dragon's teeth. And he forbids
me to make any more attempts, and positively
refuses to give up the Golden Fleece, whether I
slay the dragon or no."

"Yes, Jason," said the princess, "and I can
tell you more. Unless you set sail from Colchis
before to-morrow's sunrise, the king means to
burn your fifty-oared galley, and put yourself
and your forty-nine brave comrades to the sword.
But be of good courage. The Golden Fleece
you shall have, if it lies within the power of my
enchantments to get it for you. Wait for me
here an hour before midnight."

At the appointed hour, you might again have

seen Prince Jason and the Princess Medea, side by side, stealing through the streets of Colchis, on their way to the sacred grove, in the centre of which the Golden Fleece was suspended to a tree. While they were crossing the pasture ground, the brazen bulls came towards Jason, lowing, nodding their heads, and thrusting forth their snouts, which, as other cattle do, they loved to have rubbed and caressed by a friendly hand. Their fierce nature was thoroughly tamed; and, with their fierceness, the two furnaces in their stomachs had likewise been extinguished, insomuch that they probably enjoyed far more comfort in grazing and chewing their cuds than ever before. Indeed, it had heretofore been a great inconvenience to these poor animals, that, whenever they wished to eat a mouthful of grass, the fire out of their nostrils had shrivelled it up, before they could manage to crop it. How they contrived to keep themselves alive is more than I can imagine. But now, instead of emitting jets of flame and streams of sulphurous vapor, they breathed the very sweetest of cow breath.

After kindly patting the bulls, Jason followed Medea's guidance into the Grove of Mars, where the great oak trees, that had been growing for

centuries, threw so thick a shade that the moon-
beams struggled vainly to find their way through
it.   Only here and there a glimmer fell upon the
leaf-strewn earth, or now and then a breeze
stirred the boughs aside, and gave Jason a
glimpse of the sky, lest, in that deep obscurity,
he might forget that there was one, overhead.
At length, when they had gone farther and farther into the heart of the duskiness, Medea
squeezed Jason's hand.

"Look yonder," she whispered.   "Do you
see it?"

Gleaming among the venerable oaks, there
was a radiance, not like the moonbeams, but
rather resembling the golden glory of the setting
sun.   It proceeded from an object, which appeared to be suspended at about a man's height
from the ground, a little farther within the wood.

"What is it?" asked Jason.

"Have you come so far to seek it," exclaimed
Medea, "and do you not recognize the meed of
all your toils and perils, when it glitters before
your eyes?   It is the Golden Fleece."

Jason went onward a few steps farther, and then
stopped to gaze.   O, how beautiful it looked,
shining with a marvellous light of its own, that

inestimable prize, which so many heroes had longed to behold, but had perished in the quest of it, either by the perils of their voyage, or by the fiery breath of the brazen-lunged bulls.

"How gloriously it shines!" cried Jason, in a rapture. "It has surely been dipped in the richest gold of sunset. Let me hasten onward, and take it to my bosom."

"Stay," said Medea, holding him back. "Have you forgotten what guards it?"

To say the truth, in the joy of beholding the object of his desires, the terrible dragon had quite slipped out of Jason's memory. Soon, however, something came to pass, that reminded him what perils were still to be encountered. An antelope, that probably mistook the yellow radiance for sunrise, came bounding fleetly through the grove. He was rushing straight towards the Golden Fleece, when suddenly there was a frightful hiss, and the immense head and half the scaly body of the dragon was thrust forth, (for he was twisted round the trunk of the tree on which the fleece hung,) and seizing the poor antelope, swallowed him with one snap of his jaws.

After this feat, the dragon seemed sensible

that some other living creature was within reach, on which he felt inclined to finish his meal. In various directions he kept poking his ugly snout among the trees, stretching out his neck a terrible long way, now here, now there, and now close to the spot where Jason and the princess were hiding behind an oak. Upon my word, as the head came waving and undulating through the air, and reaching almost within arm's length of Prince Jason, it was a very hideous and uncomfortable sight. The gape of his enormous jaws was nearly as wide as the gateway of the king's palace.

" Well, Jason," whispered Medea, (for she was ill natured, as all enchantresses are, and wanted to make the bold youth tremble,) " what do you think now of your prospect of winning the Golden Fleece?"

Jason answered only by drawing his sword, and making a step forward.

" Stay, foolish youth," said Medea, grasping his arm. " Do not you see you are lost, without me as your good angel? In this gold box I have a magic potion, which will do the dragon's business far more effectually than your sword."

The dragon had probably heard the voices; for swift as lightning, his black head and forked tongue came hissing among the trees again, darting full forty feet at a stretch. As it approached, Medea tossed the contents of the gold box right down the monster's wide-open throat. Immediately, with an outrageous hiss and a tremendous wriggle, — flinging his tail up to the tip-top of the tallest tree, and shattering all its branches as it crashed heavily down again, — the dragon fell at full length upon the ground, and lay quite motionless.

"It is only a sleeping potion," said the enchantress to Prince Jason. "One always finds a use for these mischievous creatures, sooner or later; so I did not wish to kill him outright. Quick! Snatch the prize, and let us begone. You have won the Golden Fleece."

Jason caught the fleece from the tree, and hurried through the grove, the deep shadows of which were illuminated as he passed by the golden glory of the precious object that he bore along. A little way before him, he beheld the old woman whom he had helped over the stream, with her peacock beside her. She clapped her hands for joy, and beckoning him to make haste,

disappeared among the duskiness of the trees.
Espying the two winged sons of the North Wind,
(who were disporting themselves in the moonlight, a few hundred feet aloft,) Jason bade them
tell the rest of the Argonauts to embark as
speedily as possible.   But Lynceus, with his
sharp eyes, had already caught a glimpse of him,
bringing the Golden Fleece, although several
stone walls, a hill, and the black shadows of the
grove of Mars, intervened between.   By his advice, the heroes had seated themselves on the
benches of the galley, with their oars held perpendicularly, ready to let fall into the water.

As Jason drew near, he heard the Talking
Image calling to him with more than ordinary
eagerness, in its grave, sweet voice : —

"Make haste, Prince Jason! For your life,
make haste!"

With one bound, he leaped aboard.   At sight
of the glorious radiance of the Golden Fleece, the
nine and forty heroes gave a mighty shout, and
Orpheus, striking his harp, sang a song of triumph, to the cadence of which the galley flew
over the water, homeward bound, as if careering
along with wings !

BIOGRAPHICAL STORIES.

<table>
<tr><td>BENJAMIN WEST.</td><td>OLIVER CROMWELL.</td></tr>
<tr><td>SIR ISAAC NEWTON.</td><td>BENJAMIN FRANKLIN.</td></tr>
<tr><td>SAMUEL JOHNSON.</td><td>QUEEN CHRISTINA.</td></tr>
</table>

This small volume and others of a similar character, from the same hand, have not been composed without a deep sense of responsibility. The author regards children as sacred, and would not, for the world, cast any thing into the fountain of a young heart that might imbitter and pollute its waters. And, even in point of the reputation to be aimed at, juvenile literature is as well worth cultivating as any other. The writer, if he succeed in pleasing his little readers, may hope to be remembered by them till their own old age — a far longer period of literary existence than is generally attained by those who seek immortality from the judgments of full-grown men.

BIOGRAPHICAL STORIES.

CHAPTER I.

When Edward Temple was about eight or nine years old he was afflicted with a disorder of the eyes. It was so severe, and his sight was naturally so delicate, that the surgeon felt some apprehensions lest the boy should become totally blind. He therefore gave strict directions to keep him in a darkened chamber, with a bandage over his eyes. Not a ray of the blessed light of heaven could be suffered to visit the poor lad.

This was a sad thing for Edward. It was just the same as if there were to be no more sunshine, nor moonlight, nor glow of the cheerful fire, nor light of lamps. A night had begun which was to continue perhaps for months — a longer and drearier night than that which voyagers are compelled to endure when their ship is icebound, throughout the winter, in the Arctic Ocean. His dear father and mother, his brother George, and the sweet face of little Emily Robinson must all vanish and leave him in utter darkness and solitude. Their voices and footsteps, it is true, would be heard around him; he would feel his mother's embrace and the kind pressure of all their hands; but still it would seem as if they were a thousand miles away.

And then his studies, — they were to be entirely given up. This was another grievous trial; for Edward's memory hardly went back to the period when he had not known how to read. Many and many a holiday had he spent at his book, poring over its pages until the deepening twilight confused the print and made all the letters run into long words. Then would he press his hands across his eyes and wonder why they pained him so; and when the candles were lighted, what was the reason that they burned so dimly, like the moon in a foggy night? Poor little fellow! So far as his eyes were concerned he was already an old man, and needed a pair of spectacles almost as much as his own grandfather did.

And now, alas! the time was come when even grandfather's spectacles could not have assisted Edward to read. After a few bitter tears, which only pained his eyes the more, the poor boy submitted to the surgeon's orders. His eyes were bandaged, and, with his mother on one side and his little friend

Emily on the other, he was led into a darkened chamber.

"Mother, I shall be very miserable!" said Edward, sobbing.

"O, no, my dear child!" replied his mother, cheerfully. "Your eyesight was a precious gift of Heaven, it is true; but you would do wrong to be miserable for its loss, even if there were no hope of regaining it. There are other enjoyments besides what come to us through our eyes."

"None that are worth having," said Edward.

"Ah, but you will not think so long," rejoined Mrs. Temple, with tenderness. "All of us — your father, and myself, and George, and our sweet Emily — will try to find occupation and amusement for you. We will use all our eyes to make you happy. Will they not be better than a single pair?"

"I will sit by you all day long," said Emily, in her low, sweet voice, putting her hand into that of Edward.

"And so will I, Ned," said George, his elder brother, "school time and all, if my father will permit me."

Edward's brother George was three or four years older than himself — a fine, hardy lad, of a bold and ardent temper. He was the leader of his comrades in all their enterprises and amusements. As to his proficiency at study there was not much to be said. He had sense and ability enough to have made himself a

scholar, but found so many pleasanter things to do
that he seldom took hold of a book with his whole
heart.   So fond was George of boisterous sports and
exercises that it was really a great token of affection
and sympathy when he offered to sit all day long in
a dark chamber with his poor brother Edward.

As for little Emily Robinson, she was the daughter of one of Mr. Temple's dearest friends.   Ever
since her mother went to heaven (which was soon
after Emily's birth) the little girl had dwelt in the
household where we now find her.   Mr. and Mrs.
Temple seemed to love her as well as their own children; for they had no daughter except Emily; nor
would the boys have known the blessing of a sister
had not this gentle stranger come to teach them what
it was.   If I could show you Emily's face, with her
dark hair smoothed away from her forehead, you
would be pleased with her look of simplicity and
loving kindness, but might think that she was somewhat too grave for a child of seven years old.   But
you would not love her the less for that.

So brother George and this loving little girl were
to be Edward's companions and playmates while he
should be kept prisoner in the dark chamber.   When
the first bitterness of his grief was over he began to
feel that there might be some comforts and enjoyments in life even for a boy whose eyes were covered with a bandage.

"I thank you, dear mother," said he, with only a few sobs; "and you, Emily; and you too, George. You will all be very kind to me, I know. And my father, — will not he come and see me every day?"

"Yes, my dear boy," said Mr. Temple; for, though invisible to Edward, he was standing close beside him. "I will spend some hours of every day with you. And as I have often amused you by relating stories and adventures while you had the use of your eyes, I can do the same now that you are unable to read. Will this please you, Edward?"

"O, very much," replied Edward.

"Well, then," said his father, "this evening we will begin the series of Biographical Stories which I promised you some time ago."

CHAPTER II.

WHEN evening came. Mr. Temple found Edward considerably revived in spirits and disposed to be resigned to his misfortune. Indeed, the figure of the boy, as it was dimly seen by the firelight, reclining in a well-stuffed easy chair, looked so very comfortable that many people might have envied him. When a man's eyes have grown old with gazing at the ways of the world, it does not seem such a terrible misfortune to have them bandaged.

Little Emily Robinson sat by Edward's side with the air of an accomplished nurse. As well as the duskiness of the chamber would permit she watched all his motions and each varying expression of his face, and tried to anticipate her patient's wishes before his tongue could utter them. Yet it was noticeable that the child manifested an indescribable awe and disquietude whenever she fixed her eyes on the bandage; for, to her simple and affectionate heart, it seemed as if her dear friend Edward was separated from her because she could not see his eyes. A friend's eyes tell us many things which could never be spoken by the tongue.

George, likewise, looked awkward and confused, as stout and healthy boys are accustomed to do in the society of the sick or afflicted. Never having felt pain or sorrow, they are abashed, from not knowing how to sympathize with the sufferings of others.

"Well, my dear Edward," inquired Mrs. Temple, "is your chair quite comfortable? and has your little nurse provided for all your wants? If so, your father is ready to begin his stories."

"O, I am very well now," answered Edward, with a faint smile. "And my ears have not forsaken me, though my eyes are good for nothing. So pray, dear father, begin."

It was Mr. Temple's design to tell the children a series of true stories, the incidents of which should be taken from the childhood and early life of eminent people. Thus he hoped to bring George, and Edward, and Emily into closer acquaintance with the famous persons who have lived in other times by showing that they also had been children once. Although Mr. Temple was scrupulous to relate nothing but what was founded on fact, yet he felt himself at liberty to clothe the incidents of his narrative in a new coloring, so that his auditors might understand them the better.

"My first story," said he, "shall be about a painter of pictures.

"Dear me!" cried Edward, with a sigh. "I am afraid I shall never look at pictures any more."

"We will hope for the best," answered his father. "In the mean time, you must try to see things within your own mind."

Mr. Temple then began the following story:—

BENJAMIN WEST.

Born 1738. Died 1820.

In the year 1738 there came into the world, in the town of Springfield, Pennsylvania, a Quaker infant, from whom his parents and neighbors looked for wonderful things. A famous preacher of the Society of Friends had prophesied about little Ben, and foretold that he would be one of the most remarkable characters that had appeared on the earth since the days of William Penn. On this account the eyes of many people were fixed upon the boy. Some of his ancestors had won great renown in the old wars of England and France; but it was probably expected that Ben would become a preacher, and would convert multitudes to the peaceful doctrines of the Quakers. Friend West and his wife were thought to be very fortunate in having such a son.

Little Ben lived to the ripe age of six years without doing any thing that was worthy to be told in history. But one summer afternoon, in his seventh year, his mother put a fan into his hand and bade him keep the flies away from the face of a little babe who lay fast asleep in the cradle. She then left the room.

The boy waved the fan to and fro and drove away the buzzing flies whenever they had the impertinence to come near the baby's face. When they had all flown out of the window or into distant parts of the room, he bent over the cradle and delighted himself with gazing at the sleeping infant. It was, indeed, a very pretty sight. The little personage in the cradle slumbered peacefully, with its waxen hands under its chin, looking as full of blissful quiet as if angels were singing lullabies in its ear. Indeed, it must have been dreaming about heaven; for, while Ben stooped over the cradle, the little baby smiled.

"How beautiful she looks!" said Ben to himself. "What a pity it is that such a pretty smile should not last forever!"

Now Ben, at this period of his life, had never heard of that wonderful art by which a look, that appears and vanishes in a moment, may be made to last for hundreds of years. But, though nobody had told him of such an art, he may be said to have invented it for himself. On a table near at hand there were pens and paper, and ink of two colors, black and red. The boy seized a pen and sheet of paper, and, kneeling down beside the cradle, began to draw a likeness

of the infant.   While he was busied in this manner
he heard his mother's step approaching, and hastily
tried to conceal the paper.

"Benjamin, my son, what hast thou been doing?'
inquired his mother, observing marks of confusion in
his face.

At first Ben was unwilling to tell; for he felt as
if there might be something wrong in stealing the
baby's face and putting it upon a sheet of paper.
However, as his mother insisted, he finally put the
sketch into her hand, and then hung his head, expecting to be well scolded.   But when the good lady
saw what was on the paper, in lines of red and black
ink, she uttered a scream of surprise and joy.

"Bless me!" cried she.   "It is a picture of little
Sally!"

And then she threw her arms round our friend
Benjamin, and kissed him so tenderly that he never
afterwards was afraid to show his performances to
his mother.

As Ben grew older, he was observed to take vast
delight in looking at the hues and forms of Nature.
For instance, he was greatly pleased with the blue
violets of spring, the wild roses of summer, and the
scarlet cardinal flowers of early autumn.   In the de-
cline of the year, when the woods were variegated
with all the colors of the rainbow, Ben seemed to desire nothing better than to gaze at them from morn

till night. The purple and golden clouds of sunset were a joy to him. And he was continually endeavoring to draw the figures of trees, men, mountains, houses, cattle, geese, ducks, and turkeys, with a piece of chalk, on barn doors or on the floor.

In these old times the Mohawk Indians were still numerous in Pennsylvania. Every year a party of them used to pay a visit to Springfield, because the wigwams of their ancestors had formerly stood there. These wild men grew fond of little Ben, and made him very happy by giving him some of the red and yellow paint with which they were accustomed to adorn their faces. His mother, too, presented him with a piece of indigo. Thus he now had three colors, — red, blue, and yellow, — and could manufacture green by mixing the yellow with the blue. Our friend Ben was overjoyed, and doubtless showed his gratitude to the Indians by taking their likenesses in the strange dresses which they wore, with feathers, tomahawks, and bows and arrows.

But all this time the young artist had no paint brushes; nor were there any to be bought, unless he had sent to Philadelphia on purpose. However, he was a very ingenious boy, and resolved to manufacture paint brushes for himself. With this design he laid hold upon — what do you think? Why, upon a respectable old black cat, who was sleeping quietly by the fireside

"Puss," said little Ben to the cat, "pray give me some of the fur from the tip of thy tail?"

Though he addressed the black cat so civilly, yet Ben was determined to have the fur, whether she were willing or not. Puss, who had no great zeal for the fine arts, would have resisted if she could; but the boy was armed with his mother's scissors, and very dexterously clipped off fur enough to make a paint brush. This was of so much use to him that he applied to Madame Puss again and again, until her warm coat of fur had become so thin and ragged that she could hardly keep comfortable through the winter. Poor thing! she was forced to creep close into the chimney corner, and eyed Ben with a very rueful physiognomy. But Ben considered it more necessary that he should have paint brushes than that puss should be warm.

About this period friend West received a visit from Mr. Pennington, a merchant of Philadelphia, who was likewise a member of the Society of Friends. The visitor, on entering the parlor, was surprised to see it ornamented with drawings of Indian chiefs, and of birds with beautiful plumage, and of the wild flowers of the forest. Nothing of the kind was ever seen before in the habitation of a Quaker farmer.

"Why, friend West," exclaimed the Philadelphia merchant, "what has possessed thee to cover thy walls with all these pictures? Where on earth didst thou get them?"

Then friend West explained that all these pictures were painted by little Ben, with no better materials than red and yellow ochre and a piece of indigo, and with brushes made of the black cat's fur.

"Verily," said Mr. Pennington, "the boy hath a wonderful faculty. Some of our friends might look upon these matters as vanity; but little Benjamin appears to have been born a painter; and Providence is wiser than we are."

The good merchant patted Benjamin on the head, and evidently considered him a wonderful boy. When his parents saw how much their son's performances were admired, they, no doubt, remembered the prophecy of the old Quaker preacher respecting Ben's future eminence. Yet they could not understand how he was ever to become a very great and useful man merely by making pictures.

One evening, shortly after Mr. Pennington's return to Philadelphia, a package arrived at Springfield, directed to our little friend Ben.

"What can it possibly be?" thought Ben, when it was put into his hands. "Who can have sent me such a great square package as this?"

On taking off the thick brown paper which enveloped it, behold! there was a paint box, with a great many cakes of paint and brushes of various sizes. It was the gift of good Mr. Pennington. There were likewise several squares of canvas such as artists use

for painting pictures upon, and, in addition to all
these treasures, some beautiful engravings of landscapes.   These were the first pictures that Ben had
ever seen except those of his own drawing.

What a joyful evening was this for the little artist!
At bedtime he put the paint box under his pillow,
and got hardly a wink of sleep; for, all night long,
his fancy was painting pictures in the darkness.   In
the morning he hurried to the garret, and was seen
no more till the dinner hour; nor did he give himself time to eat more than a mouthful or two of food
before he hurried back to the garret again.   The
next day, and the next, he was just as busy as ever;
until at last his mother thought it time to ascertain
what he was about.   She accordingly followed him
to the garret.

On opening the door, the first object that presented
itself to her eyes was our friend Benjamin, giving
the last touches to a beautiful picture.   He had cop-
ied portions of two of the engravings, and made one
picture out of both, with such admirable skill that it
was far more beautiful than the originals.   The grass,
the trees, the water, the sky, and the houses were all
painted in their proper colors.   There, too, were the
sunshine and the shadow, looking as natural as life.

" My dear child, thou hast done wonders! " cried
his mother.

The good lady was in an ecstasy of delight.   And

well might she be proud of her boy; for there were touches in this picture which old artists, who had spent a lifetime in the business, need not have been ashamed of. Many a year afterwards, this wonderful production was exhibited at the Royal Academy in London.

When Benjamin was quite a large lad he was sent to school at Philadelphia. Not long after his arrival he had a slight attack of fever, which confined him to his bed. The light, which would otherwise have disturbed him, was excluded from his chamber by means of closed wooden shutters. At first it appeared so totally dark that Ben could not distinguish any object in the room. By degrees, however, his eyes became accustomed to the scanty light.

He was lying on his back, looking up towards the ceiling, when suddenly he beheld the dim apparition of a white cow moving slowly over his head! Ben started, and rubbed his eyes in the greatest amazement.

"What can this mean?" thought he.

The white cow disappeared; and next came several pigs, which trotted along the ceiling and vanished into the darkness of the chamber. So lifelike did these grunters look that Ben almost seemed to hear them squeak.

"Well, this is very strange!" said Ben to himself.

When the people of the house came to see him, Benjamin told them of the marvellous circumstance which had occurred. But they would not believe him

"Benjamin, thou art surely out of thy senses!" cried they. "How is it possible that a white cow and a litter of pigs should be visible on the ceiling of a dark chamber?"

Ben, however, had great confidence in his own eyesight, and was determined to search the mystery to the bottom. For this purpose, when he was again left alone, he got out of bed and examined the window shutters. He soon perceived a small chink in one of them, through which a ray of light found its passage and rested upon the ceiling. Now, the science of optics will inform us that the pictures of the white cow and the pigs, and of other objects out of doors, came into the dark chamber through this narrow chink, and were painted over Benjamin's head. It is greatly to his credit that he discovered the scientific principle of this phenomenon, and by means of it constructed a camera obscura, or magic lantern, out of a hollow box. This was of great advantage to him in drawing landscapes.

Well, time went on, and Benjamin continued to draw and paint pictures until he had now reached the age when it was proper that he should choose a business for life. His father and mother were in considerable perplexity about him. According to the ideas of the Quakers, it is not right for people to spend their lives in occupations that are of no real and sensible advantage to the world. Now, what advantage could the world expect from Benjamin's pictures? This was a difficult question; and, in order to set their minds at rest, his parents determined to consult the preachers and wise men of their society. Accordingly, they all assembled in the meeting house, and discussed the matter from beginning to end.

Finally they came to a very wise decision. It seemed so evident that Providence had created Benjamin to be a painter, and had given him abilities which would be thrown away in any other business, that the Quakers resolved not to oppose his inclination. They even acknowledged that the sight of a beautiful picture might convey instruction to the mind and might benefit the heart as much as a good book or a wise discourse. They therefore committed the youth to the direction of God, being well assured that he best knew what was his proper sphere of usefulness. The old men laid their hands upon Benjamin's head and gave him their blessing, and the women kissed him affectionately. All consented that he should go forth into the world and learn to be a painter by studying the best pictures of ancient and modern times.

So our friend Benjamin left the dwelling of his parents, and his native woods and streams, and the good Quakers of Springfield, and the Indians who had given him his first colors; he left all the places and persons whom he had hitherto known, and returned to them no more. He went first to Philadelphia and afterwards to Europe. Here he was no ticed by many great people, but retained all the sobriety and simplicity which he had learned among the Quakers. It is related of him, that, when he was presented at the court of the Prince of Parma, he kept his hat upon his head even while kissing the Prince's hand.

When he was twenty-five years old he went to London and established himself there as an artist. In due course of time he acquired great fame by his pictures, and was made chief painter to King George III. and president of the Royal Academy of Arts. When the Quakers of Pennsylvania heard of his success, they felt that the prophecy of the old preacher as to little Ben's future eminence was now accomplished. It is true, they shook their heads at his pictures of battle and bloodshed, such as the Death of Wolfe, thinking that these terrible scenes should not be held up to the admiration of the world

But they approved of the great paintings in which he represented the miracles and sufferings of the Redeemer of mankind. King George employed him to adorn a large and beautiful chapel at Windsor Castle with pictures of these sacred subjects. He likewise painted a magnificent picture of Christ Healing the Sick, which he gave to the hospital at Philadelphia. It was exhibited to the public, and produced so much profit that the hospital was enlarged so as to accommodate thirty more patients. If Benjamin West had done no other good deed than this, yet it would have been enough to entitle him to an honorable remembrance forever. At this very day there are thirty poor people in the hospital who owe all their comforts to that same picture.

We shall mention only a single incident more. The picture of Christ Healing the Sick was exhibited at the Royal Academy in London, where it covered a vast space and displayed a multitude of figures as large as life. On the wall, close beside this admirable picture, hung a small and faded landscape. It was the same that little Ben had painted in his father's garret, after receiving the paint box and engravings from good Mr. Pennington.

He lived many years in peace and honor, and died in 1820, at the age of eighty-two. The story of his life is almost as wonderful as a fairy tale ; for there are few stranger transformations than that of a little unknown Quaker boy, in the wilds of America, into the most distinguished English painter of his day. Let us each make the best use of our natural abilities as Benjamin West did ; and, with the blessing of Providence, we shall arrive at some good end. As for fame it is but little matter whether we acquire it or not.

"Thank you for the story, my dear father," said Edward, when it was finished. "Do you know that it seems as if I could see things without the help of my eyes ? While you were speaking I have seen little Ben, and the baby in its cradle. and the Indians,

and the white cow, and the pigs, and kind Mr. Pennington, and all the good old Quakers, almost as
plainly as if they were in this very room."

"It is because your attention was not disturbed by
outward objects," replied Mr. Temple. "People,
when deprived of sight, often have more vivid ideas
than those who possess the perfect use of their eyes.
I will venture to say that George has not attended to
the story quite so closely."

"No, indeed," said George; "but it was a very
pretty story for all that. How I should have laughed
to see Ben making a paint brush out of the black
cat's tail! I intend to try the experiment with Emily's kitten."

"O, no, no, George!" cried Emily, earnestly.
"My kitten cannot spare her tail."

Edward being an invalid, it was now time for him
to retire to bed. When the family bade him good
night he turned his face towards them, looking very
loath to part.

"I shall not know when morning comes," said he,
sorrowfully. "And besides, I want to hear your
voices all the time; for, when nobody is speaking, it
seems as if I were alone in a dark world."

"You must have faith, my dear child," replied his
mother. "Faith is the soul's eyesight; and when
we possess it the world is never dark nor lonely."

CHAPTER III.

THE next day Edward began to get accustomed to his new condition of life. Once, indeed, when his parents were out of the way and only Emily was left to take care of him, he could not resist the temptation to thrust aside the bandage and peep at the anxious face of his little nurse. But, in spite of the dimness of the chamber, the experiment caused him so much pain that he felt no inclination to take another look. So, with a deep sigh, he resigned himself to his fate.

" Emily, pray talk to me! " said he, somewhat impatiently.

Now, Emily was a remarkably silent little girl, and did not possess that liveliness of disposition which renders some children such excellent companions. She seldom laughed, and had not the faculty of making many words about small matters. But the love and earnestness of her heart taught her how to amuse poor Edward in his darkness. She put her knitting work into his hands.

" You must learn how to knit," said she.

" What! without using my eyes?" cried Edward

" I can knit with my eyes shut," replied Emily.

Then with her own little hands she guided Edward's fingers while he set about this new occupation. So awkward were his first attempts that any other little girl would have laughed heartily. But Emily preserved her gravity, and showed the utmost patience in taking up the innumerable stitches which he let down. In the course of an hour or two his progress was quite encouraging.

When evening came, Edward acknowledged that the day had been far less wearisome than he anticipated. But he was glad, nevertheless, when his father and mother, and George and Emily, all took their seats around his chair. He put out his hand to grasp each of their hands, and smiled with a very bright expression upon his lips.

" Now I can see you all with my mind's eye," said he. " And now, father, pray tell us another story."

So Mr Temple began.

SIR ISAAC NEWTON.

Born 1642.   Died 1727.

On Christmas day, in the year 1642, Isaac New ton was born at the small village of Woolsthorpe, in

England. Little did his mother think, when she beheld her new-born babe, that he was destined to explain many matters which had been a mystery ever since the creation of the world.

Isaac's father being dead, Mrs. Newton was married again to a clergyman, and went to reside at North Witham. Her son was left to the care of his good old grandmother, who was very kind to him and sent him to school. In his early years Isaac did not appear to be a very bright scholar, but was chiefly remarkable for his ingenuity in all mechanical occupations. He had a set of little tools and saws of various sizes manufactured by himself. With the aid of these Isaac contrived to make many curious articles, at which he worked with so much skill that he seemed to have been born with a saw or chisel in hand.

The neighbors looked with vast admiration at the things which Isaac manufactured. And his old grandmother, I suppose, was never weary of talking about him.

" He'll make a capital workman one of these days," she would probably say. " No fear but what Isaac will do well in the world and be a rich man before he dies."

It is amusing to conjecture what were the anticipations of his grandmother and the neighbors about Isaac's future life. Some of them, perhaps, fancied that he would make beautiful furniture of mahogany, rosewood, or polished oak, inlaid with ivory and ebony and magnificently gilded. And then, doubtless, all the rich people would purchase these fine things to adorn their drawing rooms. Others probably thought that little Isaac was destined to be an architect, and would build splendid mansions for the nobility and gentry, and churches too, with the tallest steeples that had ever been seen in England.

Some of his friends, no doubt, advised Isaac's grandmother to apprentice him to a clockmaker; for, besides his mechanical skill, the boy seemed to have a taste for mathematics, which would be very useful to him in that profession. And then, in due time, Isaac would set up for himself, and would manufacture curious clocks, like those that contain sets of dancing figures, which issue from the dialplate when the hour is struck; or like those where a ship sails across the face of the clock, and is seen tossing up and down on the waves as often as the pendulum vibrates.

Indeed, there was some ground for supposing that Isaac would devote himself to the manufacture of clocks; since he had already made one, of a kind which nobody had ever heard of before. It was set a-going, not by wheels and weights like other clocks, but by the dropping of water. This was an object of great wonderment to all the people round about and it must be confessed that there are few boys, or men either, who could contrive to tell what a clock it is by means of a bowl of water.

Besides the water clock, Isaac made a sundial. Thus his grandmother was never at a loss to know the hour; for the water clock would tell it in the shade, and the dial in the sunshine. The sundial is said to be still in existence at Woolsthorpe, on the corner of the house where Isaac dwelt. If so, it must have marked the passage of every sunny hour that has elapsed since Isaac Newton was a boy. It marked all the famous moments of his life; it marked the hour of his death; and still the sunshine creeps slowly over it, as regularly as when Isaac first set it up.

Yet we must not say that the sundial has lasted longer than its maker; for Isaac Newton will exist long after the dial — yea, and long after the sun itself — shall have crumbled to decay.

Isaac possessed a wonderful faculty of acquiring knowledge by the simplest means. For instance, what method do you suppose he took to find out the strength of the wind? You will never guess how the boy could compel that unseen, inconstant, and ungovernable wonder, the wind, to tell him the measure of his strength. Yet nothing can be more simple. He jumped against the wind; and by the **length of** his jump he could calculate the **force of a gentle**

breeze, a brisk gale, or a tempest. Thus, even in
his boyish sports, he was continually searching out
the secrets of philosophy.

Not far from his grandmother's residence there was
a windmill which operated on a new plan. Isaac
was in the habit of going thither frequently, and
would spend whole hours in examining its various
parts. While the mill was at rest he pried into its
internal machinery. When its broad sails were set
in motion by the wind he watched the process by
which the millstones were made to revolve and
crush the grain that was put into the hopper. After
gaining a thorough knowledge of its construction he
was observed to be unusually busy with his tools.

It was not long before his grandmother and all
the neighborhood knew what Isaac had been about.
He had constructed a model of the windmill. Though
not so large, I suppose, as one of the box traps which
boys set to catch squirrels, yet every part of the mill
and its machinery was complete. Its little sails
were neatly made of linen, and whirled round very
swiftly when the mill was placed in a draught of air.
Even a puff of wind from Isaac's mouth or from a
a pair of bellows was sufficient to set the sails in
motion. And, what was most curious, if a handful
of grains of wheat were put into the little hopper,
they would soon be converted into snow-white flour.

Isaac's playmates were enchanted with his new

windmill. They thought that nothing so pretty and so wonderful had ever been seen in the whole world.

"But, Isaac," said one of them, "you have forgotten one thing that belongs to a mill."

"What is that?" asked Isaac; for he supposed that, from the roof of the mill to its foundation, he had forgotten nothing.

"Why, where is the miller?" said his friend.

"That is true — I must look out for one," said Isaac; and he set himself to consider how the deficiency should be supplied.

He might easily have made the miniature figure of a man; but then it would not have been able to move about and perform the duties of a miller. As Captain Lemuel Gulliver had not yet discovered the Island of Liliput, Isaac did not know that there were little men in the world whose size was just suited to his windmill. It so happened, however, that a mouse had just been caught in the trap; and, as no other miller could be found, Mr. Mouse was appointed to that important office. The new miller made a very respectable appearance in his dark-gray coat. To be sure, he had not a very good character for honesty, and was suspected of sometimes stealing a portion of the grain which was given him to grind. But perhaps some two-legged millers are quite as dishonest as this small quadruped.

As Isaac grew older, it was found that he had far

more important matters in his mind than the manufacture of toys like the little windmill.   All day long,
if left to himself, he was either absorbed in thought
or engaged in some book of mathematics or natural
philosophy.   At night, I think it probable, he looked
up with reverential curiosity to the stars, and wondered whether they were worlds like our own, and
how great was their distance from the earth, and
what was the power that kept them in their courses.
Perhaps, even so early in life, Isaac Newton felt a
presentiment that he should be able, hereafter, to
answer all these questions.

When Isaac was fourteen years old, his mother's
second husband being now dead, she wished her son
to leave school and assist her in managing the farm at
Woolsthorpe.   For a year or two, therefore, he tried
to turn his attention to farming.   But his mind was so
bent on becoming a scholar that his mother sent him
back to school, and afterwards to the University of
Cambridge.

I have now finished my anecdotes of Isaac Newton's boyhood.   My story would be far too long
were I to mention all the splendid discoveries which
he made after he came to be a man.   He was the first
that found out the nature of light; for, before his
day, nobody could tell what the sunshine was composed of.   You remember, I suppose, the story of an
apple's falling on his head, and thus leading him to

discover the force of gravitation, which keeps the heavenly bodies in their courses. When he had once got hold of this idea, he never permitted his mind to rest until he had searched out all the laws by which the planets are guided through the sky. This he did as thoroughly as if he had gone up among the stars and tracked them in their orbits. The boy had found out the mechanism of a windmill; the man explained to his fellow-men the mechanism of the universe.

While making these researches he was accustomed to spend night after night in a lofty tower, gazing at the heavenly bodies through a telescope. His mind was lifted far above the things of this world. He may be said, indeed, to have spent the greater part of his life in worlds that lie thousands and millions of miles away; for where the thoughts and the heart are, there is our true existence.

Did you never hear the story of Newton and his little dog Diamond? One day, when he was fifty years old, and had been hard at work more than twenty years studying the theory of light, he went out of his chamber, leaving his little dog asleep before the fire. On the table lay a heap of manuscript papers, containing all the discoveries which Newton had made during those twenty years. When his master was gone, up rose little Diamond, jumped upon the table, and overthrew the lighted candle. The papers immediately caught fire.

Just as the destruction was completed Newton opened the chamber door, and perceived that the labors of twenty years were reduced to a heap of ashes. There stood little Diamond, the author of all the mischief. Almost any other man would have sentenced the dog to immediate death. But Newton patted him on the head with his usual kindness, although grief was at his heart.

"O Diamond, Diamond," exclaimed he, "thou little knowest the mischief thou hast done!"

This incident affected his health and spirits for some time afterwards; but, from his conduct towards the little dog, you may judge what was the sweetness of his temper.

Newton lived to be a very old man, and acquired great renown, and was made a member of parliament, and received the honor of knighthood from the king. But he cared little for earthly fame and honors, and felt no pride in the vastness of his knowledge. All that he had learned only made him feel how little he knew in comparison to what remained to be known.

"I seem to myself like a child," observed he, "playing on the sea shore, and picking up here and there a curious shell or a pretty pebble, while the boundless ocean of Truth lies undiscovered before me"

At last, in 1727, when he was fourscore and five years old, Sir Isaac Newton died — or rather he ceased to live on earth. We may be permitted to believe that he is still searching out the infinite wisdom and goodness of the Creator as earnestly, and with even more success than while his spirit animated a mortal body. He has left a fame behind him which will be as endurable as if his name were written in letters of light formed by the stars upon the midnight sky.

"I love to hear about mechanical contrivances, such as the water clock and the little windmill," remarked George. "I suppose, if Sir Isaac Newton had only thought of it, he might have found out the steam engine, and railroads, and all the other famous inventions that have come into use since his day."

"Very possibly he might," replied Mr. Temple, "and no doubt a great many people would think it more useful to manufacture steam engines than to search out the system of the universe. Other great astronomers besides Newton have been endowed with mechanical genius. There was David Rittenhouse, an American, — he made a perfect little water mill when he was only seven or eight years old. But this sort of ingenuity is but a mere trifle in comparison with the other talents of such men."

"It must have been beautiful," said Edward, "to spend whole nights in a high tower as Newton did gazing at the stars, and the comets, and the meteors

But what would Newton have done had he been blind? or if his eyes had been no better than mine?"

"Why, even then, my dear child," observed Mrs. Temple, "he would have found out some way of enlightening his mind and of elevating his soul. But come; little Emily is waiting to bid you good night. You must go to sleep and dream of seeing all our faces."

"But how sad it will be when I awake!" murmured Edward.

CHAPTER IV.

In the course of the next day the harmony of our little family was disturbed by something like a quarrel between George and Edward.

The former, though he loved his brother dearly, had found it quite too great a sacrifice of his own enjoyments to spend all his play time in a darkened chamber. Edward, on the other hand, was inclined to be despotic. He felt as if his bandaged eyes entitled him to demand that every body who enjoyed the blessing of sight should contribute to his comfort and amusement. He therefore insisted that George, instead of going out to play at football, should join with himself and Emily in a game of questions and answers.

George resolutely refused, and ran out of the house. He did not revisit Edward's chamber till the evening, when he stole in, looking confused, yet somewhat sullen, and sat down beside his father's chair. It was evident, by a motion of Edward's head and a slight trembling of his lips, that he was aware of George's

entrance, though his footsteps had been almost inau-
dible. Emily, with her serious and earnest little
face, looked from one to the other, as if she longed to
be a messenger of peace between them.

Mr. Temple, without seeming to notice any of
these circumstances, began a story.

SAMUEL JOHNSON.

Born 1709. Died 1784.

"Sam," said Mr. Michael Johnson, of Lichfield,
one morning, "I am very feeble and ailing to-day.
You must go to Uttoxeter in my stead, and tend the
book stall in the market-place there."

This was spoken above a hundred years ago, by an
elderly man, who had once been a thriving bookseller
at Lichfield, in England. Being now in reduced
circumstances, he was forced to go every market day
and sell books at a stall, in the neighboring village of
Uttoxeter.

His son, to whom Mr. Johnson spoke, was a great
boy, of very singular aspect. He had an intelligent
face; but it was seamed and distorted by a scrofulous
humor, which affected his eyes so badly that sometimes he was almost blind. Owing to the same cause,
his head would often shake with a tremulous motion,
as if he were afflicted with the palsy. When Sam
was an infant, the famous Queen Anne had tried to

cure him of this disease by laying her royal hands upon his head. But though the touch of a king or queen was supposed to be a certain remedy for scrofula, it produced no good effect upon Sam Johnson.

At the time which we speak of the poor lad was not very well dressed, and wore shoes from which his toes peeped out; for his old father had barely the means of supporting his wife and children. But, poor as the family were, young Sam Johnson had as much pride as any nobleman's son in England. The fact was, he felt conscious of uncommon sense and ability, which, in his own opinion, entitled him to great respect from the world. Perhaps he would have been glad if grown people had treated him as reverentially as his schoolfellows did. Three of them were accustomed to come for him every morning; and while he sat upon the back of one, the two others supported him on each side; and thus he rode to school in triumph.

Being a personage of so much importance, Sam could not bear the idea of standing all day in Uttoxeter market offering books to the rude and ignorant country people. Doubtless he felt the more reluctant on account of his shabby clothes, and the disorder of his eyes, and the tremulous motion of his head.

When Mr. Michael Johnson spoke Sam pouted and made an indistinct grumbling in his throat; then he looked his old father in the face and answered him loudly and deliberately.

" Sir," said he, " I will not go to Uttoxeter market ! "

Mr. Johnson had seen a great deal of the lad's
obstinacy ever since his birth ; and while Sam was
younger, the old gentleman had probably used the rod
whenever occasion seemed to require. But he was
now too feeble and too much out of spirits to contend
with this stubborn and violent-tempered boy. He
therefore gave up the point at once, and prepared to
go to Uttoxeter himself.

" Well, Sam," said Mr. Johnson, as he took his hat
and staff, " if for the sake of your foolish pride you can
suffer your poor sick father to stand all day in the
noise and confusion of the market when he ought to be
in his bed, I have no more to say. But you will
think of this, Sam, when I am dead and gone."

So the poor old man (perhaps with a tear in his eye,
but certainly with sorrow in his heart) set forth towards Uttoxeter. The grayhaired, feeble, melancholy
Michael Johnson ! How sad a thing it was that he
should be forced to go, in his sickness, and toil for
the support of an ungrateful son who was too proud
to do any thing for his father, or his mother, or himself ! Sam looked after Mr. Johnson with a sullen
countenance till he was out of sight.

But when the old man's figure, as he went stooping along the street, was no more to be seen, the boy's
heart began to smite him. He had a vivid imagina-

tion, and it tormented him with the image of his father standing in the market-place of Uttoxeter and offering his books to the noisy crowd around him. Sam seemed to behold him arranging his literary merchandise upon the stall in such a way as was best calculated to attract notice. Here was Addison's Spectator, a long row of little volumes; here was Pope's translation of the Iliad and Odyssey; here were Dryden's poems, or those of Prior. Here, likewise, were Gulliver's Travels, and a variety of little gilt-covered children's books, such as Tom Thumb, Jack the Giant Queller, Mother Goose's Melodies, and others which our great-grand parents used to read in their childhood. And here were sermons for the pious, and pamphlets for the politicians, and ballads, some merry and some dismal ones, for the country people to sing.

Sam, in imagination, saw his father offer these books, pamphlets, and ballads, now to the rude yeomen who perhaps could not read a word; now to the country squires, who cared for nothing but to hunt hares and foxes; now to the children, who chose to spend their coppers for sugar plums or gingerbread rather than for picture books. And if Mr. Johnson should sell a book to man, woman, or child, it would cost him an hour's talk to get a profit of only sixpence.

"My poor father!" · thought Sam to himself. 'How his head will ache! and how heavy his heart will be! I am almost sorry that I did not do as he bade me."

Then the boy went to his mother, who was busy about the house. She did not know of what had passed between Mr. Johnson and Sam.

"Mother," said he, "did you think father seemed very ill to-day?"

"Yes, Sam," answered his mother, turning with a flushed face from the fire, where she was cooking their scanty dinner. "Your father did look very ill; and it is a pity he did not send you to Uttoxeter in his stead. You are a great boy now, and would rejoice, I am sure, to do something for your poor father, who has done so much for you."

The lad made no reply. But again his imagination set to work and conjured up another picture of poor Michael Johnson. He was standing in the hot sunshine of the market-place, and looking so weary, sick, and disconsolate, that the eyes of all the crowd were drawn to him. "Had this old man no son," the people would say among themselves, "who might have taken his place at the book stall while the father kept his bed?" And perhaps, — but this was a terrible thought for Sam! — perhaps his father would faint away and fall down in the market-place, with his gray hair in the dust and his venerable face as deathlike as that of a corpse. And there would be the bystanders gazing earnestly at Mr. Johnson and whispering, "Is he dead? Is he dead?"

And Sam shuddered as he repeated to himself " Is he dead ? "

" O, I have been a cruel son ! " thought he, within his own heart. " God forgive me ! God forgive me ! "

But God could not yet forgive him ; for he was not truly penitent. Had he been so, he would have hastened away that very moment to Uttoxeter, and have fallen at his father's feet, even in the midst of the crowded market-place. There he would have confessed his fault, and besought Mr. Johnson to go home and leave the rest of the day's work to him. But such was Sam's pride and natural stubbornness that he could not bring himself to this humiliation. Yet he ought to have done so, for his own sake, for his father's sake, and for God's sake.

After sunset old Michael Johnson came slowly home and sat down in his customary chair. He said nothing to Sam; nor do I know that a single word ever passed between them on the subject of the son's disobedience. In a few years his father died, and left Sam to fight his way through the world by him-- self. It would make our story much too long were I to tell you even a few of the remarkable events of Sam's life. Moreover, there is the less need of this, because many books have been written about that poor boy, and the fame that he acquired, and all that he did or talked of doing after he came to be a man

But one thing I must not neglect to say. From his boyhood upward until the latest day of his life he never forgot the story of Uttoxeter market. Often when he was a scholar of the University of Oxford, or master of an academy at Edial, or a writer for the London booksellers, — in all his poverty and toil and in all his success, — while he was walking the streets without a shilling to buy food, or when the greatest men of England were proud to feast him at their table, — still that heavy and remorseful thought came back to him, "I was cruel to my poor father in his illness!" Many and many a time, awake or in his dreams, he seemed to see old Michael Johnson standing in the dust and confusion of the market-place and pressing his withered hand to his forehead as if it ached.

Alas! my dear children, it is a sad thing to have such a thought as this to bear us company through life.

Though the story was but half finished, yet, as it was longer than usual, Mr. Temple here made a short pause. He perceived that Emily was in tears, and Edward turned his half-veiled face towards the speaker with an air of great earnestness and interest. As for George, he had withdrawn into the dusky shadow behind his father's chair.

CHAPTER V.

In a few moments Mr. Temple resumed the story, as follows:—

SAMUEL JOHNSON.

CONTINUED.

Well, my children, fifty years had passed away since young Sam Johnson had shown himself so hardhearted towards his father. It was now market day in the village of Uttoxeter.

In the street of the village you might see cattle dealers with cows and oxen for sale, and pig drovers with herds of squeaking swine, and farmers with cartloads of cabbages, turnips, onions, and all other produce of the soil. Now and then a farmer's redfaced wife trotted along on horseback, with butter and cheese in two large panniers. The people of the village, with country squires, and other visitors from the neighborhood, walked hither and thither, trading, jesting, quarrelling and making just such a bustle as their fathers and grandfathers had made half a century before.

In one part of the street there was a puppet show, with a ridiculous merryandrew, who kept both grown people and children in a roar of laughter. On the opposite side was the old stone church of Uttoxeter, with ivy climbing up its walls and partly obscuring its Gothic windows.

There was a clock in the gray tower of the ancient church, and the hands on the dialplate had now almost reached the hour of noon. At this busiest hour of the market a strange old gentleman was seen making his way among the crowd. He was very tall and bulky, and wore a brown coat and smallclothes, with black worsted stockings and buckled shoes. On his head was a three-cornered hat, beneath which a bushy gray wig thrust itself out, all in disorder. The old gentleman elbowed the people aside, and forced his way through the midst of them with a singular kind of gait, rolling his body hither and thither, so that he needed twice as much room as any other person there.

"Make way, sir!" he would cry out, in a loud, harsh voice, when somebody happened to interrupt his progress. "Sir, you intrude your person into the public thoroughfare!"

"What a queer old fellow this is!" muttered the people among themselves, hardly knowing whether to laugh or to be angry.

But when they looked into the venerable stranger's face, not the most thoughtless among them dared to offer him the least impertinence. Though his features were scarred and distorted with the scrofula, and though his eyes were dim and bleared, yet there was something of authority and wisdom in his look, which impressed them all with awe. So they stood aside to let him pass; and the old gentleman made his way across the market-place, and paused near the corner of the ivy-mantled church. Just as he reached it the clock struck twelve.

On the very spot of ground where the stranger now stood some aged people remembered that old Michael Johnson had formerly kept his book stall. The little children who had once bought picture books of him were grandfathers now.

"Yes; here is the very spot!" muttered the old gentleman to himself.

There this unknown personage took his stand and removed the three-cornered hat from his head. It was the busiest hour of the day. What with the hum of human voices, the lowing of cattle, the squeaking of pigs, and the laughter caused by the merryandrew, the market-place was in very great confusion. But the stranger seemed not to notice it any more than if the silence of a desert were around him. He was rapt in his own thoughts. Sometimes he raised his furrowed brow to heaven, as if in prayer; sometimes he bent his head, as if an insupportable weight of sorrow were upon him. It increased the awfulness of his aspect that there was a motion of his head and an almost continual tremor throughout his frame, with singular twitchings and contortions of his features.

The hot sun blazed upon his unprotected head; but he seemed not to feel its fervor. A dark cloud swept across the sky and raindrops pattered into the market-place; but the stranger heeded not the shower. The people began to gaze at the mysterious old gentleman with superstitious fear and wonder. Who could he be? Whence did he come? Wherefore was he standing bareheaded in the market-place? Even the schoolboys left the merryandrew and came to gaze, with wide-open eyes, at this tall, strange-looking old man.

There was a cattle drover in the village who had recently made a journey to the Smithfield market, in London. No sooner had this man thrust his way through the throng and taken a look at the unknown personage than he whispered to one of his acquaintances,—

"I say, neighbor Hutchins, would ye like to know who this old gentleman is?"

"Ay, that I would," replied neighbor Hutchins, "for a queerer chap I never saw in my life. Somehow it makes me feel small to look at him. He's more than a common man."

" You may well say so," answered the cattle drover. " Why, that's the famous Doctor Samuel Johnson, who they say is the greatest and learnedest man in England. I saw him in London streets, walking with one Mr. Boswell."

Yes ; the poor boy, the friendless Sam, with whom we began our story, had become the famous Doctor Samuel Johnson. He was universally acknowledged as the wisest man and greatest writer in all England. He had given shape and permanence to his native language by his Dictionary. Thousands upon thousands of people had read his Idler, his Rambler, and his Rasselas. Noble and wealthy men and beautiful ladies deemed it their highest privilege to be his companions. Even the King of Great Britain had sought his acquaintance, and told him what an honor he considered it that such a man had been born in his dominions. He was now at the summit of literary renown.

But all his fame could not extinguish the bitter remembrance which had tormented him through life. Never, never had he forgotten his father's sorrowful and upbraiding look. Never, though the old man's troubles had been over so many years, had he forgiven himself for inflicting such a pang upon his heart. And now, in his old age, he had come hither to do penance, by standing at noonday, in the market-place of Uttoxeter, on the very spot where Michael Johnson had once kept his book stall. The aged and illustrious man had done what the poor boy refused to do. By thus expressing his deep repentance and humiliation of heart, he hoped to gain peace of conscience and the forgiveness of God.

My dear children, if you have grieved (I will not say your parents, but if you have grieved) the heart of any human being who has a claim upon your love, then think of Samuel Johnson's penance. Will it not be better to redeem the error now than to endure the agony of remorse for fifty years? Would you not rather say to a brother, " I have erred; forgive me ! " than perhaps to go hereafter and shed bitter tears upon his grave ?

Hardly was the story concluded when George hastily arose, and Edward likewise, stretching forth his hands into the darkness that surrounded him to find his brother. Both accused themselves of unkindness ; each besought the other's forgiveness ; and having done so, the trouble of their hearts vanished away like a dream.

" I am glad! I am so glad ! " said Emily, in a low, earnest voice. " Now I shall sleep quietly to-night."

" My sweet child," thought Mrs. Temple as she kissed her, " mayest thou never know how much strife there is on earth ! It would cost thee many a night's rest."

CHAPTER VI.

ABOUT this period Mr. Temple found it necessary to take a journey, which interrupted the series of Biographical Stories for several evenings. In the interval, Edward practised various methods of employing and amusing his mind.

Sometimes he meditated upon beautiful objects which he had formerly seen, until the intensity of his recollection seemed to restore him the gift of sight and place every thing anew before his eyes. Sometimes he repeated verses of poetry which he did not know to be in his memory until he found them there just at the time of need. Sometimes he attempted to solve arithmetical questions which had perplexed him while at school.

Then, with his mother's assistance, he learned the letters of the string alphabet, which is used in some of the institutions for the blind in Europe. When one of his friends gave him a leaf of St. Mark's Gospel, printed in embossed characters, he endeavored to read it by passing his fingers over the letters as blind children do.

His brother George was now very kind, and spent so much time in the darkened chamber that Edward often insisted upon his going out to play. George told him all about the affairs at school, and related many amusing incidents that happened among his comrades, and informed him what sports were now in fashion, and whose kite soared the highest, and whose little ship sailed fleetest on the Frog Pond. As for Emily, she repeated stories which she had learned from a new book called THE FLOWER PEOPLE, in which the snowdrops, the violets, the columbines, the roses, and all that lovely tribe are represented as telling their secrets to a little girl. The flowers talked sweetly, as flowers should; and Edward almost fancied that he could behold their bloom and smell their fragrant breath.

Thus, in one way or another, the dark days of Edward's confinement passed not unhappily. In due time his father returned; and the next evening, when the family were assembled, he began a story.

"I must first observe, children," said he, "that some writers deny the truth of the incident which I am about to relate to you. There certainly is but little evidence in favor of it. Other respectable writers, however, tell it for a fact; and, at all events, it is an interesting story, and has an excellent moral.'

So Mr. Temple proceeded to talk about the early days of

OLIVER CROMWELL.

BORN 1599. DIED 1658.

Not long after King James I. took the place of Queen Elizabeth on the throne of England, there lived an English knight at a place called Hinchinbrooke. His name was Sir Oliver Cromwell. He spent his life, I suppose, pretty much like other English knights and squires in those days, hunting hares and foxes and drinking large quantities of ale and wine. The old house in which he dwelt had been occupied by his ancestors before him for a good many years. In it there was a great hall, hung round with coats of arms and helmets, cuirasses and swords, which his forefathers had used in battle, and with horns of deer and tails of foxes which they or Sir Oliver himself had killed in the chase.

This Sir Oliver Cromwell had a nephew, who had been called Oliver, after himself, but who was generally known in the family by the name of little Noll. His father was a younger brother of Sir Oliver. The child was often sent to visit his uncle, who probably found him a troublesome little fellow to take care of. He was forever in mischief, and always running into some danger or other, from which he seemed to escape only by miracle.

Even while he was an infant in the cradle a strange accident had befallen him. A huge ape, which was kept in the family, snatched up little Noll in his fore paws and clambered with him to the roof of the house. There this ugly beast sat grinning at the affrighted spectators, as if it had done the most praiseworthy thing imaginable. Fortunately, however, he brought the child safe down again; and the event was afterwards considered an omen that Noll would reach a very elevated station in the world.

One morning, when Noll was five or six years old, a royal messenger arrived at Hinchinbrooke with tidings that King James was coming to dine with Sir Oliver Cromwell. This was a high honor, to be sure, but a very great trouble ; for all the lords and ladies, knights, squires, guards and yeomen, who waited on the king, were to be feasted as well as himself ; and more provisions would be eaten and more wine drunk in that one day than generally in a month. However, Sir Oliver expressed much thankfulness for the king's intended visit, and ordered his butler and cook to make the best preparations in their power. So a great fire was kindled in the kitchen ; and the neighbors knew by the smoke which poured out of the chimney that boiling, baking, stewing, roasting, and frying were going on merrily.

By and by the sound of trumpets was heard approaching nearer and nearer ; and a heavy, old-fashioned coach, surrounded by guards on horseback, drove up to the house. Sir Oliver, with his hat in his hand, stood at the gate to receive the king. His majesty was dressed in a suit of green not very new: he had a feather in his hat and a triple ruff round his neck, and over his shoulder was slung a hunting horn instead of a sword. Altogether he had not the most dignified aspect in the world; but the spectators gazed at him as if there was something superhuman and divine in his person. They even shaded their eyes with their hands, as if they were dazzled by the glory of his countenance.

"How are ye, man?" cried King James, speaking in a Scotch accent; for Scotland was his native country. "By my crown, Sir Oliver, but I am glad to see ye!"

The good knight thanked the king; at the same time kneeling down while his majesty alighted. When King James stood on the ground, he directed Sir Oliver's attention to a little boy who had come with him in the coach. He was six or seven years old, and wore a hat and feather, and was more richly dressed than the king himself. Though by no means an ill-looking child, he seemed shy, or even sulky; and his cheeks were rather pale, as if he had been kept moping within doors, instead of being sent out to play in the sun and wind.

"I have brought my son Charlie to see ye," said

the king. " I hope, Sir Oliver, ye have a son of your own to be his playmate."

Sir Oliver Cromwell made a reverential bow to the little prince, whom one of the attendants had now taken out of the coach. It was wonderful to see how all the spectators, even the aged men with their gray beards, humbled themselves before this child. They bent their bodies till their beards almost swept the dust. They looked as if they were ready to kneel down and worship him.

The poor little prince! From his earliest infancy not a soul had dared to contradict him ; every body around him had acted as if he were a superior being ; so that, of course, he had imbibed the same opinion of himself. He naturally supposed that the whole kingdom of Great Britain and all its inhabitants had been created solely for his benefit and amusement. This was a sad mistake ; and it cost him dear enough after he had ascended his father's throne.

" What a noble little prince he is! " exclaimed Sir Oliver, lifting his hands in admiration. " No, please your majesty, I have no son to be the playmate of his royal highness ; but there is a nephew of mine some where about the house. He is near the prince's age, and will be but too happy to wait upon his royal highness."

" Send for him, man! send for him! " said the king.

But, as it happened, there was no need of sending for Master Noll. While King James was speaking, a rugged, boldfaced, sturdy little urchin thrust himself through the throng of courtiers and attendants and greeted the prince with a broad stare. His doublet and hose (which had been put on new and clean in honor of the king's visit) were already soiled and torn with the rough play in which he had spent the morning. He looked no more abashed than if King James were his uncle and the prince one of his customary playfellows.

This was little Noll himself.

"Here, please your majesty, is my nephew," said Sir Oliver, somewhat ashamed of Noll's appearance and demeanor. "Oliver, make your obeisance to the king's majesty."

The boy made a pretty respectful obeisance to the king; for in those days children were taught to pay reverence to their elders. King James, who prided himself greatly on his scholarship, asked Noll a few questions in the Latin grammar, and then introduced him to his son. The little prince, in a very grave and dignified manner, extended his hand, not for Noll to shake, but that he might kneel down and kiss it.

"Nephew," said Sir Oliver, "pay your duty to the prince."

"I owe him no duty," cried Noll, thrusting aside the prince's hand with a rude laugh. "Why should I kiss that boy's hand?"

All the courtiers were amazed and confounded, and Sir Oliver the most of all. But the king laughed heartily, saying, that little Noll had a stubborn English spirit, and that it was well for his son to learn betimes what sort of a people he was to rule over.

So King James and his train entered the house; and the prince, with Noll and some other children, was sent to play in a separate room while his majesty was at dinner. The young people soon became acquainted; for boys, whether the sons of monarchs or of peasants, all like play, and are pleased with one another's society. What games they diverted themselves with I cannot tell. Perhaps they played at ball — perhaps at blindman's buff — perhaps at leap frog — perhaps at prison bars. Such games have been in use for hundreds of years; and princes as well as poor children have spent some of their happiest hours in playing at them.

Meanwhile King James and his nobles were feasting with Sir Oliver in the great hall. The king sat in a gilded chair, under a canopy, at the head of a long table. Whenever any of the company addressed him, it was with the deepest reverence. If the attendants offered him wine or the various delicacies of the festival, it was upon their bended knees. You would have thought, by these tokens of worship, that the monarch was a supernatural being; only he seemed to have quite as much need of those vulgar matters, food and drink, as any other person at the table. But fate had ordained that good King James should not finish his dinner in peace.

All of a sudden there arose a terrible uproar in the room where the children were at play. Angry shouts and shrill cries of alarm were mixed up together; while the voices of elder persons were likewise heard, trying to restore order among the children. The king and every body else at table looked aghast; for perhaps the tumult made them think that a general rebellion had broken out.

"Mercy on us!" muttered Sir Oliver; "that graceless nephew of mine is in some mischief or other. The naughty little whelp!"

Getting up from table, he ran to see what was the matter, followed by many of the guests, and the king among them. They all crowded to the door of the play room.

On looking in, they beheld the little Prince Charles, with his rich dress all torn and covered with the dust of the floor. His royal blood was streaming from his nose in great abundance. He gazed at Noll with a mixture of rage and affright, and at the same time a puzzled expression, as if he could not understand how any mortal boy should dare to give him a beating. As for Noll, there stood his sturdy little figure, bold as a lion, looking as if he were ready to fight, not only the prince, but the king and kingdom too.

"You little villain!" cried his uncle. "What have you been about? Down on your knees, this instant, and ask the prince's pardon. How dare you lay your hands on the king's majesty's royal son?"

"He struck me first," grumbled the valiant little Noll; "and I've only given him his due."

Sir Oliver and the guests lifted up their hands in astonishment and horror. No punishment seemed severe enough for this wicked little varlet, who had dared to resent a blow from the king's own son. Some of the courtiers were of opinion that Noll should be sent prisoner to the Tower of London and brought to trial for high treason. Others, in their great zeal for the king's service, were about to lay hands on the boy and chastise him in the royal presence.

But King James, who sometimes showed a good deal of sagacity, ordered them to desist.

"Thou art a bold boy," said he, looking fixedly at little Noll; "and, if thou live to be a man, my son Charlie would do wisely to be friends with thee."

"I never will!" cried the little prince, stamping his foot.

"Peace, Charlie, peace!" said the king; then addressing Sir Oliver and the attendants, "Harm not the urchin; for he has taught my son a good lesson, is Heaven do but give him grace to profit by it Hereafter, should he be tempted to tyrannize over the stubborn race of Englishmen, let him remember little Noll Cromwell and his own bloody nose."

So the king finished his dinner and departed ; and for many a long year the childish quarrel between Prince Charles and Noll Cromwell was forgotten. The prince, indeed, might have lived a happier life, and have met a more peaceful death, had he remembered that quarrel and the moral which his father drew from it. But when old King James was dead, and Charles sat upon his throne, he seemed to forget that he was but a man, and that his meanest subjects were men as well as he. He wished to have the property and lives of the people of England entirely at his own disposal. But the Puritans, and all who loved liberty, rose against him, and beat him in many battles, and pulled him down from his throne.

Throughout this war between the king and nobles on one side and the people of England on the other there was a famous leader, who did more towards the ruin of royal authority than all the rest. The contest seemed like a wrestling match between King Charles and this strong man. And the king was overthrown.

When the discrowned monarch was brought to trial, that warlike leader sat in the judgment hall. Many judges were present besides himself ; but he alone had the power to save King Charles or to doom him to the scaffold. After sentence was pronounced, this victorious general was entreated by his own children, on their knees, to rescue his majesty from death.

"No!" said he, sternly. "Better that one man should perish than that the whole country should be ruined for his sake. It is resolved that he shall die!"

When Charles, no longer a king, was led to the scaffold, his great enemy stood at a window of the royal palace of Whitehall. He beheld the poor victim of pride, and an evil education, and misused power, as he laid his head upon the block. He looked on with a steadfast gaze while a black-veiled executioner lifted the fatal axe and smote off that anointed head at a single blow.

"It is a righteous deed," perhaps he said to himself. "Now Englishmen may enjoy their rights."

At night, when the body of Charles was laid in the coffin, in a gloomy chamber, the general entered, lighting himself with a torch. Its gleam showed that he was now growing old; his visage was scarred with the many battles in which he had led the van; his brow was wrinkled with care and with the continual exercise of stern authority. Probably there was not a single trait, either of aspect or manner, that belonged to the little Noll who had battled so stoutly with Prince Charles. Yet this was he!

He lifted the coffin lid, and caused the light of his

torch to fall upon the dead monarch's face. Then, probably, his mind went back over all the marvellous events that had brought the hereditary King of England to this dishonored coffin, and had raised himself, a humble individual, to the possession of kingly power. He was a king, though without the empty title or the glittering crown.

"Why was it," said Cromwell to himself, or might have said, as he gazed at the pale features in the coffin, — "why was it that this great king fell, and that poor Noll Cromwell has gained all the power of the realm?"

And, indeed, why was it?

King Charles had fallen, because, in his manhood the same as when a child, he disdained to feel that every human creature was his brother. He deemed himself a superior being, and fancied that his subjects were created only for a king to rule over. And Cromwell rose, because, in spite of his many faults, he mainly fought for the rights and freedom of his fellow-men ; and therefore the poor and the oppressed all lent their strength to him.

"Dear father, how I should hate to be a king!" exclaimed Edward.

"And would you like to be a Cromwell?" inquired his father.

"I should like it well," replied George; "only I

would not have put the poor old king to death. I would have sent him out of the kingdom, or perhaps have allowed him to live in a small house near the gate of the royal palace. It was too severe to cut off his head."

"Kings are in such an unfortunate position," said Mr. Temple, "that they must either be almost deified by their subjects, or else be dethroned and beheaded. In either case it is a pitiable lot."

"O, I had rather be blind than be a king!" said Edward.

"Well, my dear Edward," observed his mother, with a smile, "I am glad you are convinced that your own lot is not the hardest in the world."

CHAPTER VII

IT was a pleasant sight, for those who had eyes, to see how patiently the blinded little boy now submitted to what he had at first deemed an intolerable calamity. The beneficent Creator has not allowed our comfort to depend on the enjoyment of any single sense. Though he has made the world so very beautiful, yet it is possible to be happy without ever beholding the blue sky, or the green and flowery earth, or the kind faces of those whom we love. Thus it appears that all the external beauty of the universe is a free gift from God over and above what is necessary to our comfort. How grateful, then, should we be to that divine Benevolence, which showers even superfluous bounties upon us!

One truth, therefore, which Edward's blindness had taught him was, that his mind and soul could dispense with the assistance of his eyes. Doubtless, however, he would have found this lesson far more difficult to learn had it not been for the affection of those around him. His parents, and George and Emily, aided him to bear his misfortune; if possible, they would have lent him their own eyes. And this too, was a good lesson for him. It taught him how dependent on one another God has ordained us to be, insomuch that all the necessities of mankind should incite them to mutual love.

So Edward loved his friends, and perhaps all the world, better than he ever did before. And he felt grateful towards his father for spending the evenings in telling him stories — more grateful, probably, than any of my little readers will feel towards me for so carefully writing these same stories down.

"Come, dear father," said he, the next evening, "now tell us about some other little boy who was destined to be a famous man."

"How would you like a story of a Boston boy?' asked his father.

"O, pray let us have it!" cried George, eagerly. "It will be all the better if he has been to our schools and has coasted on the Common, and sailed boats in the Frog Pond. I shall feel acquainted with him then."

"Well, then," said Mr. Temple, "I will introduce you to a Boston boy whom all the world became acquainted with after he grew to be a man."

The story was as follows : —

BENJAMIN FRANKLIN.

Born 1706. Died 1790.

In the year 1716, or about that period, a boy used to be seen in the streets of Boston who was known

among his schoolfellows and playmates by the name
of Ben Franklin. Ben was born in 1706 ; so that
he was now about ten years old. His father, who
had come over from England, was a soap boiler and
tallow chandler, and resided in Milk Street, not far
from the Old South Church.

Ben was a bright boy at his book, and even a
brighter one when at play with his comrades. He
had some remarkable qualities which always seemed
to give him the lead, whether at sport or in more
serious matters. I might tell you a number of amusing anecdotes about him. You are acquainted, I
suppose, with his famous story of the WHISTLE, and
how he bought it with a whole pocket full of coppers
and afterwards repented of his bargain. But Ben
had grown a great boy since those days, and had
gained wisdom by experience ; for it was one of his
peculiarities, that no incident ever happened to him
without teaching him some valuable lesson. Thus
he generally profited more by his misfortunes than
many people do by the most favorable events that
could befall them.

Ben's face was already pretty well known to the
inhabitants of Boston. The selectmen and other
people of note often used to visit his father, for the
sake of talking about the affairs of the town or prov-
ince. Mr. Franklin was considered a person of great
wisdom and integrity, and was respected by all who

knew him, although he supported his family by the humble trade of boiling soap and making tallow candles.

While his father and the visitors were holding deep consultations about public affairs, little Ben would sit on his stool in a corner, listening with the greatest interest, as if he understood every word. Indeed, his features were so full of intelligence that there could be but little doubt, not only that he understood what was said, but that he could have expressed some very sagacious opinions out of his own mind. But in those days boys were expected to be silent in the presence of their elders. However, Ben Franklin was looked upon as a very promising lad, who would talk and act wisely by and by.

"Neighbor Franklin," his father's friends would sometimes say, "you ought to send this boy to college and make a minister of him."

"I have often thought of it," his father would reply; "and my brother Benjamin promises to give him a great many volumes of manuscript sermons, in case he should be educated for the church. But I have a large family to support, and cannot afford the expense."

In fact, Mr. Franklin found it so difficult to provide bread for his family, that, when the boy was ten years old, it became necessary to take him from school. Ben was then employed in cutting candle wicks into equal lengths and filling the moulds with tallow , and many families in Boston spent their evenings by the light of the candles which he had helped to make. Thus, you see, in his early days, as well as in his manhood, his labors contributed to throw light upon dark matters.

Busy as his life now was, Ben still found time to keep company with his former schoolfellows. He and the other boys were very fond of fishing, and spent many of their leisure hours on the margin of the mill pond, catching flounders, perch, eels, and tomcod, which came up thither with the tide. The place where they fished is now, probably, covered with stone pavements and brick buildings, and thronged with people and with vehicles of all kinds. But at that period it was a marshy spot on the outskirts of the town, where gulls flitted and screamed overhead and salt meadow grass grew under foot.

On the edge of the water there was a deep bed of clay, in which the boys were forced to stand while they caught their fish. Here they dabbled in mud and mire like a flock of ducks.

" This is very uncomfortable," said Ben Franklin one day to his comrades, while they were standing mid-leg deep in the quagmire.

" So it is," said the other boys. " What a pity we have no better place to stand ! "

If it had not been for Ben, nothing more would

have been done or said about the matter. But it was not in his nature to be sensible of an inconvenience without using his best efforts to find a remedy. So, as he and his comrades were returning from the water side, Ben suddenly threw down his string of fish with a very determined air.

" Boys," cried he, " I have thought of a scheme which will be greatly for our benefit and for the public benefit."

It was queer enough, to be sure, to hear this little chap — this rosy-cheeked, ten-year-old boy — talking about schemes for the public benefit! Nevertheless, his companions were ready to listen, being assured that Ben's scheme, whatever it was, would be well worth their attention. They remembered how sagaciously he had conducted all their enterprises ever since he had been old enough to wear smallclothes.

They remembered, too, his wonderful contrivance of sailing across the mill pond by lying flat on his back in the water and allowing himself to be drawn along by a paper kite. If Ben could do that, he might certainly do any thing.

"What is your scheme, Ben? — what is it ? " cried they all.

It so happened that they had now come to a spot of ground where a new house was to be built. Scattered round about lay a great many large stones which were 'o be used for the cellar and foundation.

Ben mounted upon the highest of these stones, so that he might speak with the more authority.

" You know, lads," said he, " what a plague it is to be forced to stand in the quagmire yonder — over shoes and stockings (if we wear any) in mud and water. See! I am bedaubed to the knees of my smallclothes; and you are all in the same pickle. Unless we can find some remedy for this evil, our fishing business must be entirely given up. And, surely. this would be a terrible misfortune!"

" That it would! that it would!" said his comrades, sorrowfully.

" Now, I propose," continued Master Benjamin, " that we build a wharf, for the purpose of carrying on our fisheries. You see these stones. The workmen mean to use them for the underpinning of a house ; but that would be for only one man's advantage. My plan is to take these same stones and carry them to the edge of the water and build a wharf with them. This will not only enable us to carry on the fishing business with comfort and to better advantage, but it will likewise be a great convenience to boats passing up and down the stream. Thus, instead of one man, fifty, or a hundred, or a thousand, besides ourselves, may be benefited by these stones. What say you, lads? Shall we build the wharf?"

Ben's proposal was received with one of those uproarious shouts wherewith boys usually express their delight at whatever completely suits their views. Nobody thought of questioning the right and justice of building a wharf with stones that belonged to another person.

"Hurrah! hurrah!" shouted they. "Let's set about it."

It was agreed that they should all be on the spot that evening and commence their grand public enterprise by moonlight. Accordingly, at the appointed time, the whole gang of youthful laborers assembled, and eagerly began to remove the stones. They had not calculated how much toil would be requisite in this important part of their undertaking. The very first stone which they laid hold of proved so heavy that it almost seemed to be fastened to the ground. Nothing but Ben Franklin's cheerful and resolute spirit could have induced them to persevere.

Ben, as might be expected, was the soul of the enterprise. By his mechanical genius, he contrived methods to lighten the labor of transporting the stones, so that one boy, under his directions, would perform as much as half a dozen if left to themselves. Whenever their spirits flagged he had some joke ready, which seemed to renew their strength, by setting them all into a roar of laughter. And when, after an hour or two of hard work, the stones were transported to the water side, Ben Franklin was the engineer to superintend the construction of the wharf.

The boys, like a colony of ants, performed a great deal of labor by their multitude, though the individual strength of each could have accomplished but little. Finally, just as the moon sank below the horizon, the great work was finished.

"Now, boys," cried Ben, "let's give three cheers and go home to bed. To-morrow we may catch fish at our ease."

"Hurrah! hurrah! hurrah!" shouted his comrades.

Then they all went home in such an ecstasy of delight that they could hardly get a wink of sleep.

The story was not yet finished; but George's impatience caused him to interrupt it.

"How I wish that I could have helped to build that wharf!" exclaimed he. "It must have been glorious fun. Ben Franklin forever, say I."

"It was a very pretty piece of work," said Mr. Temple. "But wait till you hear the end of the story."

"Father," inquired Edward, "whereabouts in Boston was the mill pond on which Ben built his wharf?"

"I do not exactly know," answered Mr. Temple; "but I suppose it to have been on the northern verge of the town, in the vicinity of what are now called Merrimack and Charlestown Streets. That thronged portion of the city was once a marsh. Some of it, in fact, was covered with water."

CHAPTER VIII.

As the children had no more questions to ask, Mr. Temple proceeded to relate what consequences ensued from the building of Ben Franklin's wharf.

BENJAMIN FRANKLIN.

Continued.

In the morning, when the early sunbeams were gleaming on the steeples and roofs of the town and gilding the water that surrounded it, the masons came, rubbing their eyes, to begin their work at the foundation of the new house. But, on reaching the spot, they rubbed their eyes so much the harder. What had become of their heap of stones?

"Why, Sam," said one to another, in great perplexity, "here's been some witchcraft at work while we were asleep. The stones must have flown away through the air!"

"More likely they have been stolen!" answered Sam.

" But who on earth would think of stealing a heap of stones?" cried a third. "Could a man carry them away in his pocket?"

The master mason, who was a gruff kind of man, stood scratching his head, and said nothing at first. But, looking carefully on the ground, he discerned innumerable tracks of little feet, some with shoes and some barefoot. Following these tracks with his eye, he saw that they formed a beaten path towards the water side.

"Ah, I see what the mischief is," said he, nodding his head. "Those little rascals, the boys, — they have stolen our stones to build a wharf with!"

The masons immediately went to examine the new structure. And to say the truth, it was well worth looking at, so neatly and with such admirable skill had it been planned and finished. The stones were put together so securely that there was no danger of their being loosened by the tide, however swiftly it might sweep along. There was a broad and safe platform to stand upon, whence the little fishermen might cast their lines into deep water and draw up fish in abundance. Indeed, it almost seemed as if Ben and his comrades might be forgiven for taking the stones, because they had done their job in such a workmanlike manner.

"The chaps that built this wharf understood their business pretty well," said one of the masons. "I should not be ashamed of such a piece of work myself."

But the master mason did not seem to enjoy the joke. He was one of those unreasonable people who care a great deal more for their own rights and privileges than for the convenience of all the rest of the world.

"Sam," said he, more gruffly than usual, "go call a constable."

So Sam called a constable, and inquiries were set on foot to discover the perpetrators of the theft. In the course of the day warrants were issued, with the signature of a justice of the peace, to take the bodies of Benjamin Franklin and other evil-disposed persons who had stolen a heap of stones. If the owner of the stolen property had not been more merciful than the master mason, it might have gone hard with our friend Benjamin and his fellow-laborers. But, luckily for them, the gentleman had a respect for Ben's father, and, moreover, was amused with the spirit of the whole affair. He therefore let the culprits off pretty easily.

But, when the constables were dismissed, the poor boys had to go through another trial, and receive sentence, and suffer execution, too, from their own fathers. Many a rod, I grieve to say, was worn to the stump on that unlucky night.

As for Ben, he was less afraid of a whipping than

of his father's disapprobation. Mr. Franklin, as I have mentioned before, was a sagacious man, and also an inflexibly upright one. He had read much for a person in his rank of life, and had pondered upon the ways of the world, until he had gained more wisdom than a whole library of books could have taught him. Ben had a greater reverence for his father than for any other person in the world, as well on account of his spotless integrity as of his practical sense and deep views of things.

Consequently, after being released from the clutches of the law, Ben came into his father's presence with no small perturbation of mind.

"Benjamin, come hither," began Mr. Franklin, in his customary solemn and weighty tone.

The boy approached and stood before his father's chair, waiting reverently to hear what judgment this good man would pass upon his late offence. He felt that now the right and wrong of the whole matter would be made to appear.

"Benjamin," said his father, "what could induce you to take property which did not belong to you?"

"Why, father," replied Ben, hanging his head at first, but then lifting his eyes to Mr. Franklin's face, "if it had been merely for my own benefit, I never should have dreamed of it. But I knew that the wharf would be a public convenience. If the owner of the stones should build a house with them, nobody will enjoy any advantage except himself.   Now, I made use of them in a way that was for the advantage of many persons.   I thought it right to aim at doing good to the greatest number."

"My son," said Mr. Franklin, solemnly, "so far as it was in your power, you have done a greater harm to the public than to the owner of the stones."

"How can that be, father?" asked Ben.

"Because, answered his father, "in building your wharf with stolen materials, you have committed a moral wrong.   There is no more terrible mistake than to violate what is eternally right for the sake of a seeming expediency.   Those who act upon such a principle do the utmost in their power to destroy all that is good in the world."

"Heaven forbid!" said Benjamin.

"No act," continued Mr. Franklin, "can possibly be for the benefit of the public generally which involves injustice to any individual.   It would be easy to prove this by examples.   But, indeed, can we suppose that our all-wise and just Creator would have so ordered the affairs of the world that a wrong act should be the true method of attaining a right end?   It is impious to think so.   And I do verily believe, Benjamin, that almost all the public and private misery of mankind arises from a neglect of this great truth — that evil can produce only evil — that good ends must be wrought out by good means."

"I will never forget it again," said Benjamin, bowing his head.

"Remember," concluded his father, "that, whenever we vary from the highest rule of right, just so far we do an injury to the world. It may seem otherwise for the moment; but, both in time and in eternity, it will be found so."

To the close of his life Ben Franklin never forgot this conversation with his father; and we have reason to suppose that, in most of his public and private career, he endeavored to act upon the principles which that good and wise man had then taught him.

After the great event of building the wharf, Ben continued to cut wick yarn and fill candle moulds for about two years. But, as he had no love for that occupation, his father often took him to see various artisans at their work, in order to discover what trade he would prefer. Thus Ben learned the use of a great many tools, the knowledge of which afterwards proved very useful to him. But he seemed much inclined to go to sea. In order to keep him at home, and likewise to gratify his taste for letters, the lad was bound apprentice to his elder brother, who had lately set up a printing office in Boston.

Here he had many opportunities of reading new books and of hearing instructive conversation. He exercised himself so successfully in writing composition, that, when no more than thirteen or fourteen years old, he became a contributor to his brother's newspaper. Ben was also a versifier, if not a poet. He made two doleful ballads — one about the shipwreck of Captain Worthilake ; and the other about the pirate Black Beard, who, not long before, infested the American seas.

When Ben's verses were printed, his brother sent him to sell them to the townspeople wet from the press. " Buy my ballads ! " shouted Benjamin, as he trudged through the streets with a basket full on his arm. " Who'll buy a ballad about Black Beard ? A penny apiece ! a penny apiece ! Who'll buy my ballads ? "

If one of those roughly composed and rudely printed ballads could be discovered now, it would be worth more than its weight in gold.

In this way our friend Benjamin spent his boyhood and youth, until, on account of some disagreement with his brother, he left his native town and went to Philadelphia. He landed in the latter city, a homeless and hungry young man, and bought threepence worth of bread to satisfy his appetite. Not knowing where else to go, he entered a Quaker meeting house, sat down, and fell fast asleep. He has not told us whether his slumbers were visited by any dreams. But it would have been a strange dream, indeed, and an incredible one, that should have foretold how great a man he was destined to become, and how much he would be honored in that very city where he was now friendless and unknown.

So here we finish our story of the childhood of Benjamin Franklin. One of these days, if you would know what he was in his manhood, you must read his own works and the history of American independence.

" Do let us hear a little more of him! " said Edward; "not that I admire him so much as many other characters; but he interests me, because he was a Yankee boy."

" My dear son," replied Mr. Temple, " it would require a whole volume of talk to tell you all that is worth knowing about Benjamin Franklin. There is a very pretty anecdote of his flying a kite in the midst of a thunder storm, and thus drawing down the lightning from the clouds and proving that it was the same thing as electricity. His whole life would be an interesting story, if we had time to tell it."

" But, pray, dear father, tell us what made him so famous," said George. " I have seen his portrait a great many times. There is a wooden bust of him in one of our streets; and marble ones, I suppose, in some other places. And towns, and ships of war, and steamboats, and banks, and academies, and children are often named after Franklin. Why should he have grown so very famous?"

" Your question is a reasonable one, George," answered his father. " I doubt whether Franklin's philosophical discoveries, important as they were, or even his vast political services, would have given him all the fame which he acquired. It appears to me that Poor Richard's Almanac did more than any thing else towards making him familiarly known to the public. As the writer of those proverbs which Poor Richard was supposed to utter, Franklin became the counsellor and household friend of almost every family in America. Thus it was the humblest of all his labors that has done the most for his fame."

" I have read some of those proverbs," remarked Edward ; " but I do not like them. They are all about getting money or saving it."

" Well," said his father, " they were suited to the condition of the country ; and their effect, upon the whole, has doubtless been good — although they teach men but a very small portion of their duties."

CHAPTER IX.

HITHERTO Mr. Temple's narratives had all been about boys and men. But, the next evening, he bethought himself that the quiet little Emily would perhaps be glad to hear the story of a child of her own sex. He therefore resolved to narrate the youthful adventures of Christina, of Sweden, who began to be a queen at the age of no more than six years. If we have any little girls among our readers, they must not suppose that Christina is set before them as a pattern of what they ought to be. On the contrary, the tale of her life is chiefly profitable as showing the evil effects of a wrong education, which caused this daughter of a king to be both useless and unhappy. Here follows the story.

QUEEN CHRISTINA.

Born 1626. Died 1689.

In the royal palace at Stockholm, the capital city of Sweden, there was born, in 1626, a little princess

The king, her father, gave her the name of Christina, in memory of a Swedish girl with whom he had been in love. His own name was Gustavus Adolphus; and he was also called the Lion of the North, because he had gained greater fame in war than any other prince or general then alive. With this valiant king for their commander, the Swedes had made themselves terrible to the Emperor of Germany and to the King of France, and were looked upon as the chief defence of the Protestant religion.

The little Christina was by no means a beautiful child. To confess the truth, she was remarkably plain. The queen, her mother, did not love her so much as she ought; partly, perhaps, on account of Christina's want of beauty, and also because both the king and queen had wished for a son, who might have gained as great renown in battle as his father had.

The king, however, soon became exceedingly fond of the infant princess. When Christina was very young she was taken violently sick. Gustavus Adolphus, who was several hundred miles from Stockholm, travelled night and day, and never rested until he held the poor child in his arms. On her recovery he made a solemn festival, in order to show his joy to the people of Sweden and express his gratitude to Heaven. After this event he took his daughter with him in all the journeys which he made throughout his kingdom.

Christina soon proved herself a bold and sturdy little girl. When she was two years old, the king and herself, in the course of a journey, came to the strong fortress of Colmar. On the battlements were soldiers clad in steel armor, which glittered in the sunshine. There were likewise great cannons, pointing their black mouths at Gustavus and little Christina, and ready to belch out their smoke and thunder; for, whenever a king enters a fortress, it is customary to receive him with a royal salute of artillery.

But the captain of the fortress met Gustavus and his daughter as they were about to enter the gateway.

"May it please your majesty," said he, taking off his steel cap and bowing profoundly, " I fear that, if we receive you with a salute of cannon, the little princess will be frightened almost to death."

Gustavus looked earnestly at his daughter, and was indeed apprehensive that the thunder of so many cannon might perhaps throw her into convulsions. He had almost a mind to tell the captain to let them enter the fortress quietly, as common people might have done, without all this head-splitting racket. But no; this would not do.

" Let them fire," said he, waving his hand. Christina is a soldier's daughter, and must learn to bear the noise of cannon."

So the captain uttered the word of command, and immediately there was a terrible peal of thunder from

the cannon, and such a gush of smoke that it enveloped the whole fortress in its volumes. But, amid
all the din and confusion, Christina was seen clapping
her little hands and laughing in an ecstasy of delight. Probably nothing ever pleased her father so
much as to see that his daughter promised to be fearless as himself. He determined to educate her exactly as if she had been a boy, and to teach her all
the knowledge needful to the ruler of a kingdom and
the commander of an army.

But Gustavus should have remembered that Providence had created her to be a woman, and that it
was not for him to make a man of her.

However, the king derived great happiness from
his beloved Christina. It must have been a pleasant
sight to see the powerful monarch of Sweden playing
in some magnificent hall of the palace with his merry
little girl. Then he forgot that the weight of a kingdom rested upon his shoulders. He forgot that the
wise Chancellor Oxenstiern was waiting to consult
with him how to render Sweden the greatest nation
of Europe. He forgot that the Emperor of Germany
and the King of France were plotting together how
they might pull him down from his throne.

Yes; Gustavus forgot all the perils, and cares, and
pompous irksomeness of a royal life; and was as happy, while playing with his child, as the humblest
peasant in the realm of Sweden. How gayly did

they dance along the marble floor of the palace, this valiant king, with his upright, martial figure, his war-worn visage, and commanding aspect, and the small, round form of Christina, with her rosy face of childish merriment! Her little fingers were clasped in her father's hand, which had held the leading staff in many famous victories. His crown and sceptre were her playthings. She could disarm Gustavus of his sword, which was so terrible to the princes of Europe.

But, alas! the king was not long permitted to enjoy Christina's society. When she was four years old Gustavus was summoned to take command of the allied armies of Germany, which were fighting against the emperor. His greatest affliction was the necessity of parting with his child; but people in such high stations have but little opportunity for domestic happiness. He called an assembly of the senators of Sweden and confided Christina to their care, saying, that each one of them must be a father to her if he himself should fall in battle.

At the moment of his departure Christina ran towards him and began to address him with a speech which somebody had taught her for the occasion. Gustavus was busied with thoughts about the affairs of the kingdom, so that he did not immediately attend to the childish voice of his little girl. Christina, who did not love to be unnoticed, immediately stopped short and pulled him by the coat.

"Father," said she, "why do not you listen to my speech?"

In a moment the king forgot every thing except that he was parting with what he loved best in all the world. He caught the child in his arms, pressed her to his bosom, and burst into tears. Yes; though he was a brave man, and though he wore a steel corselet on his breast, and though armies were waiting for him to lead them to battle, still his heart melted within him, and he wept. Christina, too, was so afflicted that her attendants began to fear that she would actually die of grief. But probably she was soon comforted; for children seldom remember their parents quite so faithfully as their parents remember them.

For two years more Christina remained in the palace at Stockholm. The queen, her mother, had accompanied Gustavus to the wars. The child, therefore, was left to the guardianship of five of the wisest men in the kingdom. But these wise men knew better how to manage the affairs of state than how to govern and educate a little girl so as to render her a good and happy woman.

When two years had passed away, tidings were brought to Stockholm which filled every body with triumph and sorrow at the same time. The Swedes had won a glorious victory at Lutzen. But, alas! the warlike King of Sweden, the Lion of the North, the father of our little Christina, had been slain at the foot of a great stone, which still marks the spot of that hero's death.

Soon after this sad event, a general assembly, or congress, consisting of deputations from the nobles, the clergy, the burghers, and the peasants of Sweden, was summoned to meet at Stockholm. It was for the purpose of declaring little Christina to be Queen of Sweden and giving her the crown and sceptre of her deceased father. Silence being proclaimed, the Chancellor Oxenstiern arose.

"We desire to know," said he, "whether the people of Sweden will take the daughter of our dead king, Gustavus Adolphus, to be their queen."

When the chancellor had spoken, an old man, with white hair and in coarse apparel, stood up in the midst of the assembly. He was a peasant, Lars Larrson by name, and had spent most of his life in laboring on a farm.

"Who is this daughter of Gustavus?" asked the old man. "We do not know her. Let her be shown to us."

Then Christina was brought into the hall and placed before the old peasant. It was strange, no doubt, to see a child — a little girl of six years old — offered to the Swedes as their ruler instead of the brave king, her father, who had led them to victory so many times. Could her baby fingers wield a

sword in war? Could her childish mind govern **the**
nation wisely in peace?

But the Swedes do not appear to have asked themselves these questions. Old Lars Larrson took
Christina up in his arms and gazed earnestly into
her face. He had known the great Gustavus well;
and his heart was touched when he saw the likeness
which the little girl bore to that heroic monarch.

"Yes," cried he, with the tears gushing down his
furrowed cheeks; "this is truly the daughter of our
Gustavus! Here is her father's brow! — here is his
piercing eye! She is his very picture! This child
shall be our queen!"

Then all the proud nobles of Sweden, and the rev-
erend clergy, and the burghers, and the peasants,
knelt down at the child's feet and kissed her hand.

"Long live Christina, Queen of Sweden!" shouted
they.

Even after she was a woman grown Christina remembered the pleasure which she felt in seeing all
these men at her feet and hearing them acknowledge
her as their supreme ruler. Poor child! she was yet
to learn that power does not insure happiness. As
yet, however, she had not any real power. All the
public business, it is true, was transacted in her name;
but the kingdom was governed by a number of the
most experienced statesmen, who were called a regency.

But it was considered necessary that the little queen should be present at the public ceremonies, and should behave just as if she were in reality the ruler of the nation. When she was seven years of age, some ambassadors from the Czar of Muscovy came to the Swedish court. They wore long beards, and were clad in a strange fashion, with furs and other outlandish ornaments; and as they were inhabitants of a half-civilized country, they did not behave like other people. The Chancellor Oxenstiern was afraid that the young queen would burst out a-laughing at the first sight of these queer ambassadors, or else that she would be frightened by their unusual aspect.

"Why should I be frightened?" said the little queen. "And do you suppose that I have no better manners than to laugh? Only tell me how I must behave, and I will do it."

Accordingly, the Muscovite ambassadors were introduced; and Christina received them and answered their speeches with as much dignity and propriety as if she had been a grown woman.

All this time, though Christina was now a queen, you must not suppose that she was left to act as she pleased. She had a preceptor, named John Mathias, who was a very learned man and capable of instructing her in all the branches of science. But there was nobody to teach her the delicate graces and gentle virtues of a woman. She was surrounded almost

entirely by men, and had learned to despise the
society of her own sex.   At the age of nine years
she was separated from her mother, whom the Swedes
did not consider a proper person to be intrusted with
the charge of her.   No little girl who sits by a New
England fireside has cause to envy Christina in the
royal palace at Stockholm.

Yet she made great progress in her studies.   She
learned to read the classical authors of Greece and
Rome, and became a great admirer of the heroes and
poets of old times.   Then, as for active exercises, she
could ride on horseback as well as any man in her
kingdom.   She was fond of hunting, and could shoot
at a mark with wonderful skill.   But dancing was
the only feminine accomplishment with which she
had any acquaintance.

She was so restless in her disposition that none of
her attendants were sure of a moment's quiet neither
day nor night.   She grew up, I am sorry to say, a
very unamiable person, ill tempered, proud, stubborn,
and, in short, unfit to make those around her happy
or to be happy herself.   Let every little girl, who
has been taught self-control and a due regard for the
rights of others, thank Heaven that she has had better instruction than this poor little Queen of Sweden

At the age of eighteen Christina was declared free
to govern the kingdom by herself without the aid
of a regency.   At this period of her life she was a

young woman of striking aspect, a good figure, and intelligent face, but very strangely dressed. She wore a short habit of gray cloth, with a man's vest over it, and a black scarf around her neck; but no jewels nor ornaments of any kind.

Yet, though Christina was so negligent of her appearance, there was something in her air and manner that proclaimed her as the ruler of a kingdom. Her eyes, it is said, had a very fierce and haughty look. Old General Wrangel, who had often caused the enemies of Sweden to tremble in battle, actually trembled himself when he encountered the eyes of the queen. But it would have been better for Christina if she could have made people love her, by means of soft and gentle looks, instead of affright-ing them by such terrible glances.

And now I have told you almost all that is amus-ing or instructive in the childhood of Christina. Only a few more words need be said about her; for it is neither pleasant nor profitable to think of many things that she did after she grew to be a woman.

When she had worn the crown a few years, she began to consider it beneath her dignity to be called a queen, because the name implied that she belonged to the weaker sex. She therefore caused herself to be proclaimed KING; thus declaring to the world that she despised her own sex and was desirous of being ranked among men. But in the twenty-eighth year

of her age Christina grew tired of royalty, and resolved to be neither a king nor a queen any longer.
She took the crown from her head with her own
hands, and ceased to be the ruler of Sweden. The
people did not greatly regret her abdication; for she
had governed them ill, and had taken much of their
property to supply her extravagance.

Having thus given up her hereditary crown, Christina left Sweden and travelled over many of the countries of Europe. Every where she was received
with great ceremony, because she was the daughter
of the renowned Gustavus and had herself been a
powerful queen. Perhaps you would like to know
something about her personal appearance in the latter
part of her life. She is described as wearing a man's
vest, a short gray petticoat, embroidered with gold
and silver, and a black wig, which was thrust awry
upon her head. She wore no gloves, and so seldom
washed her hands that nobody could tell what had
been their original color. In this strange dress, and,
I suppose, without washing her hands or face, she
visited the magnificent court of Louis XIV.

She died in 1689. None loved her while she lived,
nor regretted her death, nor planted a single flower
upon her grave. Happy are the little girls of America, who are brought up quietly and tenderly at the
domestic hearth, and thus become gentle and delicate
women! May none of them ever lose the loveliness

of their sex by receiving such an education as that of Queen Christina!

Emily, timid, quiet, and sensitive, was the very reverse of little Christina. She seemed shocked at the idea of such a bold and masculine character as has been described in the foregoing story.

"I never could have loved her," whispered she to Mrs. Temple; and then she added, with that love of personal neatness which generally accompanies purity of heart, "It troubles me to think of her unclean hands!"

"Christina was a sad specimen of womankind indeed," said Mrs. Temple. "But it is very possible for a woman to have a strong mind, and to be fitted for the active business of life, without losing any of her natural delicacy. Perhaps some time or other Mr. Temple will tell you a story of such a woman."

It was now time for Edward to be left to repose. His brother George shook him heartily by the hand, and hoped, as he had hoped twenty times before, that to-morrow or the next day Ned's eyes would be strong enough to look the sun right in the face.

"Thank you, George," replied Edward, smiling; "but I am not half so impatient as at first. If my bodily eyesight were as good as yours, perhaps I could not see things so distinctly with my mind's eye. But now there is a light within which shows

me the little Quaker artist, Ben West, and Isaac
Newton with his windmill, and stubborn Sam Johnson,
and stout Noll Cromwell, and shrewd Ben Franklin, and little Queen Christina, with the Swedes
kneeling at her feet.   It seems as if I really saw
these personages face to face.   So I can bear the
darkness outside of me pretty well."

When Edward ceased speaking, Emily put up her
mouth and kissed him as her farewell for the night.

"Ah, I forgot!" said Edward, with a sigh.   "I
cannot see any of your faces.   What would it sig-
nify to see all the famous people in the world, if I
must be blind to the faces that I love?"

"You must try to see us with your heart, my
dear child," said his mother.

Edward went to bed somewhat dispirited; but,
quickly falling asleep, was visited with such a pleasant dream of the sunshine and of his dearest friends
that he felt the happier for it all the next day.   And
we hope to find him still happy when we meet again.

www.ingramcontent.com/pod-product-compliance
Lightning Source LLC
Chambersburg PA
CBHW030953110726
47900CB00004B/1257